The Dilemma *of* Charlotte Farrow

Books by Olivia Newport

AVENUE OF DREAMS

The Pursuit of Lucy Banning

The Dilemma of Charlotte Farrow

“Newport’s latest novel, *The Dilemma of Charlotte Farrow*, provides an enthralling examination of the complex class and gender barriers in nineteenth-century Chicago. Second in the Avenue of Dreams series, this book will find swarms of devoted fans rooting for Charlotte Farrow, a mother forced to make excruciating choices in a world where women have limited options. The storyline is not only unique but also framed by a delicately designed backdrop of both luxury and longing. With timeless themes, Newport gives voice to women across the ages who have found themselves fighting for what matters most, and in the end, readers will join the battle cry.”

—**Julie Cantrell**, *New York Times* and *USA Today* bestselling author of *Into the Free*

“In the character of Charlotte Farrow, Olivia Newport gives voice to the countless thousands of women in domestic service who were seen but rarely heard. Set with exacting detail in Chicago during the World’s Columbian Exposition, Charlotte’s tale of courage and struggle will keep you on the edge of your seat from the first page to the last.”

—**William Tyre**, executive director and curator, Glessner House Museum

Praise for *The Pursuit of Lucy Banning*

“Hats off to Olivia Newport and the debut novel *The Pursuit of Lucy Banning*. The characters are compelling, and Chicago’s history comes alive on each page. Readers will feel like they’ve been transported back to 1892.”

—**Andrea Boeshaar**, author of Seasons of Redemption series

"Lucy Banning is my kind of heroine, pushing against the strictures of her times of the 1890s. Her love and caring wraps around your heart as it does those who need her and even to those who wish her harm. A fine read from this first-time author."

—**Lauraine Snelling**, author of the Red River of the North series and the Wild West Wind series

"With attention to historical detail and an artful sense of place, Olivia Newport gives readers a fascinating glimpse into the way the wealthy interpreted the 1893 World's Fair—and the roles of women in the world. *The Pursuit of Lucy Banning* is a compassionate coming-of-age romance with a spunky, determined heroine and a Happily Ever After that's satisfyingly sweet."

—*USA Today*, *Happily Ever After* blog

"In a new historical series, Avenue of Dreams, readers head to the Chicago World's Fair of 1893 where they will be treated to the grandeur and charm of the wealthy and the not-so-wealthy. In this story thick with secrets and lies, Newport's characters are by turn charming, conniving, or trying to be true to themselves in spite of what society expects of them."

—*RT Book Reviews*

AVENUE OF DREAMS • BOOK 2

The Dilemma of Charlotte Farrow

A Novel

OLIVIA NEWPORT

Revell
a division of Baker Publishing Group
Grand Rapids, Michigan

Published by Revell
a division of Baker Publishing Group
P.O. Box 6287, Grand Rapids, MI 49516-6287
www.revellbooks.com

Printed in the United States of America

Library of Congress Cataloging-in-Publication Data
Newport, Olivia.
The dilemma of Charlotte Farrow : a novel / Olivia Newport.
p. cm. — (Avenue of dreams ; bk. 2)
ISBN 978-0-8007-2039-1 (pbk.)
1. Young women—Fiction. 2. Upper class women—Fiction. 3. World's Columbian Exposition (1893 : Chicago, Ill.)—Fiction. 4. Christian fiction. 5. Love stories. I. Title.
PS3614.E686D55 2012
813'.6—dc23 2012031654

This book is a work of fiction. Names, characters, places, and incidents are the product of the author's imagination or are used fictitiously.

13 14 15 16 17 18 19 7 6 5 4 3 2 1

Remembering my dad,
who loved me and wanted me
to be happy.

1

Kiss Henry for me."

Momentarily startled by hearing the words aloud, Charlotte Farrow glanced around, seeking assurance the moment was private.

"Don't worry." Lucy's green eyes glowed above her amber broadcloth traveling suit. "No one is listening to us."

At the back of the large carriage along the curb in front of the Banning mansion, the cab driver strapped the last trunk in place. Will Edwards slapped it in approval. In the other direction, Mr. Penard, the household butler, disappeared around the side of the house.

Charlotte reached for the hand of Lucy Banning Edwards and gripped fingers of friendship. "I'm going to miss you so much. Two months married and already off on an adventure."

Lucy laughed. "I never wanted a big fussy wedding, but Will promised my parents a proper honeymoon if they would let us get married quickly in June. But I couldn't very well leave the women's exhibit at the world's fair in the lurch, could I?"

Charlotte nodded. "You promised your services through July."

"This was our first opportunity. Two whole months alone with Will—I can't wait."

"It's not the honeymoon that bothers me, Miss Lucy." Shyness washed over the maid. "But then three months in New Jersey—that's so far away!"

"Will could hardly refuse the assignment. His firm was gracious to offer it and allow him to be near his mother through the holidays."

"Of course, it's perfect for Will. Still, I can't imagine being here without you." With one hand Charlotte fiddled with a strand of hair the color of damp hay. It had worked its way loose from the knot at the back of her neck, as it did most days.

"You'll be fine," Lucy assured her. "Be patient with Sarah. I've spoken to Penard and Mrs. Fletcher about her, but she's sure to make them think I've gone round the bend. I know she lacks polish, but she just needs some time."

"I'll do my best."

"We'll be moving around France at impulse, but after I get back from Europe, it will be simple enough to exchange letters. I'll let you know the address in New Jersey as soon as Will arranges accommodations."

"I've never had a proper letter."

Lucy leaned her head in close. "Charlotte, I know you have your reasons for keeping quiet about your life before you arrived on Prairie Avenue. I can only imagine what great sacrifices you've made for Henry. But this is your home now. I'll be back, and I expect to find you right here."

Charlotte nodded.

"On Thursday my family will return from the lake house," Lucy continued, "and the routine will go back to normal.

Leo will bring people home to dinner, and Richard will be back in school in a few weeks. I suspect Oliver and Pamela may make an announcement soon. You'll hardly notice I'm gone."

"I know I'll be busy."

Lucy straightened her simple beige hat with one brown feather. "And when the family gets back, Archie Shepard will be back as well. If you ask me, he'll be glad to see you."

Charlotte shook her head at the thought of the young coachman. "No, Miss Lucy, there's nothing between us."

A carriage slowed at the corner of Eighteenth Street and Prairie Avenue in front of the Glessners' Chicago home, three lots to the north and across the street from the Bannings. Bride and maid lifted their glances together at the visitors, craning their necks for a view down the block. The driver dropped out of his seat and opened the door to allow the tourists to roam for a few minutes.

"More gawkers." Lucy sighed. "They come from all over the country to see the world's fair, and then stop by Prairie Avenue to stare at us as if we're a sideshow on the Midway."

Charlotte did not respond. While the gapers who paraded through the neighborhood on a daily basis made her smooth her apron and adjust her cap if she happened to be outside, she understood their fascination. Her reaction had not been so different when she first arrived nearly a year ago. Life on Prairie Avenue was like nothing she had ever imagined.

"The Glessners must be getting tired of these cab drivers treating their address like a bus stop." Lucy tugged at her white gloves. "I suppose I've seen my last gawker, though! The fair will be over weeks before I come home."

"Mrs. Edwards, I believe we have a train to catch." Will

Edwards grinned. "If we miss the boat out of New York to France, we may have to go to England instead."

"I'm coming." Lucy squeezed Charlotte's hand one last time.

Charlotte waved as the carriage pulled away, then walked around the side of the Banning house to the female servants' entrance. With the family finishing a month in Lake Forest, away from the blistering August temperatures in Chicago, she slipped into a serene house.

Tall and clean-shaven, Mr. Penard looked up from the wide-planked table where he had spread his papers. "The family will be home the day after tomorrow," he said, as if Charlotte were not well aware. "I have a number of items to go over with you tonight."

"Yes, sir. I thought we would have a cold supper, if that meets your approval. The day is so warm still."

"Yes, that will be fine. You'll be back to helping Mrs. Fletcher with full meals soon enough."

Charlotte moved to the icebox for a liberal leftover portion of beef she had roasted the day before to serve to Will and Lucy Edwards. With bread, cheese, apples, and cucumber slices, the three servants sharing a meal tonight would be more than satisfied.

"Where is Sarah?" Penard looked up and scanned the room.

"The last I saw her, she was headed to the courtyard to bring the sheets in off the line." Charlotte lifted the sharpest knife in the kitchen from a drawer and laid it beside the roast on the butcher block. "They weren't dry before the laundress left. We'll make the beds tomorrow."

"Satisfactory." Penard laid his fountain pen down and laced his fingers together behind his head. "I must admit, Charlotte, that when you arrived here last October, I had my doubts about you. But you have learned well, and you've been quite trustworthy this summer to keep the house in order while the family is gone."

"Thank you, Mr. Penard." Charlotte glanced at the butler, who had already turned his attention back to his lists. She had Lucy to thank for arranging to leave Charlotte in Chicago while the family went to the lake. No one else had any notion why it was imperative she remain in the city.

"Along with the beds, the parlor must have a final dusting." Penard pressed his lips together in thought. "And you can show Sarah how to polish the silver satisfactorily."

"I'll be happy to."

"I do wish we had arranged for Sarah to join the staff a little sooner. I'm uncertain how quickly she is going to learn the way things must be done here. The assistant director at St. Andrew's assures me she's bright and capable."

Charlotte set three apples in a row on the counter. "Perhaps she needs time to adjust."

"Mrs. Edwards felt it would do her good to have some work experience, and I accepted the girl on her behalf."

"She has recommended other girls to families nearby, and I haven't heard of any who didn't work out."

Penard gave a half grunt. "If Sarah is grateful for her position, it is not evident. I wonder if Mrs. Edwards was fully aware of her temperament."

"It's just different from the orphanage, sir." Charlotte turned to take the cloth off a chunk of Wisconsin cheese on the counter. "She's used to helping with chores. Miss Lucy

. . . I mean, Mrs. Edwards says all the orphans at St. Andrew's have their responsibilities, and Sarah's been there six years."

"Yes, I understand they all must do for themselves in their setting, but does Sarah understand what it means to do for a family such as the Bannings? The work requires a distinctive demeanor."

"Mrs. Edwards says Sarah will sort herself out with a little patience." Charlotte drew the knife through the meat, slicing the beef as thinly as she could manage. One of the first things she had learned in the Banning kitchen was that Mr. Penard was a stickler about the thickness of his meat cuts.

Penard ordered his papers carefully. "I think I'll take these upstairs to my rooms to review the household accounts. If you need me, you know where to find me. You may notify me when the meal is ready." He tucked his chair under the table, then left the room, going up the stairs off the kitchen.

It seemed to Charlotte that Sarah ought to be back with the sheets by now. The linens would have to be ironed tonight if the maids were going to prepare the bedrooms tomorrow. Putting the knife down, Charlotte crossed the kitchen to the servants' hall that led to several interconnected workrooms as well as a door opening onto the courtyard. The Banning house jutted out at angles that surrounded three sides, and the row house next door closed in the fourth side except for a passage accommodating delivery carts. Clearly the brick used on this view of the house was less expensive than the stone walls facing Prairie Avenue, but Charlotte savored the enclosure. Something about it felt safe. The family spent little time outside. The winters were too cold, and in the summer they escaped to the lake house. Certain the Bannings would not step into the rear courtyard, Penard allowed the staff to set out pots of flowers and enjoy the lush patch of grass. Charlotte often lingered outside in the evening to inhale the night air before retiring to her stifling third-floor room.

Charlotte exhaled. Despite her defense of Sarah's abilities to Penard, she had her own doubts. In the day and a half since she had come from St. Andrew's Orphanage to the Bannings', sixteen-year-old Sarah Cummings had not completed a single task as requested. Charlotte already was aggravated at perpetually checking up on her and finding work half done. But she had promised Lucy to do her best with Sarah.

Sheets flapped in the wind above an empty basket, and Sarah was nowhere in sight. With a sigh, Charlotte reached for the first clothespin and began to pull the sheets off the line.

"Charlotte!"

Charlotte stilled her hands. Had she actually heard the hoarse whisper? That voice should not be on Banning property. She spun around, a sheet draped over her shoulder. Out of the shadows against the courtyard wall stepped a middle-aged woman holding a baby.

"Mrs. Given! What are you doing here?"

"I've been waiting for almost thirty minutes, hoping you would come out. He was sleeping, but now he's awake and I don't think I can keep him quiet. I was about to give up and knock at the back door."

Shock swelled through Charlotte as the little boy's hands reached for her eagerly. Swiftly she wrestled out of the sheet across her shoulders, dumping it in the basket, and took the baby in her own arms. She cooed in a low voice to keep him quiet. Looking up again, she whispered, "Mrs. Given, what's going on?"

"I have to leave town." The older woman stuffed the baby's

quilt and a small bundle in Charlotte's arms. "I'm on my way to the train now."

"But what about Henry? I can't keep him here. You know that."

Mrs. Given covered her eyes with one hand as her shoulders heaved once. "I have a family emergency. I truly have no choice. I can't take him, and I have to go. You'll have to work something out. I'm sorry I couldn't bring more of his things, but it was too much to manage on the streetcar."

Charlotte held the child tightly, wrapping him in the quilt he loved—her grandmother's quilt. He snuggled happily against her chest, tucking his head under her chin in his favorite way.

"You know I can't have him here!" Charlotte's eyes moved from left to right, scanning the courtyard. "Mr. Penard will dismiss me if he discovers I have a child." Without Lucy, Charlotte had no advocate. "What about your neighbor? Doesn't she sometimes help you watch him?"

"For an hour or two," Mrs. Given answered, "but I can't ask her to take on the care of a child when I don't know when I'll be back—or even if I'll be able to return."

"Please, Mrs. Given—"

The woman was resolute. "I've had two telegrams saying that I must come now. My sister wired the fare this morning. I'm sure St. Andrew's will take the boy, but I don't have time to see to that for you."

"You know I don't want him at St. Andrew's. That's why he's with you."

"I'm sorry. I have to be on the next train to Omaha." Brushing a strand of gray hair out of her face, Mary Given softened. "He's a lovely child, Charlotte, and you're a devoted mother. You'll always do what's best for him."

Within a few seconds, Charlotte was left standing in the courtyard with a laundry basket at her feet and an eleven-month-old boy squirming in her arms. Suddenly feeling weak, she set her son in the basket and watched absently as he pulled a corner of the sheet over his head and giggled. Her knees trembled. Uncertain they would support her slight weight, Charlotte crouched next to the basket and laid her hand on the child's feathery brown hair.

A shadow crossed her vision. Sarah.

"Where did that baby come from?" the girl demanded to know.

2

Charlotte sprang to her feet, startling the baby, who wailed in reflex.

"Charlotte, where did that baby come from?" Sarah paced swiftly around the yard in several directions, peering into every angle of the courtyard. "Did someone leave him in the laundry basket?"

"I came out to see what was taking you so long with the sheets," Charlotte mumbled.

"I took a little break." Sarah's hands went to her hips, her elbows jutting out. "I'm entitled. I was just coming back to get them. Why would someone leave a brat here? What are we supposed to do with it?"

The little boy took a deep breath and wailed again.

"He's not an 'it.' He's a little boy." Charlotte picked him up. "I suppose the first thing is to make him feel safe." She patted her son's back, right between the shoulders the way he liked it. The baby settled.

"Does Mr. Penard know he's here?" Sarah asked.

"How could he? We only just discovered him." So far she was speaking truth.

Sarah glanced toward the back door. "Is Mr. Penard in the kitchen?"

"He went up to his rooms. You still need to get the sheets off the line. Start at the far end."

Sarah shook her head. "I may be new to being in service, but I know we can't have a baby in the house without the butler knowing about it."

"Of course not. I do not propose we deceive Mr. Penard about the baby's presence." Charlotte's knees did not match her firmness of voice. "He'll have to decide what to do. I'll take the baby inside, and you get the sheets."

Sarah rolled her eyes but grabbed at a sheet.

Inside the kitchen, Charlotte inspected the space. This was no room for a crawling baby. Instinctively she kissed the top of her son's head. She turned three wooden chairs on their sides and arranged them against one wall, then put a folded tablecloth on the floor in the midst of the makeshift pen. Charlotte saw her son every Thursday and every other Sunday afternoon. She knew he was resourceful enough to climb his way out of this cage, but it had to suffice for at least a few minutes. She settled him among the chairs and handed him a wooden spoon to play with. He examined it happily with fingers and tongue.

The door slammed behind Sarah as she appeared with the laundry basket wedged against one hip. The girl strode across the room and dropped the basket overflowing with thick white sheets on one end of the table. "You haven't told him yet, have you?"

"I've only just got the baby settled." Charlotte moved toward the dish shelves. "I've got to get Mr. Penard's supper ready. He'll be down soon enough to see for himself."

"I'm going to tell him now." Sarah demanded Charlotte's gaze.

Charlotte's eyes did not flicker. "If you want to climb all the way up there to tell, go ahead."

As Sarah flounced up the narrow back stairs to the butler's apartment, Charlotte picked up the knife again and sliced more beef, working her lips in and out with the motion of the knife.

Soon enough she heard the urgent rhythm of double footsteps descending the stairs, Mr. Penard's larger feet pounding each step, followed by Sarah's smaller, lighter step. Charlotte glanced at the baby, who dropped the spoon and turned his head toward the sound on the stairs.

Mr. Penard appeared, his sleeves rolled up and his vest open. "I understand we have an unexpected situation."

"Yes, sir." Regardless of her lungs' protest, Charlotte held her breath and shoulders steady.

Mr. Penard's eyes moved to the child playing among the chairs. "Mrs. Edwards is well known for her tireless efforts on behalf of the children at St. Andrew's. It would seem someone in need has learned of her work and decided to trust a child to her care."

Sarah scoffed. "Why didn't they just take it to the orphanage?"

Penard and the baby inspected each other. The child grinned and banged his spoon against the side of a chair, his blue eyes wide and welcoming. Eventually Penard squatted for a closer look. "He seems to be well cared for. His circumstances cannot have been overly desperate."

"Perhaps there was an emergency." Charlotte picked up a fresh knife to slice bread. She weighed her words carefully.

She did not want to tell an outright lie, but she could not possibly tell the truth.

"He's here now and we have to deal with him," Mr. Penard said.

"He's probably getting hungry at this time of day. The food is ready."

"Doesn't a child of this age require a special diet?" Mr. Penard asked. "Sarah, what did the babies in the orphanage eat?"

The girl shrugged. "Soft foods."

"I noticed he has quite a few teeth." Charlotte spoke calmly, quelling the tremble in her hand. "I'm sure he can handle bread and some bits of apple and cheese."

"Why don't we just take it to St. Andrew's?" Sarah crossed her arms and with a foot nudged the edge of one of the chairs penning the child. "They have people there who know what to do with a baby, no matter what time of day. You just have to knock on the front door. They don't ask a lot of questions."

"No." Mr. Penard stood to his full height again. "We'll keep him here for the time being."

Turning to keep her face out of view, Charlotte breathed relief.

"If someone left him here for the attentions of Mrs. Edwards," Mr. Penard continued emphatically, "we must respect that it should be the family's decision to respond to this situation."

"Do you seriously expect they are going to want a baby?" Sarah eyed the child.

Penard scowled. "Miss Cummings, I suggest you learn your place before the family returns. It is your role to do what you're asked and to anticipate the family's needs and desires within reason. It is expressly *not* your role to make decisions on their behalf. We will keep the child until Thursday at least, and give Mr. and Mrs. Banning time to consider the situation and advise their wishes under these unusual circumstances."

"I'm going to feed him." Charlotte snuck in a smile at her son. "There's no telling when he ate last. Babies can get cranky rapidly when they get hungry."

"You seem well versed in the needs of children," Mr. Penard observed.

"I have three younger brothers." Charlotte laid a plate of bread on the table alongside the beef.

"I believe that's the first glimpse I've ever had into your personal history. Your experience certainly proves relevant."

Charlotte quickly transferred the remaining elements of the meal to the table, then leaned over the chairs and extracted the baby. Moving to the table, she settled him in her lap and broke some bread into small bites on a plate. He reached for a piece, put it in his mouth, and began working his jaw. Charlotte crumbled up some cheese as well.

Mr. Penard sat in his usual place at the head of the servants' table. Sarah sat across from Charlotte and began to fill her plate.

Mr. Penard cleared his throat. Sarah looked up, then put her hands in her lap.

"You are aware that it is our custom to give thanks before each meal," Mr. Penard chastised. "Certainly you learned to pray at the orphanage."

Sarah sighed yet again. Charlotte ignored her, stilled Henry's hands, and bowed her head for the prayer she knew Penard would offer. Every meal around the servants' table began with an expression of thanksgiving and penitence, whether or not individual members of the staff felt such sentiments.

Today, if she were to pray at all, Charlotte would have been inclined to request divine assistance in quelling her panic.

"This certainly disturbs our plan." Mr. Penard served himself a generous stack of sliced beef. "It is now Tuesday evening, and we have a great deal to accomplish by noon on Thursday, when the family is due to arrive. Obviously the child will require considerable attention."

"I don't mind taking care of him." Charlotte restrained herself from putting a protective arm around the baby, instead letting him wiggle in her lap.

Mr. Penard shook his head. "You're more familiar with the household. It will be far more efficient to have you concentrate on getting the house ready and leave it to Sarah to look after the child and help you as she is able."

Charlotte blanched.

Sarah protested. "Nobody at St. Andrew's said I would be taking care of a brat."

"Miss Cummings!" Penard's rebuke was sharp. "I remind you once again to learn your place. You will not speak to me that way. When you are part of a staff such as the one that serves the Bannings, you will do as you are asked for the good of the family. That is your priority."

"Mr. Penard, I really don't mind looking after the baby." Charlotte put a hand on Henry's head. "He seems to like me." The baby gave a drooling smile and reached for Charlotte's face.

"That much is true," Mr. Penard agreed. "Nevertheless, I feel it is a wise use of your experience in the household for you to focus on preparations for the family. Surely Sarah has sufficient experience with younger children at St. Andrew's to keep track of one child for a few days. Is that clear to both of you?"

Charlotte swallowed hard. "Yes, sir."

Sarah sighed petulantly. "Yes, sir."

Sarah held the baby a foot away from her body as she stomped upstairs two hours later. If Penard was so concerned about this brat, why didn't he take it to his room? After living in a dormitory for the last six years, Sarah finally had her own room, and now, after just two short nights, she had to share it with a baby. What if it didn't even sleep through the night?

She clutched the creature in one arm and with the other hand turned the glass knob to open her bedroom door.

"What are you doing in here?" Sarah stared at Charlotte, who was kneeling on the floor.

"I thought I could make a pallet for the baby." Charlotte spread a blanket over two thick quilts.

"But it's *my* room!"

"And you're lucky you don't have to share it with one of the other maids." Charlotte smoothed the blanket and tucked under a corner. "I'm just trying to be helpful. I can see you're not eager to look after him."

"Just because I don't want to doesn't mean I'm incompetent. I can make the best of the situation as well as you can."

"He might try to crawl."

"I know that." In truth, the idea had not crossed Sarah's mind.

"You'll have to watch him, but this way you won't have to worry about rolling over on him in bed."

"I was never going to let it sleep in my bed." When Charlotte reached for the baby, Sarah gladly released her hold.

"I brought the blankets down from the attic," Charlotte explained. "The Bannings haven't used them in years and won't miss them. It's enough layers to make him comfortable. I found some old diapers in the nursery boxes too."

"Growing up in an orphanage doesn't mean I like changing diapers."

"Don't be so dramatic. I'll do it this time. I helped with my brothers all the time." Laying the baby down on the makeshift pallet, Charlotte changed its diaper. Behind her, Sarah silently watched the steps. She was not going to repeat them any more often than absolutely required, and she certainly was not going to admit she was unsure of the procedure.

"I don't know why Penard didn't just let you take it." Sarah sprawled across her bed. "Maybe you should have it for the night anyway. Penard would never know."

"I would be happy to." Charlotte laid the quilt next to the baby on the floor. "But someone has to iron the sheets tonight, and Mr. Penard has assigned the task to me."

"He doesn't trust me," Sarah said.

"You're new. He has to get to know you and see you at work. He was the same way with me last year."

Sarah felt Charlotte's gaze and met it.

"Have you ever ironed a sheet?" Charlotte asked.

"It sounds like a ridiculous notion to me."

Charlotte nodded. "We didn't iron them where I came from, either, but Mr. Penard runs a meticulous household."

Sarah scoffed. "You sound as if you're afraid to cross him." So far Sarah Cummings had not detected much about Charlotte Farrow to interest her. The maid seemed to have not an ounce of spunk.

"He's the butler." Charlotte stroked the baby's cheek with

a forefinger, moving up and down in steady rhythm. "He has charge of the household. He takes his responsibilities seriously."

"So you think I should 'learn my place' too?" Sarah sat up, her eyes wide.

"What I think is that steady jobs are hard to come by," Charlotte said evenly. "Even many of the finest households have cut back on their staff. The Banning house has been a good place to work, and I intend to hang on to my position."

"So you're leaving it with me while you go off to show what a submissive servant you are?" Sarah stood up and peered down at the small intruder.

"Why don't you try calling him a boy, rather than 'it'?" Charlotte glanced up at the overhead bulb. "If you turn off the electric light, he'll go to sleep easily enough."

"Am I supposed to sit here and watch it sleep?"

Charlotte shrugged. "Try to rest yourself. Tomorrow will be a busy day. We'll all be up early."

"What if it wakes up during the night?"

"I don't think *he* will," Charlotte responded. "If you need help, I'll be just across the hall."

"After you iron the sheets."

"After I iron the sheets."

"So go."

"Good night. Let me know if you need something."

Charlotte flipped the light switch, and the room fell dim in the summer evening light sifting through the muslin curtains.

With Charlotte out of the room, Sarah blew out her breath. She never wanted to come to this place. How long were they going to make her stay?

In the hall, Charlotte leaned against a wall and pressed a fist into her mouth. She would be up for hours ironing those sheets. How could Penard think Sarah was prepared to take care of a baby? Charlotte could not imagine Penard would have ever agreed to engage Sarah if Lucy had not urged the arrangement.

By now Lucy would be settled in a Pullman sleeping car on a train crossing northern Ohio on her way to New York. Then she would be on a ship to cross the Atlantic Ocean. Mrs. Given was on a train hurtling west to Omaha.

Everyone Charlotte had dared to trust was gone.

She had been sixteen and petulant once herself. The little baby on that pallet behind the door had changed everything.

3

Charlotte could not resist a moment longer. She threw off the sheet, clammy with humidity, and swung her feet over the side of the bed. Moonlight was sufficient to guide her across the narrow room and into the hall, bringing Sarah's closed door into view. Charlotte put her hands on either side of the door frame and pressed her ear against Sarah's door.

She heard nothing. With a sigh, she considered her options. She had not allowed herself to fall asleep for a single moment, lest her baby cry out in the night and be ignored. Not since he was five weeks old had Charlotte been part of her son's nocturnal habits. She could only comfort herself with Mrs. Given's repeated reports that he had begun sleeping through the night at five months and now almost never woke before daylight broke. But would that hold true in a strange setting—on a pallet on the floor when he was used to a proper crib?

Charlotte moved one hand to the doorknob and twisted it slowly, knowing the wood swollen with summer heat and dampness would likely stick. A glance confirmed Sarah had not reacted to the slight pop. Charlotte gazed at her son sleeping on his back, sucking his left thumb and clenching the corner of his quilt with his right fist. She knew the corner. Her grandmother had claimed the blue calico of the corner was her favorite in the mosaic of color. Henry liked to grasp the thickness of the seam in that spot.

He was fine. Lest Sarah waken and stir up a ruckus, Charlotte withdrew, closing the door behind her.

In her own room, Charlotte opened the top drawer of her narrow dresser and removed the velvet bag Lucy had given her months ago. When Charlotte acquired the bag, she had a single Christmas coin to put in it. Now it held assorted coins, but not of much value. She dumped them into her hand, knowing as she did so that they were far from sufficient. Time was of the essence. She needed to collect her August wages before anyone found out the truth about the baby. If she did not have to hold back anything for Mrs. Given, she could add more to the pile than usual.

The entire farmhouse Charlotte had grown up in, cobbled together over several generations, was not much bigger than a few third floor servants' rooms, and it was a lifetime away from Prairie Avenue.

Henry's lifetime.

Charlotte's parents and three younger brothers lived in a farmhouse outside Greenville that had been in the family since before the Civil War. Despite the town's proximity to St. Louis, Charlotte had never actually visited the city, arriving instead in Chicago, three hundred miles away, with a newborn in her arms.

Her own parents had never seen Henry. His birth had been quick and much easier than she had been given to believe a first birth would be. Born several weeks early, he was on the small side. Mercifully, his father was away from home on a run to check his stills and to deliver bootleg to waiting customers. Feeling magnanimous, he had arranged for a girl even younger than Charlotte's twenty years to come in for a few hours each day and do the heavy work around the house for the cumbersome weeks of late pregnancy. Charlotte had known from her first look at the girl that she would be useless in a crisis, and the girl had lived up to the assessment. When Charlotte's water broke and labor began in earnest, she had to explain every little thing to be done.

Henry was suckling at Charlotte's breast when the girl said good night. Charlotte was not sorry to see her go. She had a limited number of hours before the girl would be back at noon the next day. As soon as she had gone, Charlotte got out of the bed where she had given birth, cleaned up what the girl had been too horrified to deal with, and packed a few tattered personal items, her grandmother's Bible and some food in one carpetbag and the baby quilt in another. All Charlotte's preparations had to be moved up a few weeks, but she had managed it. By then, though, the urge to rest overwhelmed her. She only woke again when the baby cried. Feeding him for the first time was a struggle, but she finally got him settled in the second carpetbag.

Charlotte left the rundown house on the outskirts of Greenville—a full thirty minutes before the girl would arrive and discover her missing—and headed for an abandoned hunter's cabin. As far as Charlotte could determine, she was the only one who had been in the cabin for years. After resting a few days and getting used to the baby, she was on a train to Chicago. Never for an instant had she considered returning to Greenville or anywhere near it.

For now, the baby was safe. She would have perhaps two

more days before Mr. Penard handed her son over to the family—two days before she would have to make an impossible decision.

By daylight, Charlotte was in the kitchen whisking a bowl of eggs into froth and buttering thick slices of bread to fry along with generous servings of bacon. Mr. Penard had specifically requested a hearty breakfast because the day would be demanding, especially now that it was uncertain Sarah would be available to help with the housework. Charlotte also squeezed several oranges and arranged sprigs of red and green grapes on three plates. For the baby, she took top milk from the jar the milkman had left the day before, warmed it on the stove, and stirred in some oatmeal to cook.

Wiping her hands on a dish towel, Charlotte stepped over to the open stairway and cocked her head. She was certain she had heard movement echoing down the shaft a few minutes earlier. Listening a moment longer, she was satisfied Sarah had wakened and would be down to breakfast on time—hopefully with the baby. By the time the griddle was hot enough for the eggs, bread, and bacon, Mr. Penard had descended the stairs in his dark navy morning coat, ready for an official day. Sarah appeared as Charlotte set the platter of scrambled eggs and toast on the table.

This time Sarah sat stiffly for the prayer. Charlotte wondered if the ache in her own heart counted as prayer.

"How did the child sleep?" Penard transferred eggs onto his plate.

"I didn't hear a peep out of him all night." Sarah bit ravenously into a piece of fried bread, the baby on her lap.

"I made him some oatmeal." Charlotte slid the small bowl and a spoon toward Sarah.

"I'll feed him as soon as I'm finished." Sarah swatted away the little hand reaching for her toast.

Charlotte swallowed her objections to Sarah's priorities, but the baby was not easily deterred. He squalled and spread his arms for Charlotte across the table.

"Sarah, why don't you attend to the child first?" Mr. Penard nodded toward the boy. "We have a great deal to discuss, and I don't intend to be talking over his cries."

Sarah dropped her toast and picked up the spoon. "Can't it just feed itself? At the orphanage we didn't coddle the little ones."

"It's oatmeal. Just think of the mess he'll make that you'll have to clean up. For now it's easier if you feed him."

At least Sarah had the sense to be gentle as she aimed a spoonful of oatmeal at the baby's mouth. He eagerly parted his lips to receive the nourishment, even as his face cracked with a grin for Charlotte.

"You must have a way with children, Charlotte." Mr. Penard waved a fork between his fingers toward the child. "This one seems particularly smitten with you."

Charlotte answered quickly. "He's a sweet child."

Sarah frowned across the table as she offered the baby another bite.

"Let's get down to business," Mr. Penard said. "I assume the bedding is all in order."

"Yes, sir." Charlotte nibbled a grape, which was about all she could manage this morning.

"Sarah, do you anticipate the child will require a nap later this morning?"

The girl shrugged. "How should I know what a strange baby does?"

"Most children this age nap twice a day," Charlotte supplied.

Mr. Penard nodded. "Then while he sleeps, Sarah, you may dust the parlor and polish the dining room table. Charlotte can show you where everything is. I'll polish the silver myself."

Sarah chomped on her bread again.

"Sarah, it is appropriate for you to acknowledge that I've spoken to you." Mr. Penard's tone was flat but his meaning clear.

Sarah eyes flickered. "Yes, sir."

"Just be sure to check on him frequently," Charlotte said. "He might wake up frightened in a strange place. It will be difficult to hear him if he cries."

The butler turned his attention to Charlotte. "Mrs. Fletcher has provided a list of the meat cuts she would like to have available in the kitchen upon her arrival tomorrow. You will visit the butcher's shop and make the arrangements for delivery in the morning."

"Certainly." Henry was reaching for food again. Sarah seemed in no hurry to satisfy him. When she finally moved the spoon toward the child's mouth again, Charlotte permitted herself another grape.

"And then there is the green grocer's," Penard continued. "Mrs. Fletcher asks that you use your best judgment and select a colorful variety. Three bushels should be sufficient to begin with. Since all the coachmen are still in Lake Forest, I have arranged a day driver to be at your disposal for the morning. You may use the service carriage."

"Thank you, sir." Charlotte's heart quickened. Using a

carriage would allow her to complete the errands more quickly and come home to her son—or at least come home to the house where someone else was caring for her son.

Sarah sniffed its diaper and decided the mess was not urgent enough to attend to. It was acting tired finally, none too soon to suit her. She had been with it for four hours already. Why old Penard did not just give the stupid brat to the stupid kitchen maid, she could not fathom. Charlotte actually seemed to want to take care of the baby, after all.

As Sarah laid it on the pallet in her room, blue eyes stared at her and she looked at them for the first time. It wasn't such a bad face when she thought about it. Not thin and sallow like so many of the babies who turned up at the orphanage. Sometimes it took weeks of tedious feeding to make them look human. The baby did not seem to miss wherever it had come from. Sarah would have thought it would be squalling for the mother who had abandoned it. As its blue eyes fluttered and closed in slumber, Sarah considered whether it would be so awful to look after it for a few days. She would be Nanny Sarah, and that was a far cry from the scullery maid she was hired to be, or whatever sort of maid Charlotte Farrow fancied herself to be.

Nanny Sarah. That might not be terrible—at least until she could figure out another release from this unbearable captivity.

It was soundly sleeping now, breathing deep and regular, thumb in mouth. Sarah made sure not to leave any personal items on the floor. She had no idea how long it would sleep, and she did not like Charlotte telling her what to do, but inevitably she would have to run up and down the stairs to check on it. She had not yet seen it crawl, but Charlotte seemed to think it would. Certainly she was not going to sit there and stare at it during what might be a long nap. She backed out of the room and closed the door quietly behind her.

Sarah had hoped to simply sneak out to the courtyard and let old Penard think she was upstairs with the creature, but he was there at the bottom of the stairs waiting for her with a cotton rag in one hand and a tin of vegetable oil soap in the other. Sarah recognized it as a basic tool for cleaning tables. Occasionally some church ladies would decide to serve the poor by polishing the tables at St. Andrew's, and the older girls would end up doing the work while the ladies drank tea the cook brewed for them. Sarah did not like the way the soap smelled, nor the memories it evoked.

Keeping conversation to a minimum, Sarah took the supplies and moved through the butler's pantry that separated the kitchen from the dining room. She slowed her steps enough to take in the floor-to-ceiling cabinetry, framed in wood with glass doors, and the deep sink with its own faucet and running water. The black and white floor tiles were a smaller size of the same pattern the kitchen featured.

Sarah had seen little of the house so far, other than the cursory tour Mr. Penard had given on the afternoon she arrived. In addition to the kitchen and workrooms, the downstairs held a spacious dining room, a broad foyer, the parlor, the master bedroom, and Mr. Banning's private study. If the baby had not yet awakened when she finished polishing table, chairs, and sideboard, she was supposed to also do the round mahogany table in the foyer and the side tables in the parlor. The marble staircase off the foyer led to the remainder of the family and guest bedrooms, but Sarah was not to use those stairs.

Sarah pried open the tin, dipped the rag in, and began rubbing haphazardly at the long oak dining room table. Her eyes lifted to the parted drapes adorning the windows looking out on Prairie Avenue. Broad bands of buff-colored taffeta trimmed in gold beads swept back claret-toned velvet from the centers of the wide windows. Mirror image pale blue swags topped the oak-framed windows. Sarah, however, was not looking at the draperies. The rubbing motion slowed as her gaze followed the movements of the strangers outside.

The men in their gray suits and striped vests lacked the bearing of the men Sarah had seen coming and going from Prairie Avenue homes in the last two days, and the women's dresses were closer to her own garb than the latest 1893 fashions the women of Prairie Avenue boasted. Unabashed children stared and pointed—all of them fairgoers lured into creating a spectacle of themselves as they absorbed the spectacle that was Prairie Avenue.

Across the street, a neighbor glided along the short walkway to her waiting carriage, never once turning her head to acknowledge the presence of spectators. Sarah's lips turned up at one end. The woman showed her class with every step. Someday, Sarah thought, she would be the one to show her class. She was not going to spend her life in service.

The Pullman carriage rolled by just then. Mr. Penard had pointed it out to her two days earlier with a caution not to gawk. As if she would ever gawk, as if she would ever accept that she did not deserve to travel in such a carriage herself.

"Sarah, I suspect you may be daydreaming."

Mr. Penard's voice from his pantry fractured her reverie. Sarah dipped the rag in the tin once again and rubbed the tabletop more convincingly. Someday she would prove that she was better than this.

"Good morning, Mr. Mason." Charlotte spoke brightly to the butcher, who was more likely to produce choice cuts if she indulged in conversation.

"Good morning, Miss Farrow. Am I to understand by your presence that the family returns soon?"

Charlotte nodded. "Tomorrow, midday. I have a list of the meats Mrs. Fletcher wants delivered."

Mr. Mason smiled, set his hands on his hips, and looked at the ceiling. "Let's see. If I know your Mrs. Fletcher, the list asks for two racks of lamb, eight lamb kidneys, three beef roasts with no more than half an inch of fat, calves livers, four chickens, a large goose, and a Virginia ham."

Charlotte laughed. "She also wonders if you have a wild turkey."

"She knows it takes an extra day to get one of those, but I'll try to work my magic."

"So we can expect your delivery by ten in the morning?"

"Nine-thirty."

"Thank you, Mr. Mason."

Charlotte returned to the Banning service carriage with the hired driver. It was far from the family's best—hardly more than an enamel-coated work cart complete with scratches—but she was grateful for its efficiencies, and in the summer she appreciated the open top. She shared the space with three empty bushel baskets, which would be filled within minutes at the shop of the only green grocer Mrs. Fletcher would tolerate. Then she could go home again to make the beds. At least there she might have some notion of whether her son was being properly looked after. She did not care if she did not leave the house again as long as he was there.

Charlotte did not trust Sarah Cummings with a child—anyone's child, but particularly not hers. The fact that the girl could freely take Henry out of her sight and Charlotte could not protest nearly provoked her to sobs. Yet she refused to cry. No one could know Henry was hers. If anyone suspected the truth, she and Henry would be put out on the street summarily. Mr. Penard would no longer feel obliged to discover the will of the Bannings regarding the baby. The household staff was his to deal with as he saw fit, and Charlotte knew perfectly well he would not tolerate a maid with a child. Even after nearly a year of faithful service in the Banning household, Charlotte did not take her position for granted.

As the laden cart rumbled back toward Prairie Avenue, Charlotte sat upright in her seat, determined not to give in to the looming despair that crushed her chest.

4

Logically Charlotte could tell herself it did not matter how often she checked the time. The hands of the clock did not move any faster. Still, she glanced at the timepiece on the kitchen mantel over and over. The family was due back any minute now, and the house was as ready as it could be. Charlotte and Sarah sat in the spotless kitchen, hesitant to move lest their shifting cause disorder they would not have time to remedy. The baby amused himself on a blanket on the kitchen floor. Charlotte watched him in her peripheral vision, not permitting herself a full-face gaze.

One more night had passed with her son slumbering across the hall, but still Charlotte had no plan for how to withstand the blustering storm when the truth leaped from her heart to the Bannings' faces. And surely a storm was coming if she did not simply take her son and leave. She missed Lucy Banning Edwards keenly. Lucy would have known what to do.

"What was that?" Sarah jumped up from the table and lurched toward the door leading from the kitchen into the servants' hallway.

Charlotte followed. "The servants' carriage must be here. That means the family will be right behind." Looking past

Sarah through the window, she saw the carriage pull up alongside the servants' entrance. Sarah flounced into the hall without looking back at the baby playing happily on the blanket. Relishing the private moment, Charlotte smiled broadly at her son, who responded by leaning to one side to get to his knees and beginning to crawl toward her. In an expert movement and with a giggle of delight, he left the confines of the blanket.

"Oh no, you don't!" Charlotte swooped in to pick him up. She snuck in a kiss and settled him on her hip just as she heard the voices in the servants' hall. From the sounds, she concluded that Karl, an under-coachman, had driven one of the smaller carriages and brought home the cook, the parlor maid, the ladies' maid, and a groom. Footsteps and chatter filled the hall.

Mrs. Fletcher appeared in the kitchen and stopped in her tracks. "That's a baby!"

"Yes, it is." Charlotte forced herself not to smile with pride and said the words—technically true—she had carefully rehearsed. "He turned up in the yard on Tuesday."

"What do you mean, 'turned up'?"

Sarah pushed her way past the glut of staff still shedding belongings in the hall and burst into the kitchen. "We found him in the laundry basket in the courtyard. I've been put in charge of him." She reached possessively for the baby and transferred him to her own hip.

Mrs. Fletcher raised an eyebrow at the slender stranger in her kitchen. "I assume you are Sarah Cummings."

"Yes, and I'm to be the nanny."

"My understanding is you were to begin as a scullery maid and be of some help with the never-ending work in the kitchen."

"That was before this situation arose."

Mrs. Fletcher's gaze sputtered toward Charlotte. "Where is Mr. Penard? I can't have this child underfoot in my kitchen."

"I'm right here." Mr. Penard pushed open the door from his butler's pantry. "I'm afraid we have no alternative for the moment. I will of course speak to Mr. and Mrs. Banning as soon as they are settled."

"Why should they concern themselves with an abandoned child?" Mrs. Fletcher's face bore only confusion at the notion.

Charlotte glanced up and flickered a smile at the familiar faces she had not seen in a month. By now Elsie, the ladies' maid, and Lina, the new parlor maid, had removed their hats. They stood wordlessly with Karl, the under-coachman.

"My suspicion is that the child was left for Mrs. Edwards," Mr. Penard explained to the onlookers. "It is not our place to decide his disposition. I will speak to the Bannings tomorrow morning after breakfast. In the meantime, none of you will make any reference to his presence within earshot of the family. Is that clear?"

Charlotte scanned the group, seeing nods all around. This was not an edict any of them would want to violate. A few more hours. One more night at best.

"Your arrival can only mean we are to expect the family within the hour," Mr. Penard said. "I have never known Mr. Banning to be imprecise in his travel arrangements. Please sort yourselves out immediately and take up your posts. This is not a half day off for any of you."

Mrs. Fletcher sighed, looked back at Sarah, and said flatly, "I'm sure he's a charming child, but the kitchen is a dangerous place for a baby. If you fancy yourself a nanny, then I expect you will keep him out of my way."

Sarah's eyes flashed. "I grew up at St. Andrew's. I know a thing or two about babies!"

"Then do a thing or two about this one."

Archie Shepard pulled on the reins to slow the duo of Belgian draft horses as he turned onto Prairie Avenue. The entourage had made good time traveling down from Lake Forest, arriving within a few minutes of the time Mr. Penard expected them. Archie drove the largest Quinby carriage, carrying Samuel and Flora Banning and Mrs. Banning's sister, Violet Newcomb. Behind him was a carriage with the top down, allowing the three Banning brothers—Oliver, Leo, and Richard—to enjoy the open air. Only Richard had spent the entire month in Lake Forest. Though Oliver and Leo had careers and social lives to attend to, all three had spent the final week with their parents and returned together. A third coach carried luggage and household supplies not needed in Lake Forest during the winter. The family might return to the lake for the odd weekend before the weather turned completely, but the summer holiday was ended.

To Archie, the house looked just as it had a month earlier, with its solid oak front door embedded in stone facing. In many respects it was a welcome sight. But Archie was already missing the cooler air that blew around the Bannings' lake house. He had lived in Chicago his entire life, yet the August heat and humidity wilted him every summer, especially when he was required to wear a full livery.

Archie swung down from the bench atop the carriage and reached for the door.

"Every year at the end of the summer, I am amazed at

how grateful I am to return home," Flora Banning said when Archie pulled the door open.

Archie offered his hand, and she took it to aid her exit.

"I do wonder if I ought to go directly to my own home." Violet Newcomb shifted in the seat and leaned toward the door herself.

"Nonsense," Flora answered. "It's Thursday. The entire family makes a point to be home for dinner on Thursdays."

"But we've been together for a month, Flora, and before that we had all the flurry of Lucy's wedding. A few quiet days would be welcome."

"I insist you come inside," Flora said. "We've been in the carriage for hours. Mrs. Fletcher can prepare some refreshment and you can have a satisfying dinner before Archie takes you home. Tomorrow will be soon enough for your own staff to resume their duties."

Archie now offered his hand to Miss Newcomb, who smiled at him as she took it. "Thank you, Archie."

Samuel Banning emerged from the carriage and immediately checked his pocket watch. "We're right on time. Penard should have everything ready. Perhaps I'll telephone the office."

Flora swatted at her husband's arm. "Samuel, you promised me you'd finish the week on holiday. You can go back to that dreary law office on Monday."

"It's not dreary to me, my dear."

Despite Samuel's gentle rebuff, Archie could see his employer had no serious intent to return to his office prematurely.

"Why are these people loitering?" Flora wrinkled her nose at the gaggle of onlookers gathered on the corner of Eighteenth and Prairie to climb back into their carriage. "I'm of a mind to tell them all to go home and leave us alone."

"Pay them no mind at all, dear." Samuel took his wife's arm. "It's all part of the promotion of the world's fair. It will be over soon enough."

With the family on their way to the front door, where Mr. Penard already stood waiting to attend their wishes, Archie secured the carriage door, climbed to the driver's seat, and clicked his tongue. He would have to drive around the block to enter the coach house from the most efficient direction, and then he would have to oversee the grooms to ensure the horses were properly cooled and brushed. His recent promotion to head coachman pleased him, though he believed his future was not fixed on the coach house.

His thoughts strayed to the scene that would greet him when he entered the house again after all these weeks. The slim form of Charlotte Farrow had haunted him the whole time he was away. Her face, sometimes calm but always secretive, was a careful harbor of her mysterious emotions. He had watched her for months, speaking a kind word whenever he had opportunity and noticing the flush it caused in her freckled complexion. Archie hoped she would be at her post in the kitchen when he finally stepped through the servants' hall.

Sarah had to admit that dinner preparations in the Banning house were far more complex than she anticipated. The kitchen operated on as strict a routine as the kitchen at St. Andrew's, all to serve an elaborate dinner for six, rather than an elemental meal for four hundred. The food stores Charlotte had arranged provided all the resources Mrs. Fletcher needed for cold cucumber soup, two kinds of fruit bread, baked trout, roast goose, garlic-seasoned potatoes, fresh garden greens with apricots and walnuts covered in a tangy dressing, and the family's favorite red velvet cake. The table laid with china, crystal, and sterling silver was as beautiful as anything Sarah had seen in a painting or picture book. When the family gathered, the electric lights would be turned off, and the twin candelabras rising from the floral arrangements would be lit. Polished silver would be luminous in the gleam of candles.

Sarah had managed to absent herself from much of the fuss during the meal preparation, taking the brat upstairs for an afternoon nap and opting to indulge in one herself. The creature had fussed a bit more than usual, until Sarah relented and changed his diaper. The cloths he had soiled would soon need washing or he wouldn't have a fresh one. Sarah resolved to mention this to Charlotte as she closed her eyes and dreamed of dinner.

Charlotte knew from the rhythmic patter that it was Sarah on the narrow back stairs. Besides, she was the only one missing from the assembly in the kitchen, where the servants had gathered for their evening meal. Blowing out her breath, Charlotte willed herself not to turn from the stove to gaze at her son the instant Sarah entered the room with him. Mrs. Fletcher stood next to her at the stove, basting the family's goose as Charlotte tended the chickens the staff would consume momentarily.

"What have you done with the tablecloth?" Sarah said brusquely. "I can't put it . . . him . . . directly on the floor."

Charlotte swallowed the impulse to speak sharply and did not turn toward Sarah. "The tablecloth should be right where you left it. I assure you I have not borrowed it."

"What have you made for him to eat?"

"If you mash up some potato, I'm sure he can manage," Charlotte suggested, "and you'll find bananas in the larder."

Sarah did not bother to smooth the blanket before she plopped the child down with a huff. "I would think his meal preparation was your responsibility."

Charlotte felt Mrs. Fletcher's scrutiny as she lifted a pot lid to stir the potatoes.

"You may think you are nanny," Mrs. Fletcher said to Sarah, "but I rather think you have simply been given temporary charge of a distraction. This should be resolved in the morning and the two of you will have nothing to squabble over in my kitchen."

Charlotte stifled a moan. Henry might be sent away as soon as the morning. She was not prepared to leave so soon. The thought of making her peace with St. Andrew's after all turned her stomach.

Across the table, Archie Shepard was trying to catch her eye. Charlotte recognized the effort but did not surrender to the urge to satisfy him. His eyes would ask for an explanation she could not give.

After their own meal, the staff moved smoothly into serving the family meal. Mr. Penard and Archie had both changed to white-tie formal wear to serve dinner. Charlotte was so used to seeing Archie serve soup that she no longer wondered why he continued in a footman's role once he became head coachman. In her newest, crispest white apron, Charlotte took up her post against a wall in the dining room, waiting to quietly move between courses to remove dishes to the butler's pantry. She willed color into her face as she imagined the devastation the morning could bring if no alternative dawned during the long night.

The family had finished the meat course and put their forks down. Charlotte stepped forward to remove the meat dishes as Mr. Penard carried in the garlic-seasoned potatoes. As she lifted the plate from in front of Oliver Banning, she noticed Mr. Penard had leaned hard enough against the butler's pantry door that it remained propped open—surely unintentional. In a year's time, she had never seen Mr. Penard take a wrong step. The fastidious butler would never abide anyone else's error in allowing the family to see into the place from which their food appeared. Surely he would quickly and discreetly close the door and hope none of the family had noticed.

When she moved to Miss Newcomb's place, Charlotte nearly dropped the china. The butler's pantry remained wide open to both kitchen and dining room, and toddling into the dining room, upright and independent, was a small boy with a round face, feathery brown hair, and vivid blue eyes.

His first steps!

5

Silence shrouded the dining room as all heads turned toward the child toddling with uncertain steps. Gleeful, he took four small steps into the room, then paused to adjust his balance and pivot toward the spectators. Unsuccessful, he landed on his bottom. Undeterred, he pushed himself upright once again and took a few more steps.

Charlotte stood immobilized at the table with two meat plates in her hands as thc baby's movements clearly identified her as his intended destination. Mrs. Given had never said Henry was ready to walk! Mr. Penard divested himself of the serving dish at the sideboard and turned rapidly to carry the child out of the room, closing the door to the butler's pantry behind him.

Barely breathing, Charlotte moved on to Richard's place and removed his plate.

"I'm afraid I don't understand what just happened." Flora Banning scanned the faces around the dinner table.

"Penard's got a secret baby!" Fifteen-year-old Richard twisted his lips up at one end. "Maybe he has a secret wife in the attic!"

"Don't be ridiculous, Richard." Flora pressed her lips together in a frown.

"I'm sure there's a more logical explanation," Leo said.

"Penard had better be back shortly to enlighten us." Oliver scowled in the direction of the butler's pantry.

"Yes, I will be most curious to hear what he has to say." Samuel Banning cleared his throat heavily.

Violet Newcomb, the boys' aunt, sighed. "Let's not make this more complicated than it has to be."

"Violet," Flora said, "you know perfectly well that if such an instance occurred at your house, you would demand an immediate explanation."

"But the explanation could be one of any number of things," Violet said.

"It really could be a secret wife." Richard's eyes lit with the possibility.

"Hush, Richard," Flora said. "You're not being the least bit helpful."

Charlotte's chest tightened. Breathless, she picked up one more plate and carried the stack into the butler's pantry. Setting the china in the sink, she forced herself to take a deep breath and peered into the kitchen.

"Miss Cummings!" Penard said sharply, thrusting the child at the girl with a force that made Charlotte flinch. "Have I not been sufficiently clear on your duties and the importance of executing them in a competent manner?"

Sarah's faced blanched. "I didn't know he could walk."

"That is irrelevant. If you'd been attentive to him, you would have noticed that he did in fact navigate a considerable distance by whatever means. You have placed me in a most compromised position, and you have not heard the end of this."

Penard pivoted, stormed back into the pantry, and paused long enough to straighten the sleeves of his jacket. His poise returned with the gesture. "Charlotte, please finish clearing the meat plates and I will serve the vegetables."

"Mr. Penard," Charlotte said uncertainly, "I've heard what they're saying in there. They're expecting you to explain."

"I intend to, but the meal will proceed."

"Yes, sir."

Charlotte followed Mr. Penard back into the dining room and stepped around the table to collect the remaining meat plates. Mr. Penard picked up the potato platter. Charlotte disposed of the dishes by putting them in the sink, then peeked through the space where the pantry door met its frame.

Mr. Penard smoothly offered potatoes to each member of the family, while beginning his explanation. "I regret that your homecoming meal was disturbed in that manner, and I would imagine you have questions. I will do what I can to answer them with the plain facts. On Tuesday afternoon, the maids preparing the house for your arrival discovered a child in the courtyard. He seems to have arrived without any information as to his background and circumstances, though he appears well cared for. It was my immediate belief that his arrival was somehow tied to Mrs. Edwards's well-known work on the behalf of orphaned children, and that perhaps his being left here was an appeal for her good graces.

"The no-doubt destitute mother could not have known that Miss Lucy has left for an extended period of time. Against that reality, I did not feel it was my place to discern what Mrs. Edwards would have done. My intention was to leave such a decision to the wisdom of the family, and I have assigned the new scullery maid the task of looking after him until you have opportunity to consider the matter. I had believed, of course, that the matter was not so urgent as to interrupt your meal tonight. I accept full responsibility and beg your forgiveness."

Leo pushed a fork into his potatoes. "That's quite a speech, Penard."

Oliver shifted in his chair. "I appreciate your deference to our wishes, Penard, but it seems logical to simply contact St. Andrew's. Father, if you wish, I'll attend to the matter in the morning."

"Yes, perhaps that would be the simplest disposition," Samuel agreed.

"Simplest, but not best." Violet looked around the table. "I may be sticking my nose in where it does not belong, but it seems to me that Penard has a rightful understanding of the situation."

"What are you saying, Violet?" Flora asked.

"If someone left a child here for the sake of Lucy's wisdom, then we should endeavor to apply wisdom as well."

"But Lucy's on a ship in the middle of the Atlantic," Samuel pointed out, "and not due back to US shores for eight weeks or more."

"And I am *not* going to advocate that we interrupt her long-awaited and well-deserved honeymoon with this matter." Flora was adamant. "I will not entertain discussion of a telegram."

"I know we cannot confer with Lucy." Violet casually moved a fork around her plate. "However, that does not mean we cannot do as she might wish. If this child's mother meant for him to be at the orphanage, she would have taken him directly there rather than risk being discovered on Prairie Avenue of all places."

"Mmm." Samuel twisted his mouth thoughtfully. "You make a cogent argument."

"What would it hurt to take a bit of time to consider what is truly in the best interest of the child," Violet asked, "or what might please Lucy?"

Mr. Penard had withdrawn from the table after completing his simple explanation and apology. Now he stood at the sideboard and signaled with a nearly imperceptible tilt of his head that Charlotte should bring in the green salads. Reluctant to miss a single word of the family's conversation, Charlotte nevertheless went through to the kitchen and began arranging salad greens and fruit on the plates the cook had left to chill in the icebox.

"What's going on in there?" Sarah wrestled with a wriggling Henry on her lap.

"I think he wants to walk some more. Why don't you go in the hall and let him down?" Charlotte ached to be the one to open her arms and receive the gleeful toddler at the end of his trek.

"He'll have his whole life to walk." Sarah's arms made a vise for the child now. "You tell me this minute what they're saying in there. Am I to be sent back to St. Andrew's?"

Charlotte clenched her jaw. "Are you always this self-absorbed? They are not even discussing you. It's the child who matters at the moment."

"Are they going to send him to St. Andrew's?"

"I don't think so." Charlotte relaxed with the relief she heard in her own voice. Her shoulders softened and her hands quickened. "At least, they are going to consider what's best for him in the long run."

"Are you certain they're not discussing me?"

"Quite." Charlotte balanced salad plates along her arms and moved back into the pantry.

Mr. Penard met her there and relieved some of her load. "You may clear the potato dishes," he said.

She slipped into the dining room behind him, anxious to hear the conversation as she laid salad plates on the sideboard.

"I think that would be an enviable solution to the question," Flora said conclusively.

"It would certainly seem to bring great benefit to both parties," Samuel agreed.

Charlotte's mind screamed to discover what she had missed. She glanced at the butler, wondering if he would tell her or consider the discussion none of her business. As she collected empty plates once again, she hardly allowed herself to breathe.

"How long might that take to accomplish?" Violet inquired.

Flora tilted her head to one side. "I will have to write a letter, of course, thoroughly explaining the situation. And I suppose they will want to have time to consider, or perhaps even meet the child before deciding whether to adopt him."

Adopt him!

"Perhaps we should try to discern his temperament before making such a proposal," Leo said. "If he should prove to be a difficult child, Cousin Louisa might harbor ill feelings against you."

"That's a wise suggestion." Flora nodded. "I have not seen Cousin Louisa since she was a child herself. After all, she is only a second cousin once removed."

"I think she may be our *third* cousin," Violet said mildly. "Hardly any relation at all, but a good starting point for finding a suitable home for the child."

"I have not met her husband. Her mother has made me

aware of the delicate issue of her dismay in not being able to bear a child. I certainly do not want to add to her suffering with a difficult baby."

Charlotte knew she could stop this unfolding drama only one way—claim Henry as her son and suffer the consequences of a year of duplicity. And then where would Henry be? Her own destitute circumstances would make it even more probable he would end up at the orphanage.

Plates clinked in her trembling hands as she moved into the pantry again to add them to the sink. How could she possibly think of letting them send Henry away to a stranger? But how could she possibly do better for him? Once again, she moved to the closed door for what she might discern there.

"You have little to lose by taking your time," Violet suggested. "If Lucy should contact you, then you will have opportunity for consultation after all. In the meantime, you may make every effort to evaluate the circumstances as she would herself."

"So we're really going to keep a baby in the house?" Richard's voice lilted in anticipation.

"It would seem so." Samuel Banning picked up his fork to approach the salad Penard set in front of him. "I would be remiss not to inquire who will be looking after the child during this period of investigation, and at what expense."

"If I might speak to the question, sir," Penard said, divesting himself of the last salad.

"Please."

"As you are aware, on Miss Lucy's recommendation, we have engaged a new maid to train for the kitchen. The girl is from the orphanage herself. Since she has not yet begun a full range of duties, the household would experience the least unsettledness if we simply reassign her to the child's care for the time being. She can always take up her kitchen training at a later date."

Charlotte's heart fell, though she hardly expected anything else. Sarah would be caring for her son. At least he was not being sent away in the morning, or even in the next few weeks.

"We shall have to open the nursery and nanny's quarters," Flora said. "Charlotte can oversee that endeavor in the morning. I believe she's familiar with the resources available in the attic to outfit the rooms. The girl can look after him there. There may even be an old nursemaid's uniform."

"Then it's settled." Samuel dabbed his beard with his napkin. "I hope now we can return to a peaceful meal."

Mr. Penard bowed slightly. "I deeply regret the intrusion and offer my sincerest apologies. You will be pleased to know that Mrs. Fletcher has baked a red velvet cake for your homecoming."

"Lucy's favorite." Violet nodded in pleasure. "We shall have to enjoy it on her behalf."

Charlotte eased out her breath, hoping for some relief of the pressure in her chest as she gripped the edge of the sink. She had not felt this ill in many months, but in between the waves assaulting her stomach came the realization that she had received the gift of time.

A hand on her shoulder made her gasp.

"Charlotte," Archie Shepard said, "are you all right?"

6

Sarah set the baby on the cloth on the kitchen floor and turned a couple of chairs on their sides around him.

Mrs. Fletcher scowled. "What makes you think that's going to make him stay put?"

"I have to put him somewhere, and this is what we did before. Is breakfast ready yet?"

"I do not plan my menus around the needs of an infant. We're serving sausages, sweet rolls, and fruit."

"He doesn't have enough teeth for that," Sarah said. "He should have oatmeal again, I suppose."

Mrs. Fletcher gestured toward the stove. "Help yourself."

"But I haven't learned to cook yet. You were supposed to teach me. That's why they sent me here." Sarah glanced around the kitchen. "Where's Charlotte?" Sarah asked. That stupid maid would not let him starve.

"I've sent her to the cellar for the day's vegetables."

"Maybe I'll just mash another banana then, and stir in some milk. We do have fresh milk, don't we?"

Mrs. Fletcher sighed but did not answer.

Sarah opened the icebox and removed a jar of milk. "We must instruct the milkman to increase the daily order. Babies drink a lot of milk, and this one will be here for a few weeks at least."

The cook spun and planted her fists on her hips. "You will not tell me how to manage my kitchen."

"I simply asked for milk for the baby." Jar and bowl in hand, Sarah withdrew to the other end of the kitchen, a safe distance from the spatula Mrs. Fletcher wielded in one fist. "I suppose you were here in the days when there was a nursery. I do hope the furniture in the attic is suitable."

"It was good enough for the Banning children," Mrs. Fletcher muttered. "I've no doubt it will do for a temporary arrangement for a foundling."

"He'll need a proper high chair for feedings, and a carpet to play on. Of course, my bed will be in the room next to his—not in the servants' quarters."

The baby clattered against his chair-cage. The chair he used to pull himself up slid under his slight weight, and he tumbled to the floor in a wail.

"Take him out of that ridiculous contraption," Mrs. Fletcher demanded. "You saw with your own eyes that the child can walk. You can't confine him for your convenience." She stepped across the room and picked up both chairs, roughly replacing them at the table and leaving the way wide open for the child to go wherever he wanted.

"Fine!" Sarah abandoned the bowl and milk. "I'll take him with me to find a banana." She snatched the howling child from the floor and stomped into the back hall, passing Archie the coachman as he arrived in search of his breakfast.

"How are things in the coach house on this first morning back?" Mrs. Fletcher asked from her post at the stove.

"A fair bit better than they are in here, from the looks of that girl." Archie scratched under his chin.

"She's still learning her place, and if you ask me, that high-minded butler has confused the question by putting the child in her care."

"Is that why she's come to the house," Archie asked, "to learn her place?"

"She is only here because Mrs. Edwards asked us to keep the girl at least until she returned to Chicago. But as long as she's here, she will only make herself miserable by ignoring the order of things."

Archie glanced into the empty hall after the girl. "Mrs. Edwards generally has a sound reason when she arranges these things."

"Mrs. Edwards is on a boat in the middle of the ocean."

"Yes, with her husband, who is not from Prairie Avenue, because Mrs. Edwards dares to disrupt the order of things as well."

Mrs. Fletcher turned to inspect him. "Since when have you become the troublemaker?"

Archie met her gaze. "I'm not a troublemaker. For the time being, I'm just a coachman hungry for his breakfast."

"Has Mr. Penard spoken to you about the furniture in the attic?" Mrs. Fletcher dropped a knife through the center of a large sweet roll fresh from the oven.

"Only in passing."

"You'll have to go up there and see what Charlotte wants for the nursery."

"I thought Sarah was to be in the nursery."

"She is. But for some reason Mrs. Banning put Charlotte in charge of setting things up. I expect Mr. Penard will ask you to carry things down for her."

"I'll be happy to. I'll get Karl to help. Karl has a stronger back than the rest of the grooms put together." Archie considered the opportunity to change the subject. "Charlotte seemed troubled last night. How is she this morning?"

Mrs. Fletcher shrugged and dropped a pair of sausages on the sizzling griddle. "She was up before dawn doing just what she was supposed to be doing." She glanced over her shoulder at the door to the hall. "It does seem it's taking her overly long to bring the vegetables up."

"I think having the baby here has affected her somehow," Archie said cautiously. "Has she said anything to you about why it would be troublesome for her to have a baby around?"

"We don't discuss our personal lives. She has never seemed interested."

Archie nodded. "That's my experience too. I inquired last night when it seemed to me she might collapse, but she would not answer me."

"You're exaggerating. Why would she collapse over a baby? Once she gets the nursery set up, she won't even have anything to do with him."

Archie suspected that was precisely what bothered Charlotte, but he held his tongue.

"All I know is I've lost both my kitchen maids for the day," Mrs. Fletcher groused, "with a mountain of food to prepare for the weekend."

Charlotte came in from the hallway with a basket of vegetables hanging over her arm. "I'm sorry I took so long, Mrs. Fletcher." She laid the produce on the counter.

Archie waited to see if she would offer more explanation for her tardiness, but she did not.

"The laundress is coming today," Mrs. Fletcher announced.

"I only just learned she is Karl's sister. In any event, she'll come in two days a week from now on. You'll be glad to know you won't have to iron any more sheets for a while."

Charlotte shrugged. "I didn't mind so much."

"I'm going to the workroom to see if the water is heating up satisfactorily. You can mind the sausages."

"Yes, ma'am." Charlotte moved to the array of sausage slices and began arranging them on the griddle.

Archie moved toward her, but she seemed to step away. "Charlotte, I only meant to be helpful last night."

"I know." She did not look at him. "You needn't bother about it."

"You must know how I feel about you."

His voice was low, but the words paralyzed her nevertheless. It happened every time he came near enough for her to smell his scent or to feel the brush of air against her skin that his movements caused. Her breath stalled every time, and every time she forced it out in an even flow. His hand followed hers as she reached for more meat, his fingers brushing against hers.

"I've made no secret these last few months," Archie said, "that I have come to admire you. I only hope to understand you as well."

Charlotte picked up a spatula and flipped several sausages. "You've been most kind to me, Archie."

He had first held her hand last Christmas Eve, eight months ago, while singing a carol at church, and she had pulled away after only a few seconds. Longing for his touch now would accomplish nothing.

"I have not been nearly as kind as I would like to be," Archie murmured, standing behind her at the stove, "if only you would allow me."

She could never tell him. Never. "I think our breakfast is nearly ready. Would you mind calling up the stairs to the other maids, and let the grooms know?"

"You can ask me to do anything, Charlotte Farrow," he said. "Anything."

No. Never.

The staff breakfast behind her, Charlotte moved on to the dining room to ensure all was ready for the family's breakfast. The coffee finished perking just as Leo entered and took his seat.

"Your newspaper, sir." Charlotte laid the paper in front of him.

"Sausage and fruit will be sufficient, and coffee of course." Leo unfolded the newspaper. "Let's see what the commentators have to say about the World's Columbian Exposition today. The news in Lake Forest always seemed stale." He scanned his paper. "We missed Illinois Day at the fair yesterday. Five thousand members of the Illinois National Guard marched down the Midway Plaisance, followed by warriors from around the globe. Governor Altgeld himself led the parade. That must have been a sight."

"Yes, sir." Charlotte murmured in the same way she always did when family members spoke to her.

Leo dropped his newspaper. "Charlotte, the rumor around the house is that you're afraid to go up in Mr. Ferris's wheel at the fair." Leo grinned at the maid.

"I admit it makes me a bit nervous, sir." Charlotte dipped her head.

"I'm an engineer and I believe the construction is sound. Lucy's husband is an architect, and he believes it's safe. Don't you trust us?"

"Please, Mr. Leo. You put me in a difficult spot." Charlotte busied herself by needlessly lifting the flap of a breadwarmer to check on the sweet rolls.

"You still have a couple of months," Leo said. "Maybe you'll change your mind."

She doubted it. "May I bring you anything else from the kitchen?"

"No, not from the kitchen." Leo bit into a sausage. "However, I found myself awake much of the night wondering about the child. I can't help wondering about the mother who would have dropped him off here, and whether there might be some way to trace her. She may have regrets."

Questions. Fears. No regrets.

"I'm not sure what else to say, sir." Charlotte picked up the coffeepot on the sideboard and needlessly moved it about six inches.

"What did he have with him when he arrived? Perhaps there's a label in a piece of clothing or a note tucked in somewhere."

"We didn't find anything like that." Charlotte chose her words carefully to speak truth. "He arrived only with a faded quilt, a change of clothing, and a few ordinary diaper cloths."

"What became of the quilt? May I see it?"

The request startled Charlotte. "I . . . I suppose it's in Sarah's room. I believe the child sleeps with it."

"Would you mind going to get it?" Leo asked.

"Yes, sir. Right away, sir."

What could he possibly hope to tell by a quilt more than twenty years old? Charlotte scooted through the kitchen and up the back stairs, her heart beating fast. On the third floor, she paused outside Sarah's closed door and knocked softly.

"Yes?"

"It's Charlotte. Mr. Leo has asked to see the baby's quilt."

Sarah yanked the door open and glowered. "What on earth for?"

"He's hopeful he might find an idea of where it came from." Charlotte pressed into the room and gathered her grandmother's quilt from where Sarah had thrown it under the bed. Sitting upright on his pallet, Henry reached out, and Charlotte gave his hand a quick pat.

"You can't just barge in here." Sarah snatched up Henry.

"I'm following Mr. Leo's instructions." Charlotte moved out to the hall again with the quilt in hand.

Sarah followed Charlotte through the hall, down the stairs, and across the kitchen, protesting every step of the way. When she reached the butler's pantry, Charlotte stopped in her tracks and spun.

"Why are you following me?" Charlotte folded the quilt in quarters with sharp motions. "Have you fed the baby yet this morning?"

Sarah drew her shoulders back. "I was just about to."

"Now is a good time to do that." Charlotte pushed into the dining room again.

"Here it is, Mr. Leo." Charlotte offered the quilt as if on a tray.

Leo put down his newspaper and received the quilt, spreading it in his hands for examination. "It's made by a skillful needleworker. I've listened to my mother remark on quilts enough to know that these narrow rows of fabric are not easy to piece together. And it's been well mended over the years. This child came from a place where he was loved."

Yes, he did.

"But it's common calico fabric," he said, "the sort that one might buy in any mercantile around the state for working class day dresses." He shook his head. "I doubt we can determine anything from this." He handed the quilt back to Charlotte. "Thank you."

"It was good of you to try, Mr. Leo." She meant what she said—though she was relieved he had discerned nothing useful.

7

Both sleeves rolled up, Charlotte plunged an arm into the bucket of soapy water, pulled out the rag, and slapped it against the oak slats of the floor once again. Controlled circular movements while on her knees had begun to reveal the sheen hidden beneath years of disuse. Already she had swept the rooms twice to excavate the true wood surface that could be swabbed to a shine, rather than merely creating mud by adding water to dust. Her knees bore witness that she had scrubbed nearly half the floor.

Charlotte had only seen behind the door to these rooms one other time in her months in the Banning house. During Miss Lucy's engagement to Will Edwards, a few gifts of small furniture had been stored temporarily in this room, which was situated on an oddly placed half level with access to both the family bedrooms and the servants' staircase. Charlotte had heard the story then of the room's history. Richard, the youngest of the four Banning children, had left the nursery years ago, and the longtime nanny who had served the family since Oliver's birth had retired. In the intervening time, many of the items that had furnished the rooms had been stored in the attic, but a few of the larger pieces were still in the room.

Leaning back on her heels, Charlotte took stock. The wallpaper featured twisted vines of roses and had responded well to a damp rag. She had not yet removed the cloths draping the heavy shelves or dresser and mirror—pieces that undoubtedly had been too cumbersome to move to the attic—but she had peeked beneath them to admire the luster and craftsmanship of the furnishings. A quick polish was all they would need. The large room was the day nursery—or so Charlotte had been told—where the children spent their waking hours. She had deduced from the stacks of crates and trunks in the attic that the wide mahogany shelves behind brass-trimmed doors once had been stocked to overflowing with books, toys, and dolls. Lucy had preserved a few of her favorite dolls, with china heads and stuffed calico bodies, in her adult bedroom, along with the taffeta and silk dresses that fit them perfectly. Charlotte could easily imagine a broad shelf laden with whatever had made Lucy happy as a child, along with the carved train cars and tin soldiers her brothers must have played with.

Charlotte thought of the simple wooden spoon she had handed her little boy on the afternoon he arrived at the Banning house, probably the best plaything he had ever had. At Mrs. Given's house, he used to like a ball made out of strip rags wound tightly together, and pounding a tin cup against the floor was a favorite pastime. Even as she imagined him lying on the pallet in Sarah's room with his quilt—her quilt—Charlotte resisted the urge to dash to the servants' quarters and look in on her sleeping son, who was down for a late morning nap. Sarah had made quite the production out of saying how closely she was going to watch him, though Charlotte was sure Sarah was merely using the time for a nap herself.

At least Sarah had stopped calling Henry an "it." Most of the time.

No one called Henry anything but "the baby" or "the child" or "him." Charlotte did not dare speak his name aloud. She knew he would turn toward the familiar sound if she did and meet her eyes in recognition. Even if they were alone, she tried not to call him anything in particular. She could not risk that anyone might hear.

Charlotte sloshed more water on the floor. Sarah was smug about Charlotte's having been given the task to scour the nursery rooms, but the truth was Charlotte was grateful to be doing something for her son.

Behind the large dayroom were two small bedrooms. One, hardly more than an alcove, would be Henry's, and Sarah would occupy the other, which was not much larger than the servant rooms on the third floor. For the moment, Henry was safe and was likely to be with the Bannings for a few weeks. But then what?

It was the best thing for Henry, she was sure of it. Look where he was. Soon he would sleep peacefully in the Banning nursery, of all places, while people were trying to sort out what was best for him. And Charlotte could be nearby and see him every day, not just Thursdays and every other Sunday afternoon. She felt like Moses's mother, hired to take care of her own child. Her grandmother had loved that Bible story and frequently offered it as evidence that God always had a plan.

Clattering steps in the hall pulled Charlotte's gaze toward the sound. Archie and Karl carried two trunks between them, one stacked on top of the other.

"Both of these trunks are linens," Archie said. "Where do you want them?"

"Out of the way over there until I finish the floor." Charlotte pointed to a corner she had already scrubbed. "Did you see the high chair and the crib?"

"Both seem to be in working order. We'll bring them down next."

Karl brushed dust off his hands. "There's a fine-looking rocking horse up there—one of the big ones with a red mane and a leather saddle."

"Oh!" Charlotte said. "Don't you think he's small for a rocking horse?"

"He looks like a strapping boy to me," Karl responded, "and he's only going to get bigger. There's no harm in bringing it down, is there?"

"No, I suppose not." Charlotte was nervous at the thought of Sarah Cummings in charge of her baby on a rocking horse. "Thank you for the help. I don't expect either of you planned to spend your day crawling around an attic. You're to have the afternoon off, aren't you, Karl?"

The under-coachman nodded. "The Midway Plaisance is wooing me. I'm going up on the wheel today."

"Go on upstairs and sort out what to bring down next." Archie nudged Karl back toward the door. "I'll be there in a moment."

Karl left, and Archie squatted on the floor beside Charlotte. His closeness unnerved her.

"You don't have to bring everything." Charlotte swirled water in a direction that would demand she move away from Archie. "It's just one child, and he may not be here long." She could barely stand to say that aloud.

"Still," Archie said, "Sarah will be staying in these rooms, and she'll need a bed as well, and a table for her own meals."

"You're right, of course." Charlotte leaned into the rag again. "If you see a carpet, bring that as well."

"Charlotte," Archie said, "I was hoping you would agree to come out with me on your next Sunday half day. I can trade the afternoon with Karl and get a few hours myself."

Archie was nothing if not persistent. Charlotte scrubbed even harder. "I'm afraid that's not possible."

"Why not?"

"I can't explain it." She knew if she looked at him, even for a second, his shining eyes would grip her. Charlotte could not risk glimpsing Archie's eyes, much less spending her time off with him.

"I wish you'd try."

She merely shook her head and sloshed more water. Finally he stood up and left the room.

Charlotte paused, staring into the hallway and listening to his steps on the stairs. Archie Shepard was a good man. He did not deserve to get entangled with this. And she could not take that risk.

Charlotte scrubbed faster and harder. With the two bedrooms to do and furniture to consider, she could not spend all day on this floor. If these rooms were going to be her son's world, they would be the best she could make them.

Henry's world.

As Charlotte moved her bucket to the final quadrant of the room, she allowed herself to picture Henry here, in a high chair or in the crib or playing on a carpet.

His bright smile on the rocking horse—when he was bigger.

The certain meals.

The toys that would amuse him.

A safe bed.

A good school in a few years.

Security.

Choices he could make for himself.

Her throat locked with the uncertainty that she could ever give her son that kind of a childhood.

But Mrs. Banning's cousin could. She might not be as wealthy as the Bannings, but Charlotte had no doubt she was well positioned. And she wanted a child.

Maybe Charlotte's child.

Charlotte scrubbed furiously.

8

Charlotte balanced the tray against her hip with one hand and used her free hand to turn the knob on the day nursery door. Every time she did this, five times a day, her stomach tightened as she imagined what she might find on the other side. Had Sarah bathed Henry? Had she made sure he had a good nap? Was his diaper dry?

Charlotte crossed the nursery with firm steps and set the tray on the small round table draped almost to the floor with a pink-and-green-checked cloth and topped by a simple white linen square that could be changed daily.

"What have you brought me for lunch?" Sarah sniffed, then frowned.

Charlotte ignored the girl's tone as she lifted the tea towel covering Sarah's plate. "Mrs. Fletcher has been creative with leftovers again. The lamb is from Tuesday and the rice croquettes and vegetables from last night."

Sarah had moved into the nursery with the baby six days ago and spent her days as separate from the rest of the household staff as she could manage. The trays Charlotte carried up included nourishment for both Sarah and Henry. Charlotte knew Sarah always ate before feeding the baby, but at least

Henry's small bowls were scraped empty when Charlotte picked up the trays. Her son was not going hungry.

Arrangements for Henry had fallen into a routine. Though she spent most of her time in the nursery, once each afternoon Sarah carried Henry down the narrow back stairs and put him in a buggy for a stroll. Archie and Karl had come to expect the request for the buggy to be wheeled from the coach house to the servants' entrance at midafternoon. Charlotte had found a child's straw hat in the cartons of clothes Richard used to wear, and the entire staff giggled at how adorable Henry looked under the hat when he sat up in the buggy with his broad grin and iridescent blue eyes.

Charlotte took Sarah's plate off the tray and arranged a place setting at the table. She put Henry's bowl on the high chair's wooden tray.

Her son whined a little and toddled toward Charlotte, pulling on her skirt when he reached her. She glanced down at him and steeled herself not to pick him up. "I think he's hungry."

"That makes two of us." Sarah picked up a fork.

"Well, only one of you is old enough to feed the other. His rice is creamed with a bit of soft spinach." Charlotte stirred the mixture, but Sarah barely glanced at it. "There are a few bites of scraped meat he might like to try." Charlotte allowed herself to drop a hand and brush the boy's head ever so briefly.

Sarah put half a rice croquette on her fork and stuffed it in her mouth as Henry slapped a hand against the leg of the high chair. He opened his mouth and gave a cry.

"I rather think he wants to eat," Charlotte said.

"And he will." Sarah stabbed a piece of lamb.

"Mr. Penard asked me to give you a message." Charlotte

finally relented, picked up the baby, and settled him in the chair. She left the dish out of his desperate reach, though, still hoping that Sarah would choose to fulfill her responsibility to feed the baby before he upended the bowl on the floor.

"What does he want?"

"It's a request from the family, actually. Mrs. Banning has asked to see the child during tea this afternoon and interview you as to his temperament and progress."

Sarah dropped her fork. "What do they want me to say?"

Irritation welled. "Simply tell them how he is adjusting. Is he sleeping? Is he in good temper? Does he seem to like to play?"

Sarah shrugged. "He's a baby. Everyone knows not to play with babies. It only makes them cranky."

"Or it makes them happy." Charlotte could ignore her son's hunger no longer. She dipped his little spoon in the creamed rice and offered it to him.

"Nonsense."

"All you have to do is answer their questions," Charlotte said. She gave Henry another bite. "You might want to give him a bath and make sure he has fresh clothing."

"Don't tell me how to do my job."

"Maybe if you would do your job, I wouldn't have to."

"Stop feeding him. I'll do it." Sarah roughly grabbed the spoon and stabbed it into the creamed rice.

"Tea is promptly at four." Charlotte pulled the door closed behind her and leaned against it, her eyes closed. Why didn't this get easier? At least she and Henry were under the same roof.

"Charlotte?"

Archie.

Her eyes fluttered open and she tried to make them bright. "Hello, Archie."

"Are you all right?"

She met his warm brown eyes briefly, then broke the gaze. She had learned from months of experience that if she looked into his eyes for more than a few seconds, her heart would quicken and her breathing would grow shallow. She would want to reach out and touch him, and she simply could not afford to give in to such a sensation.

"Of course I'm all right," she finally managed to say. "I've just brought lunch up."

Archie glanced at the closed door. "And I suppose Sarah is just as unappreciative as she always is."

Charlotte nodded. "I don't think she cares much for the child."

Archie shrugged. "She seems to fancy herself quite the nanny."

"She's not even an under-nursemaid," Charlotte insisted, "just a girl who has been told to look after a baby temporarily. They only opened up the nursery so he wouldn't be underfoot in the kitchen."

Archie searched out her eyes again. "I think the Bannings truly are trying to determine what's best for him. His mother brought him here for a reason, and they are trying to respect her wishes somehow."

Charlotte could not form the words for a response.

"I know you miss Mrs. Edwards," Archie said softly. "She's one of the kindest people I've ever known, and I believe she's fond of you."

Charlotte nodded.

"I don't know everything that is between you, but her

parents are trying to do as Mrs. Edwards would do. The baby will have a home soon enough—perhaps a very good one. Maybe you shouldn't let yourself get so close to the situation."

If only he knew it was far too late for such advice.

"Lina could bring the trays up to the nursery." Archie raised his eyebrows.

"That's not necessary." Charlotte was not going to trade away her only opportunities to check on Henry. She pushed away from the door.

Archie reached for her arm as she brushed past, but Charlotte hastened her pace and did not look back.

Charlotte pushed the tea cart into the parlor promptly at four o'clock. Lina had come to the kitchen a few minutes ago and reported that Mrs. Banning had expressly asked that Charlotte serve the tea today. Charlotte had dashed up to the third floor to put on her evening service uniform and a proper cap, all the while scrambling for any reason why Mrs. Banning should ask for her. When she entered the parlor, she was even more dumbfounded.

No one had told her Miss Brewster was coming. She sat on the green and gold settee next to Violet Newcomb. Charlotte had never heard a complete story of how Emmaline Brewster was related to sisters Violet Newcomb and Flora Banning, but she had served Emmaline dinner a number of times earlier in the summer when she came from New Hampshire for Lucy's wedding. She had stayed with Miss Newcomb at the time, but Charlotte knew she had been up to the lake house with the family.

"Thank you, Charlotte," Flora Banning said perfunctorily.

"Hello, Charlotte." Emmaline Brewster caught the maid's eye briefly.

Charlotte curtseyed and dipped her head. "Miss Brewster. Miss Newcomb."

"Charlotte," Flora said, "Emmaline has been enjoying a few extra days in Lake Forest as the guest of family friends, but she has now decided to stay in the city for a few weeks to take in the world's fair and other cultural attractions before she goes home to New Hampshire. I have offered her Lucy's suite for her accommodations."

"Yes, ma'am." Charlotte nervously poured tea into china cups and wondered why Mrs. Banning was telling her this.

"I have a particular need which you may be able to satisfy," Emmaline said. "You will recall I was traveling with my own ladies' maid. I had to dismiss her rather abruptly because I discovered her dallying with a young man in a most unsuitable manner. Mrs. Banning has kindly given her consent for you to assist me as a ladies' maid during my stay in Chicago."

"Yes, ma'am," Charlotte said.

Violet chimed in. "I told Emmie you have some experience in the role with Lucy and assured her you know what you're doing."

"Yes, ma'am."

"I'm confident we'll get on well enough for a few weeks," Emmaline said. "I realize you have other responsibilities. Primarily I will ask for assistance in the morning and in the evening, and of course when changes of clothing are required during the day."

"I want Emmie to enjoy her time in Chicago," Violet said, "so I'm arranging some social engagements for her."

"She'll be making calls and receiving callers," Flora added.

Charlotte nodded. "Shall I come to the suite tonight?"

"I shall expect you at about ten o'clock."

Flora Banning, in her favorite floral-patterned William Morris side chair, gestured that she was ready for her tea. The cup clinked faintly as Charlotte handed it to her before turning to the tray for a plate of pastries to set before the three women.

"One more thing," Flora said. "When you go back to the kitchen, please inform Sarah that I am ready for her to bring the child. I must decide whether it would be suitable to write to my cousin Louisa. I want to reassure myself of the child's temperament before I do so."

"Yes, ma'am." Choking on trepidation, Charlotte forced her feet to move.

Did he not trust her to walk through the dining room on her own?

Sarah resented Mr. Penard's insistence that he would accompany her to her interview in the parlor. It was true she had not been in the dining room since the day the Bannings came home from the lake, but what did he think would happen if she walked through? However, she had the good sense not to provoke an argument with the butler as they crossed through the family's living space.

In the foyer, Sarah glanced at the spotless marble staircase that swept in from both sides and curved up with walnut banisters to the second story, and it occurred to her that as the nanny she should be using those front stairs rather than creeping up and down the back way like a servant. The baby wriggled in her arms, and she squeezed him more tightly. She had scrubbed him spotless not an hour ago and dressed him only ten minutes ago, and she was not going to risk a smudge now.

She glared a warning at him as she tugged his smocked pale blue cotton gown down over his belly. The black boots on his feet were far too big, but it was the best she could do with what she had found in the boxes.

Penard paused at the arched doorway that led to the parlor and bowed slightly. Behind him, Sarah dutifully bent a knee and dropped her head slightly.

"Mrs. Banning," Penard said, "the girl is here with the child."

The nanny, you mean!

Penard stepped to one side to position himself invisibly against the wall. Sarah tried to wish him away. She did not need him.

"Let me see the child, please." Mrs. Banning waved Sarah toward her. "Set him down."

Sarah slid the boy off her hip, retaining her grip on one hand to assure he stood steadily. The last thing she needed was for him to stumble in the parlor and knock over something valuable. She would be sent back to the scullery in a heartbeat if that happened. The child compliantly stood still and stared, curious, at the three women scrutinizing him.

"He's a handsome child!" Violet exclaimed. "I thought so a week ago, and I think so now."

"How have you found his temperament?" Mrs. Banning asked.

"He's very little trouble," Sarah said truthfully. "He eats well five times a day and sleeps soundly at night."

"What does he eat?"

"I have found that he is particularly fond of barley with cream." Sarah remembered that Charlotte once made that observation. "And bread is always welcome."

"No vegetables?" Violet asked.

"Today he had spinach with his rice, and he seemed most eager, ma'am." He had been so demanding that she had to forgo the last bites of her own lunch to shovel rice into him. Sarah was proud of herself for a polished rendition of events.

"Oh, he's too young for many vegetables," Flora protested. "Babies need milk and cereal, perhaps a bit of soft egg. Who prepares his meals, Sarah?"

"Mrs. Fletcher, ma'am, or Charlotte. The maid brings them up."

"On what schedule?"

Sarah tried to picture the clock over the fireplace in the nursery. When did Charlotte come? Finally it came to her. "He eats promptly at seven, ten, one, four, and seven," she said, echoing the instructions Penard had given. However, she had skipped his four o'clock feeding today to have him ready for this inspection. Any moment now he might begin to protest.

"Nothing during the night?" Mrs. Banning asked.

"No, ma'am. Feeding a child during the night is not advised."

"I'm sure you saw a lot of babies at St. Andrew's. Is there anything about the disposition of this baby that concerns you in comparison?"

"No, ma'am. Children who are well managed will be little disturbance." Sarah had no doubt she was managing this child just fine.

Mrs. Banning looked at her sister. "Then perhaps it is time

to write to Cousin Louisa and invite her to visit Chicago and meet this child. I'm sure Lucy would be pleased if we found an agreeable solution before she returns from Europe."

Sarah's thoughts leapt out of the room. If Mrs. Banning's Cousin Louisa adopted this brat, she would need a nanny. If she managed things properly the next few weeks, she might never scrub a vegetable again.

Emmaline Brewster's blue eyes glowed. The child was enchanting! Cousin Louisa was young and married. She had plenty of time to find happiness with a family. At age thirty-three, Emmaline's options had narrowed considerably. She was here. Louisa was not. She might never know the love of a man, but this child could make her long wait for happiness worthwhile. This was meant to be.

She watched as the girl picked him up and carried him from the room, followed by the butler's soft footsteps. The baby was truly captivating. His eyes and complexion even favored hers. Already she wanted to see him again.

9

"What's for supper?"

When Charlotte turned and grimaced, Archie answered with a grin. He would look at that face every chance he got, grimace or not.

"My sister and I used to nag my ma on a daily basis about what was for supper," Archie said. "The answer was always the same: 'food—and you'll eat it and be grateful.'"

"Food—and you'll eat it and be grateful," Charlotte echoed lightly. She stood at a butcher block heaped with chopped onion, turnips, and beets and dropped a knife through the end of a thick bundle of celery. On the stove were two large pots of water on the brink of boiling.

Archie shuffled toward the stove, brushing Charlotte's shoulder in the process. "Perhaps I'll have to decipher for myself."

Charlotte blew out her breath and gestured to the preparations spread around the kitchen. "Turnip soup with soda muffins, baked halibut, broiled lamb kidneys, onion custard, baked beets, tropical Waldorf salad, and apple snowballs."

Archie chuckled. "I know how much you like making apple snowballs."

"They do seem rather a lot of work, if you ask me," Charlotte said. "Coring them, stuffing the centers, rolling them in rice, wrapping in cloths, boiling, the extra butter and sugar—all so it will look like a snowball in summer. Why not just eat a fresh apple and appreciate it for what it is?"

"My ma would have liked you." Archie saw her face soften as she glanced at him out of the side of her eye. "Will the staff enjoy the same menu?"

"Pot roast instead of kidneys, no onion custard, plain old baked apples."

"Good. I like pot roast and plain old baked apples." Archie interrupted her chopping motion to snatch a walnut meant for the salad. Charlotte slapped his hand, which was what he hoped for. He caught her fingers and squeezed quickly. Charlotte did not lift her eyes, but he was close enough to hear her breathe, and he was sure the rhythm had changed. In just a few seconds Charlotte did what he expected and pulled her hand away. She dragged the back of her knife across the butcher block to corral the chopped celery.

"Is Miss Brewster making special menu requests?" Archie moved away from Charlotte.

"Not so far, but Mrs. Banning does seem determined to impress her. Mrs. Fletcher is out right now putting in orders all over town for next week's deliveries as if every day were Christmas dinner. Every night has a different list of guests."

"Which leaves you with all the work for Saturday dinner."

Charlotte glanced at the clock. "And any moment now Miss Emmaline is going to call me to help her get out of the gown she wore this afternoon. Heaven forbid she come down to dinner in the same dress. We could really use another pair of hands in the kitchen."

"That was supposed to be Sarah," Archie said. "I know someone has to take care of the baby, but I'm sorry you have to bear the brunt of the work because she's not down here."

"There's nothing to be done about it."

"I saw her out with the baby buggy not long ago, walking up and down the avenue. The fresh air seems good for the baby. He looked happy."

"I doubt that's what Sarah has on her mind," Charlotte murmured.

"One of the Pullmans' under-coachmen seemed to be paying quite a bit of attention to her."

"That would be Kenny. Their maids say she doesn't want anything to do with him."

"That much was clear." Archie chuckled. "But he was making a noble effort." He paused to pull a chair away from the table. "You look exhausted. Are you sure you can't take ten minutes to sit down?"

Charlotte glanced at the chair, then looked at Archie. "My feet are awfully achy. Maybe five."

Archie held the chair for her until she was seated. She said five minutes, but he knew it would be more like three. He sat next to her, removing his blue and yellow jacket with the brass buttons and tossing a pamphlet on the table in one smooth motion. "The beginning of September is too warm for these woolen uniforms."

Charlotte reached for the pamphlet. "What are you doing with this?"

He shrugged. "It's just a pamphlet. People are handing them out all around town."

"I know what it is, and I know who is handing them out. If Mr. Penard finds this, he'll be fit to be tied." Charlotte folded the pamphlet and pressed a crease across it. "Anarchist propaganda."

Archie was surprised to hear such a phrase out of Charlotte's gentle mouth. "That's a rather extreme position."

"That's what Mr. Penard calls it." Charlotte laid the pamphlet on her lap, half out of sight. "And ever since June when the governor pardoned the men convicted of the Haymarket riot, he has nothing kind to say about the people who stir up the workers."

"Those men were railroaded into prison. No one ever had any proof they threw that bomb into the crowd or intended to hurt anyone."

"I don't think that matters," Charlotte said. "The point is, Mr. Penard thinks of them as rabble-rousers and malcontents, and the people who hand out these pamphlets are the same lot."

"These people have a point, Charlotte. We work very long days for a pitiful wage. All they're suggesting is a measure of justice."

"But an eight-hour workday? That would be like having a half day off every day. Is that realistic?"

"It's certainly humane," Archie said. "The families of Prairie Avenue might have to hire more people and not run them half as ragged."

Charlotte turned to face him square on. "Are you unhappy being in service?"

Archie soaked up her eyes. For once she was really looking at him, her blue-gray eyes shrouded in secrets as they always were. "Unhappy? Not exactly. The Bannings are probably more reasonable than many households. But that doesn't mean I expect to be a footman or a coachman my entire life."

"A butler, then? You can work your way up, I'm sure."

"There must be something else." He shook his head. "Look at you, for instance. Up before dawn to work on meals, up and down stairs all day to the nursery, and now every evening you're waiting up half the night for a woman who needs help unbuttoning her dress. In the middle of all that, you're afraid to take ten minutes off your feet."

Charlotte sighed heavily as Archie continued.

"All this for a few hours off on Thursday and every other Sunday afternoon—if the family doesn't plan something that requires your presence, which they do without giving it a second thought. We're supposed to be grateful for the pittance they pay us."

"But we have a secure place to live and enough to eat—at a time when jobs are hard to find. Mr. Banning says we're in an economic depression."

"A place to live is not a life," Archie countered. "The butler is the only one of us who is even allowed to be married."

"But Mr. Penard's not married, and he works as hard as we do."

"He could be, though. And his rooms are a far cry more comfortable than mine or yours—enough for a family. If we were to marry . . . I mean . . . one of us . . . well, we'd have to leave our positions. We're held hostage."

Charlotte fingered the pamphlet. "Still, it's dangerous to have this literature in the house. Mr. Penard will have your head." She stood up, smoothed her work apron, and pressed the pamphlet against Archie's chest with her flat palm. "I would hate to see that happen."

Archie covered her hand with his against his beating heart. "Charlotte, if I were to leave service, I would want to take you with me."

Her eyes held a story. If only he could sort out what it was.

"It sounds to me as if you and Sarah are the ones who want out of service," she finally said.

"I don't want Sarah," he said sharply. "I want you."

She met his eyes for the longest she ever had. Why did she have such a wall around herself?

The back door opened, and Sarah bustled through with the baby.

Charlotte's abrupt movement away from Archie was not unnoticed by Sarah, who entered the kitchen with a drowsy baby in her arms. The coachman stuffed something in his pocket as he reached for his uniform jacket.

"I've left the buggy outside," she said. "You may tell Karl to put it away."

"Karl knows what to do when you come back from airing the baby." Archie buttoned his jacket. "I'm sure he'll be along without a reminder."

"The baby looks sleepy." Charlotte resumed her chopping at the butcher block but glanced at the child.

"The sun was bright, and he didn't have his hat," Sarah said. That maid had better not blame her for the warm sun.

"Is he hungry?"

Sarah sighed. "I don't know. But I'd like tea."

Archie stepped over to Sarah and took the baby from her. "So make yourself some tea."

"But Charlotte is right here."

"Charlotte is already filling in for Mrs. Fletcher, keeping up with her own work, and listening for Miss Brewster's call. Make your own tea."

Sarah stomped across the kitchen and snatched the kettle off the stove.

"He's perspiring." Archie gently wiped the baby's face with his hand.

"I told you, the sun was overly bright." Sarah took a cup down from a shelf and set it on a saucer.

"Did you at least put up the hood of the buggy?" Archie asked. "His skin is quite fair, you know."

"I didn't want to cut off the air. What's the point of airing a baby if you do that?"

She turned her head to meet his eye, but he was looking at Charlotte. What he saw in the maid, Sarah couldn't fathom.

"He needs something to drink," Archie said. "Charlotte, some milk!"

Charlotte panicked. Was Henry not simply sun-drenched and ready for his nap? Dropping her knife, she snatched a bottle from the counter and filled it with a few ounces of the milk she had mixed and sweetened for the baby's daily use. Screwing on a nipple, she moved toward Archie.

"He doesn't take his milk cold." Sarah moved to the sink to fill the kettle.

Charlotte ignored her and offered the bottle. The baby reached with a hand to help guide it to his mouth and sucked eagerly. Sarah rolled her eyes.

"You let him get too hot and thirsty," Archie said to Sarah. "Next time, use the buggy hood."

"I'll thank you not to pretend to know anything about children!" Sarah posed with her arms crossed and her weight on one foot. "Coddling them teaches poor habits."

"And neglecting them? What does that teach them?"

Charlotte could hardly believe what she was seeing—Archie standing up for her son. Except he did not even know he held her son in his arms. He simply did it because it was the right thing to do. She couldn't imagine Henry's own father ever holding him this way. Charlotte hardly knew how to respond to Archie's gentleness toward a stranger's nameless child.

"Perhaps we should sponge him off," Archie suggested.

Sarah yanked the child out of Archie's arms. "I'm quite capable of doing that."

Charlotte barely caught the bottle headed for a collision with the floor. Calmly, she handed it to Sarah. "When I get a chance, I'll bring you some tea and biscuits."

Sarah spun and left the room.

"Charlotte," Archie said, "why did you offer to bring her tea? She's—"

Charlotte cut him off. "She's taking care of a baby. I'm concerned for the child."

Archie put a hand on her shoulder. "I know I suggested a couple of days ago that perhaps you were getting too close to things. But I can see now how hard it is to watch her neglect an innocent child for her own convenience."

"She can't seem to control her tongue, but she is keeping a strict routine. That's good for the baby."

"I suppose so."

"Besides, Mrs. Edwards wants Sarah to stay on until she returns in January."

"You don't think Mrs. Edwards wants to take Sarah on at her home, do you?"

"She hasn't mentioned it." The kettle Sarah had put on the stove whistled, and Charlotte moved it off the heat.

"Perhaps it really would be the best thing for him if Mrs. Banning's cousin adopts the baby," Archie said.

Charlotte drew a jagged breath and turned away abruptly. "I have to finish chopping everything. Mrs. Fletcher will be back any moment."

The annunciator button rang. Charlotte felt Archie's gaze follow her movements even as he answered it and had a brief conversation.

He replaced the earpiece and said, "Miss Emmaline requires your assistance."

Charlotte wiped her hands on her work apron. "I'll have to go up to change my apron first."

"I don't for a minute believe that the men Leo is bringing home for dinner are really his friends." Emmaline Brewster looked in the mirror at her young ladies' maid as she prepared for bed hours later. "Have you ever seen Mr. Talon here for dinner before?"

"No, miss." Charlotte pulled the brush through Miss Emmaline's hair, knowing she would run into knots. She always did. The coppery mane was predictably stubborn. Charlotte had learned that she could tug fairly hard before Miss Emmaline would protest.

"He's some associate of Leo's from the university, but if you ask me, they did not seem to know each other very well. And he's so much older than Leo. I wouldn't be surprised to learn he was at least forty."

Charlotte merely shrugged and smiled briefly into the mirror, not knowing what to say.

"When I was your age," Emmaline said, "I suppose I didn't

mind so much being paraded around before the eligible bachelors. Everyone expected I would meet someone and marry." She paused to sigh heavily. "But at my age, it seems a pitiful endeavor. What do I need a husband for, anyway? My father left me a generous trust."

"I'm sure I couldn't say, miss."

Emmaline interrupted the brushing to turn around and look Charlotte in the face. "Have you ever thought about what it would be like to have a child?"

"Yes, miss." Charlotte set the brush down, sensing Miss Emmaline would not sit still much longer. If Miss Emmaline insisted on talking about children, Charlotte would feel like squirming herself.

"I suppose that's something all women wonder about," Emmaline murmured. "But I'm starting to think it's only a dream. With no husband at my age . . ."

"I thought perhaps the green dress for tomorrow." Charlotte steered the conversation toward something she could manage without emotion. "If I may say so, miss, it flatters your complexion when you go out calling."

"Flora makes sure I reciprocate promptly whenever I have a visitor." Emmaline sighed. "But I'm losing interest. Yes, I suppose the green will do for the morning at least." Emmaline stood up and moved to the chaise lounge. "You're very pretty, you know. I'm sure you could have a husband if you wanted one, and a baby soon enough."

Charlotte blanched. "I'm only a maid, miss."

"A maid is still a woman."

10

The parlor was pleasant enough, in Emmaline Brewster's opinion. Charming small art pieces and illustrated books created interest around the room, and a perfectly pitched grand piano beckoned anyone who would like to play. However, Emmaline thought Flora might think about adding more tolerable wing chairs. She was getting a little weary of always sitting on the slightly overstuffed settee because the other chairs looked less appealing.

After more than a week under the Banning roof, Emmaline was settling in well. Lucy's suite had every amenity she could imagine needing for the next few weeks, and the ladies' maid seemed to be competent and efficient with laying out gowns and suggesting accessories. Emmaline had first arrived in Chicago just days before Lucy's wedding in mid-June, and at the time she had stayed with Violet. The Banning house had seemed in uproar with the hastily planned wedding. After a scant two months of engagement, Lucy had married Will Edwards on a Friday morning in the presence of barely fifty witnesses at Second Presbyterian Church. The affair was hardly the society wedding her parents must have envisaged for their only daughter.

Still, Lucy had a wedding and she was only twenty-two. Emmaline was thirty-three years old—actually closer to thirty-four—and well aware that her prospects for marriage had diminished rapidly long ago. The truth was, she hardly thought of a husband anymore, but every glimpse of a friend's child opened up the gaping hole in her own life. She had never expected true love, but she had hoped that a dutiful marriage would lead to motherhood.

Emmaline looked up as Flora Banning glided through the arched doorway of the parlor.

"Emmie, dear, what are you doing in here?" Flora asked. "Hasn't Violet arranged something for you today? Shouldn't you be changing your gown for tea?"

"We've only just finished luncheon," Emmaline answered. "I can't think about tea."

Emmaline felt her hostess's stare as Flora lowered herself into a favorite side chair. Flora rummaged through a basket of needlework and selected a pillowcase she was embroidering for Lucy.

"If I didn't know better, I'd think you were reluctant to go out this afternoon," Flora said.

"Violet has some mesmerizing acquaintances," Emmaline conceded, "but I am getting a bit weary. Every day is a party, it seems."

Flora scoffed. "I'm not sure you can call that affair at the Kimballs' a party. Mr. Henderson seemed quite deranged, if you ask me, and Mr. Pullman shook my hand as if it were a dead fish. I don't know when I've been so insulted."

"At least you were not seated with a man who is vulgar on one side and one who dreams too much on the other."

"I'm sorry about that," Flora said. "I never should have

accepted the invitation on your behalf. But your tea this afternoon is with Violet. Surely it will not be so distressing."

"Perhaps not, but I rather think I will stay home and do something else today." Emmaline lifted a slender volume of poetry from the end table and ran a finger down its spine.

Flora's eyes flashed with curiosity. "I'm afraid there's not much to interest you around here."

"I plan to take some air," Emmaline said. "I thought I would ask for the baby to be brought down and take him for a stroll."

Flora dropped both pillowcase and needle. "The baby? My goodness, Emmie, what has gotten into you?"

"It's a fine day, and you feed me rather more richly than I am accustomed to on my own. A bit of a constitutional would do me good."

"Of course, dear, but I don't understand what part the baby has in your plan."

"Your butler reports that the girl takes him out every afternoon for an airing. I simply thought I would take him today." Emmaline flipped several pages in the book.

"By yourself?"

"The girl may come, of course, or I'll take Charlotte."

"I hardly think you need to trouble yourself with the child, Emmie, dear." Flora's wide eyes clouded with disbelief. "Penard has ably arranged for the child's care while he's here, and I've written to Cousin Louisa to inquire of her interest. I'm sure your time in Chicago could be put to much better use."

Emmaline sighed. If only Flora had not written to Louisa. If Louisa responded with interest—well, Emmaline was not going to think about that.

"Flora," Emmaline said, "you and Violet must face facts. If you invited me for an extended visit in hopes of finding me a husband in Chicago because I have exhausted the possibilities of New England, I think perhaps it is your time that could be put to better use."

Flora pushed aside the entire needlework basket and stood up. "We only want you to enjoy your time here. You haven't been to Chicago in over ten years. The city has so much more to offer now."

"Yes, such as a population of over one million people. Only a small percentage are eligible bachelors who might be suitable matches, but somehow Violet seems to march more than her share of them into my view."

"Emmaline, you speak harshly of our intent."

"I'm sorry, Flora. I realize you mean well." Emmaline returned the poetry book to the table. "Violet never married, and she seems quite happy with her life. Why should I not have the same hope? The two of you have conspired to have me socially engaged every night for a week. Perhaps I'd simply like a quiet afternoon."

"Of course, dear, but the child!"

"Humor me, Flora." Emmaline met Flora's green eyes and held them. "Call for the child and let me take him for a stroll. Then we'll see about tea at Violet's."

Flora sighed, but she reached for the annuciator button.

"What do you suppose that was all about?" Archie sank into a kitchen chair when the flurry of getting the baby ready for his daily airing had cleared. Archie had pushed the buggy around to the front of the house, while Penard sternly admonished Sarah about her comportment while accompanying Miss Brewster for the outing.

"I don't know what to make of it," Charlotte answered. "Miss Brewster seems pleasant enough, and she could be far more demanding than she has been. But why is she interested in the baby?"

Archie watched the wave of anxiety splash across Charlotte's face even as she tried to turn from his view. Neither did the catch in her voice escape him.

Mr. Penard pushed open the door from the butler's pantry and strode across the black and white tiles of the kitchen. "They're off. That girl had better behave herself."

Archie said nothing. Sarah Cummings had not mastered her tongue around the kitchen in her few weeks in the Banning house. It might be only a matter of time before she stepped out of place in front of a family member—or visiting relative.

"Archie, Mr. Leo has asked for you," Penard said. "Bring the open wicker carriage around immediately. He has decided not to return to his office this afternoon but to look after some personal business. You are to be at his disposal until dinner if necessary."

"Yes, sir." Archie stood up, straightened his jacket, and paced across the kitchen to the servants' hall.

A few minutes later, Archie stood beside the wicker carriage in front of the Banning house, watching Leo Banning step up and settle on the seat.

"St. Andrew's, please," Leo said. "I have some questions for Mr. Emmett."

"Yes, sir."

Archie knew the route well. Leo's sister, now honeymooning, had used it often. Deftly he swung himself up onto his seat, picked up the reins, and clicked his tongue. At the corner of Eighteenth Street, Archie steered the horse to the west, allowing it to trot to Michigan Avenue before turning south. Archie had a rough idea of how Lucy Banning Edwards spent her time at the orphanage, but he was uncertain what Leo's business was there.

Outside the orphanage a few minutes later, Archie once again stood at attention beside the carriage.

"Find a place to tie up the horse," Leo instructed as he exited the wicker transport. "No sense leaving you standing here in the sun. You might be of some assistance."

"Yes, sir."

Though he could not imagine what good he would be inside the orphanage office, Archie led the horse to a post. He knotted the reins around it, then hurried his steps to reach St. Andrew's red front door a short distance behind Leo.

Inside the hall, Leo explained his request to a young girl, who struck Archie as being only a year or two younger than Sarah. Most likely the girls would know each other, he speculated. Perhaps it was just a matter of time before this girl went into service. He scanned the wide hallway and the doors that opened off of it, imagining Sarah moving among them and wondering if she'd always had the cocky attitude she paraded around the Bannings.

"Please wait here, sir," the girl said meekly, and left them.

Quite quickly a youngish man stepped out of the offices at the back of the building and advanced toward them, straightening his jacket as he moved.

"Good afternoon, Mr. Banning," he said. "I am Simon Tewell, the assistant director of St. Andrew's. It's a privilege to have you here."

"I had hoped I might speak with Mr. Emmett," Leo said. "Perhaps the girl misunderstood."

"I'm sorry, sir," Simon said. "Our director is away on leave. I will do my best to be of assistance to you in any way possible. Perhaps you would like to come to my office to help me understand what brings you here today."

"Of course." Leo nodded. "It's good of you to see me."

"I understand Miss Sarah Cummings is in the service of your family. I hope she is proving satisfactory."

"As far as I know, yes."

Archie looked away. Leo did not see Sarah Cummings often enough to know whether she was satisfactory or not, but Archie could not hold that against him.

Leo followed Simon Tewell, and at Leo's gesture, Archie followed Leo. In the simple office, Leo sat across the pine desk from the young assistant director, and Archie stood rigidly against the wall.

"My question is theoretical at this point." Leo put his hands on his knees and leaned forward slightly. "If a small child were to be abandoned or surrendered, what kind of placement options might you arrange?"

"We would offer immediate shelter, of course." Simon Tewell's chair creaked as he shifted his weight. "Depending on the age of the child, he might be placed in the nursery or perhaps one of the dormitories. Most children seem to adjust quickly to the daily structure we provide, and we operate a first-rate school."

"I'm sure you do," Leo said. "What about a very young child, less than two years of age?"

"Occasionally Mr. Emmett has placed very young children in private settings." Simon pressed the pads of his fingers together. "But those opportunities are limited. As you can imagine, private care is more costly than caring for a group of children together."

Archie saw Leo's posture straighten. "Do you keep records of such children, Mr. Tewell?"

Tewell smiled absently and gestured. "We have a room full of records. No doubt you are aware that your sister oversees them. It's perhaps the most valuable work she does for us—other than the fact that the children adore both her and Mr. Edwards."

Leo leaned back in his chair. "So if you had a child in a private care setting, you would in fact have records. Might I ask you to show me records you have for these children? Perhaps boys around one year of age?"

Tewell's smile faded slightly. "I'm afraid we leave the records in the capable hands of Mrs. Edwards and her army of volunteers. At the moment I don't believe any of them are here. Mrs. Jamison left only a few minutes ago. I'm not at all sure I could be of any practical assistance locating a specific case. Perhaps when your sister returns—"

"Mrs. Edwards will be away for several months. The issue is more urgent than that. Would you mind if I had a look for myself?"

Archie's eyebrows raised involuntarily. It seemed Mr. Leo had brought him inside St. Andrew's to look at files about infant boys. Perhaps they would stumble on one infant boy in particular.

Sarah did not like the blush of pleasure on Emmaline Brewster's face as she carried the child up the front steps and back into the house. She wanted to snatch him away. This stranger was going to ruin everything.

She threw her shoulders back, held up her head, and lifted her skirts as she followed Miss Brewster through the front door. As long as she was tending to the child with Miss Brewster, there seemed to be no objection to Sarah's using the front door. They had been outdoors for an hour and a half. Miss Brewster had insisted on finding a bench in a grassy park with some shade. She actually lifted the brat out of the buggy and held him on her lap and played with him. Sitting on a bench several yards off, Sarah had been helpless to interfere with the indulgence. They had stayed out twice as long as usual. Now she was the one who would be left to manage a fussy coddled baby who only needed fresh air, not smiles and embraces.

"I think we've quite worn him out," Miss Brewster said once they were in the foyer. "I imagine he will nap soundly now."

"Yes, miss. Shall I take him now?"

"He might need something to eat first." Emmaline showed no sign of releasing the child. "You did say he eats at four in the afternoon, didn't you?"

"He sometimes likes a bottle." Sarah had been looking forward to putting the child directly to bed and having an undisturbed cup of tea.

"You've been very helpful, Sarah." Miss Brewster smiled in a way that unnerved Sarah. "I'll speak to Penard and make sure you are available to help with an outing every afternoon—though of course I could ask Charlotte if you are not available."

"Yes, miss." Sarah barely moved her lips. She did not need supervision in airing the child.

Finally Miss Brewster kissed the baby's head and handed him back to Sarah. "Perhaps when I have an opportunity, I'll see if he needs anything in the nursery. I would enjoy seeing him in the setting he's most familiar with."

"Yes, miss." Would she really come to the nursery? Surely old Penard would not approve.

Sarah adjusted the child in her arms as she watched Emmaline, smiling with pleasure, gracefully raise the hem of her dress just enough to glide up the marble staircase.

"Sarah, please come with me," a man's voice said behind her.

She turned to see Penard at the dining room door. Sarah exhaled and followed the butler to the kitchen.

"There's nothing here." Leo slapped a stack of papers back into the drawer they had come from. "Thank you for helping me look, Archie, but it seems like we've come to a dead end."

"Yes, sir, it would seem so."

They had looked through four filing cabinets before encountering any papers that related to infants placed in private settings. Archie was not sure exactly what they were looking for, but after nearly an hour, they had stumbled upon a drawer full of files on "placements."

"Everything we found has been resolved." Leo flipped through some loose pages. "A few babies are with wet nurses in the country, and a handful here in the city with women who have sheltered several children over the years. A woman named Mary Given looked after twins until recently, but they were graduated to the toddler dormitory here at St. Andrew's three months ago. She doesn't seem to have any others."

"No, sir," Archie said.

Leo tossed the papers on a desk. "I don't see anything that matches the boy who showed up at our house. If he were somehow connected to St. Andrew's, there would be a file on him. A caretaker should have been in touch with the orphanage to report him missing by now."

"Yes, sir,"

"So we have to conclude that a poor, desperate mother was at the end of her rope and thought my sister could help."

"I'm sure she would want to, sir."

"You're absolutely right, Archie." A fresh gleam lit in Leo's eyes. "I don't see what harm it can do to send her a telegram at the hotel in Paris. Our family always stays at the same place. If she's not there, she will have left a forwarding address at the front desk."

11

Summer waned at last. Charlotte propped both elbows behind her on the ledge and leaned back into one of the curved stone walls in the courtyard. Letting her arms dangle, she lifted her face to the afternoon sun. Not nearly as strong as even a week ago, nevertheless the streaming rays soothed her. Behind her closed eyes, she felt the breeze off the creek where she used to take refuge more than a mile from the old farmhouse. As a girl, especially after her grandmother died, she used to scurry across the fields to be out of shouting distance as quickly as possible, then slow her pace to snoop along the gurgling water spilling over the rocks. For a few prized moments, she could be away. Just away.

Rarely could she afford to indulge such a thought now.

A shadow blocked the sun's warmth, and she allowed her eyes to quiver open. "Hello, Archie."

He scowled playfully, crossing his arms and leaning one shoulder against the wall, his body angled toward her. "It's Thursday."

"I know what day of the week it is."

"So why are you here? Thursday is your afternoon and evening off, but you don't seem to be taking it lately."

Charlotte shrugged. "There's too much to do."

"There's always too much to do, and the more you're here to do it, the more you'll be taken advantage of."

"You sound like one of those people with the leaflets again."

"I happen to agree with them on that point. You deserve regular time off. We all do, with the impossible hours we keep."

"I don't really have any place to go," Charlotte said. Henry was here now. Why should she go anywhere else?

"Jump on a streetcar and go where it takes you," Archie suggested.

"And then what?"

"And then . . . whatever appeals, wherever you end up."

She laughed. "You must have me confused with someone else."

"What if I could finagle the evening off? Would you come out with me?"

She allowed herself a brief look into his brown eyes. It was tempting. But it could not be. "Who would serve the soup?"

"The new footman," Archie answered. "Remember, I'm coachman now. It's time I reminded Mr. Penard of the distinction."

"I doubt you have to remind Mr. Penard of anything," Charlotte said. "Besides, I already promised Mrs. Fletcher I would be here. She's acting rather put out these days."

"She has reason to be. She was counting on a new scullery maid, and she didn't get her. But it's not fair that you have to take up the slack. I haven't noticed Mrs. Fletcher giving up her days off."

"There you go, sounding like those labor protesters."

"I'm just looking for what's fair." Archie unfolded an arm and teased Charlotte's fingers as they hung from the ledge. "It's only two-thirty. What if I promised to have you back by five? Would you come out with me then?"

Charlotte collected both her hands and busied them in her apron. Whether she wanted to go with Archie was irrelevant. She simply couldn't, so it did no good to look in his eyes. "That doesn't seem practical. I'm sorry, Archie. I should go back inside."

Coachman or not, Archie served the soup in the Banning dining room as he had for three years. Charlotte never lifted her eyes to check for his gaze, but if she had, she was sure she would have found his eyes lowered in the demeanor Mr. Penard insisted on and which was required in every house along Prairie Avenue. Nevertheless, he followed her every move, and Charlotte knew it. She suspected that being near her was the only reason he still served at meals. Gripping dishes with more intention than usual, she resisted the sensation his gaze caused in her. After she cleared the meat plates, Charlotte stacked them carefully in the sink in the butler's pantry. By the time she returned to the dining room, the family's conversation had drifted away from the weather and the world's fair and Samuel's latest legal challenge.

"I thought perhaps Mr. Emmett would have something helpful," Leo was saying. "I know Lucy has his ear on a number of matters around the orphanage. If this child were somehow connected to St. Andrew's, he would know."

Violet toyed with her sweet potatoes à l'allemande. "Was Mr. Emmett helpful?"

Leo shook his head. "Apparently he is on leave, and his assistant did not seem overly familiar with the filing system. Archie and I had a look for ourselves."

Charlotte's stomach pinched. She hated to think what they might have found. Immediately she reminded herself that more than a week had passed since the day Leo whisked Archie out on errands. Archie had not said a suspicious word the whole week. Surely they found nothing worth mentioning.

"And what did you discover?" Violet asked.

Leo shrugged. "As it turns out, not much of anything. Obviously if an infant had gone missing from the orphanage, Mr. Tewell would have informed me when he heard the nature of my inquiry. He said nothing, and I found no record of a child matching the description of the one who turned up here. The child doesn't seem to have any connection with the orphanage at all."

"Well, of course not," Flora Banning said. "That's why he's here. Honestly, Leo, I'm not sure why you felt it was necessary to trouble yourself. The entire situation is under control. The child is being well cared for."

"Yes, clearly he is." Leo spread his hands in front of him. "However, I thought we might find his mother. She may be suffering regrets. I've only glimpsed the boy a time or two, but I left the best description I could with Mr. Tewell. If the mother should turn up looking for him, he will contact us."

"Why have you waited an entire week to say anything?" Flora pressed.

Leo hesitated. "I've sent a telegram to Lucy. I thought it might catch up with her in Paris and she could send a reply if she has some insight into the matter. I had hoped to have some word from her before speaking to you on the matter."

Flora dropped her fork. "But I've already written to Cousin Louisa! I've told her all about the child's charms, and she has sent word that she is most eager to meet the boy. I am only awaiting the details of when her husband can manage to be away from his pressing business matters. In any event, they hope to come to Chicago to visit the fair, so it would be simple enough to spend some time with the child as well."

Charlotte noticed that Emmaline Brewster had stopped eating altogether, having not even touched her sweet potato. She looked pale. Her hands were in her lap, so if Charlotte did not soon step forward and remove Miss Brewster's plate, Mr. Penard would chastise her with his eyes—and his words later. Charlotte herself was barely breathing and feared her knees would buckle if she had to hear one more word about her son's future with strangers.

"Journeying from St. Louis will take some time," Samuel observed.

"The train is efficient," Leo said.

"I only just learned that they bought a new home in a country setting," Flora said. "They hope to move in within six weeks. Greenville, I think."

Greenville!

Charlotte removed Miss Brewster's plate swiftly and took it immediately to the butler's pantry.

Archie eyed the table, flashed a glance at Mr. Penard, then somberly and quietly stepped into the butler's pantry.

"Charlotte, are you unwell?" he whispered. Bent over the sink, she looked as if her own evening meal might find its way up.

She did not speak, but Archie saw the tremor in her hands.

"Charlotte?" Archie said more urgently. He moved toward her, taking her chin in his hand and inspecting her face. "You look as if you've seen a ghost."

She would not meet his eyes.

"I'm going to tell Mr. Penard you've taken ill." He turned her around at the shoulders. "I want you to go up to bed immediately."

"But—"

"Go, Charlotte."

On Sunday morning after breakfast, Charlotte carried dishes from the dining room. Archie was finishing a cup of coffee at the kitchen table.

"Shouldn't you be pulling the carriage around for the family to go to church?" Charlotte asked. He was watching her too closely since finding her ill in the butler's pantry. She moved briskly as if to prove she was untroubled.

"Come with me." Archie locked his eyes onto hers.

"Don't be silly, Archie." Charlotte tossed a dish towel at him.

"You've only been to church one time since you got here," he said, "and that was Christmas Eve."

"I have work to do on Sunday mornings." Charlotte swished a hand in the dishwater, fishing for a rag. "The family will be expecting luncheon when they get home from church."

"What if I talk to Mrs. Fletcher?" Archie asked. "What if she says you can go?"

"She won't."

"What if she does?"

Charlotte shrugged. "Okay. I would go. But she won't."

Archie blew out of the room to find Mrs. Fletcher, and a few minutes later triumphantly announced that Charlotte should go upstairs and change her dress. She was going to church. Charlotte could not help wondering what Archie had to promise Mrs. Fletcher to get her consent, but she could not back out of her own agreement.

Now she stood beside Archie in one of the side balconies looking down on the main floor. The Bannings were sitting just where they'd sat on Christmas Eve, toward the front on the right side, in the pew for which Samuel made a generous annual contribution to the expenses of Second Presbyterian Church. Emmaline Brewster sat between Richard and Leo, and Samuel and Flora sat like bookends at opposite ends of their row. Around them were other Prairie Avenue families Charlotte recognized.

As he had on Christmas Eve, in the balcony Archie covered her hand with his and shared his hymnal with her. And now, as then, Charlotte had no voice for the hymns. The tunes might have been familiar from her childhood, but her heart could not sing.

As the speaker began his sermon on the sovereignty and providence of God, Charlotte pulled her hand out of Archie's. What was she doing letting him touch her? It would come to no good, and she would only hurt him.

The speaker intoned from Matthew's Gospel: "Therefore I say unto you, Take no thought for your life, what ye shall eat, or what ye shall drink; nor yet for your body, what ye shall put on. Is not the life more than meat, and the body than raiment? Behold the fowls of the air: for they sow not, neither do they reap, nor gather into barns; yet your heavenly Father feedeth them. Are ye not much better than they?"

Charlotte had a fleeting speculation that Jesus might have had a different perspective if he'd had a child to take care of. He made it sound so simple.

"God provides," the speaker said. "Do you trust him?"

Charlotte shook her head almost imperceptibly. Looking over the balcony banister, she noticed Emmaline Brewster leaning forward in the Banning pew, eyes wide open.

On Sunday afternoon, Emmaline entered the parlor, expecting to find Samuel and Flora, and perhaps even Violet, enjoying a leisurely afternoon and awaiting their tea. She had just returned from airing the baby, certain that he recognized her now and that the smiles aimed in her direction were intentional. It was all she could do to merely push his buggy and gaze down at him, when she wanted to scoop him up and carry him in her arms every step of the way. The small park had become a regular excuse to pause, seek respite on a bench, and pluck the child out of the pram. He toddled around, examining the bounty of nature on the ground, and brought her gifts at frequent intervals. Emmaline kept every rock and twig in a box under her bed.

After dispatching Sarah with the child and longingly watching the girl take him through to the kitchen, Emmaline looked around for any sign of the family in the dining room, foyer, and parlor. Silence greeted her. But it was nearly four. Surely they would appear for tea momentarily. Still basking in the pleasure of the outing with the baby, Emmaline seated herself in the parlor and picked up the latest copy of *The Ladies' Home Journal.*

When the telephone in the foyer rang, Emmaline merely turned another magazine page. Observation had proven that if Penard were in the house, he would answer the phone himself. Only if he were unavailable would one of the other servants pass through the family's rooms for the task. Rarely was a family member moved to action by a jangling phone. Even in her own home, Emmaline seldom answered the telephone herself.

The telephone continued to ring. Emmaline flipped another unread page. Involuntarily she glanced through the arched parlor door and across the foyer, expecting to see the form of one of the staff momentarily. No one came, and the phone continued its insistent clatter. Finally, Emmaline tossed the magazine aside and stepped into the foyer. Still she saw no one. Still the phone jangled.

Tentatively, she picked up the pewter base, raised it to her face, and removed the earpiece.

"Banning residence. Miss Emmaline Brewster speaking."

She listened carefully, her shoulders trembling.

A young female voice asked for Flora.

"No, I'm sorry, Mrs. Banning is not available to speak on the telephone. I would be happy to give her a message."

"Yes, if you would be so kind," the voice said. "This is her Cousin Louisa. I would very much like to speak to her about the baby she's keeping."

Emmaline forced even breaths.

"I'm sorry you've been troubled unnecessarily," Emmaline said at last. "I'm afraid it's all been an unfortunate misunderstanding, and the situation has been resolved."

"I don't understand," Louisa said. "Do you mean the child is not available?"

"I believe that to be the case," Emmaline said.

"Flora said nothing about this in her note. Are you sure?"

"I'm quite certain. Someone with an attachment to the child has come forward. It was entirely unforeseen, or I'm sure Flora would not have raised your hopes."

"I see."

Emmaline heard the catch in Louisa's voice at the stunning announcement. She was stunned herself at the words she had spoken.

"Good-bye then," Louisa said quietly.

"Good-bye, Louisa."

Emmaline nearly dropped the telephone as she aimed the earpiece for its hook and set the apparatus down. She inhaled deeply and let her breath out in a long controlled silent wind.

Charlotte had been up to her elbows, scrubbing pots, when she realized no one was going to answer the telephone. The family had accepted a last-minute invitation to a private recital at the home of Marshall Field and his wife. Mr. Penard had gone out on a rare personal errand while the house was empty, and several of the staff were enjoying a half day off on Sunday afternoon. Charlotte had even managed to shoo off Archie and his persistent brown eyes excavating her soul. By the time Charlotte got her hands dried off and moved through the dining room to cautiously determine that she should in fact respond to the ringing, the jarring noise stopped.

She stood with her hands on the pocket doors between the dining room and the foyer, gazing at the back of Miss Emmaline Brewster.

And she heard what she said. *Someone with an attachment to the child has come forward.*

12

He's crying!

In the hall outside the nursery the next morning, Charlotte reminded herself that small children routinely cried, and while Henry was mild-mannered, he was still a baby not yet a year old. What perturbed her was that she heard no movement from within the room to tend to the cries. She had his midmorning warmed bottle on a small tray, which she balanced in one hand as she turned the knob and opened the nursery door.

"Sarah?" she called out.

The only response was increased wailing. Charlotte set the tray down on the nearest side table and moved into the small alcove where the crib was tucked. One of her baby's legs protruded between the rails of the crib, wedging him in. The mottled red of his face made it clear he had been shrieking for some time.

"Sarah!" Charlotte called out, exasperated. She gently eased Henry's leg between the rails, then picked him up and clutched him against her. Livid, she marched into the small room next door where Sarah slept, but it was empty. Henry had been left alone in the nursery suite, and there was no telling how long he had been screaming. Pounding blood echoed through Charlotte's ears. Her instinct was to pull the baby's quilt from the crib and swaddle him in it, but she did not see the quilt. What had Sarah done with her grandmother's quilt?

Infuriated, Charlotte sat in an oak rocking chair and forced herself to calm down while she soothed her baby. Tucking his head under her chin as he always had, he seemed to settle. She stroked his reddened leg, assuring herself that no serious damage had been done. The gliding motion mollified them both.

Almost a year.

Almost a year since she had passed her twentieth birthday and a day later held her son in her arms for the first time.

Almost a year since she fled.

Almost a year since she arrived at the Banning house with her secret.

Almost a year since Lucy Banning secured a safe place for Charlotte to leave her son.

Almost a year, and what was going to happen now?

If she confessed that Henry was hers, even Lucy would not be able to manage events from an unknown location in France.

Maybe Archie was right about the long hours and low wages. Charlotte had little to show for almost a year of hard work in the Banning house—certainly not enough to look after Henry, and no place to take him where he would be safe. She had spent the year breathing her way through one day at a time, unable to think any further into the future. All that mattered was that Henry was safe for another day. And now her prospects were every bit as precarious as they had been a year ago. If she ended up in a workhouse as a consequence of neglecting to mention certain facts, she might never see Henry again.

But if she did not tell them Henry was hers, they would send him away.

Greenville. That was simply too close for comfort—she could not allow him to go to Greenville. Her own family was on a farm outside of town.

And him. *He* was there. No, Henry could not go to Greenville.

She had to find some way to keep him in Chicago.

And guard her secret.

She kissed his head. And then there was Miss Emmaline. She wanted him.

Emmaline laid the book down in her lap and leaned back in the chaise lounge in the anteroom to Lucy's suite. She had been at the Bannings' for two weeks, and so far she had been to two balls, five dinner parties, high tea at three different downtown restaurants, a symphony concert, an opera, and a private recital in the home of friends of Flora and Samuel.

She was weary. And she had yet to visit the world's fair, ostensibly the reason for an extended stay in Chicago. Next week a widower acquainted with Violet was expecting to escort Miss Emmaline Brewster of New Hampshire to the World's Columbian Exposition. She supposed there was no way to avoid going—it was the world's fair, after all, and Violet would attend as well. The truth was, Emmaline did not want to go. Her yearnings had returned to the undulating landscape of her New Hampshire estate, and the vision of a giddy little boy tumbling in the grass and squealing at the sight of the new puppy. A little boy needed a puppy. Emmaline had decided that much already.

Emmaline knew just the room she would put him in. It faced the front of the house. Morning sun shimmered through the bank of windows and danced off the walls from spring to fall. She would have the walls covered in mint green wallpaper, and she would paint seascapes with her own brushes and hang them on the walls. Her father had left her plenty of money, removing the need to marry if she did not genuinely wish to. Now it would not matter if she ever married, because she would have him.

He would need a name.

She swung her feet to the floor, stood, and moved to the vanity table, where she tucked in stray hair and pinched some color into her cheeks. Nothing was stopping her from seeing him right now if she wanted to.

Charlotte looked up sharply when the nursery door creaked open.

"Sarah?"

"No, it's me," Lina the parlor maid answered. "Mr. Penard is looking for Sarah."

Charlotte shrugged and gestured around the room with one arm. "As you can see, she's not here. I came up with the baby's bottle, and she was nowhere in sight."

"Where is she?"

"I don't know. The baby was screaming. Someone had to look after him, so I stayed."

"Mr. Penard is going to be most displeased."

"He should be." Charlotte gently adjusted Henry in her

arms. He was far from settled. "What can Sarah have been thinking?"

"That's not the problem at the moment," Lina said. "Miss Brewster is in the parlor, and she has asked to see the baby."

Charlotte's heart lurched to her throat. "But he's upset and hungry . . . and Sarah is missing."

Lina raised her eyebrows. "Someone will have to make him presentable. We can't keep Miss Brewster waiting, can we?"

"No, I suppose not."

"Then I'll tell Mr. Penard you'll bring him down." Lina turned toward the door. "But Miss Brewster is expecting a happy child."

He was a happy child—when he was looked after properly. Charlotte gathered her wits. "I'll need twenty minutes to feed him and find some fresh clothing. You make sure Mr. Penard understands that Sarah is the one who left her post!"

Twenty minutes later, Archie hung his uniform jacket on a hook in the servants' hallway off the kitchen and went in search of the pot of strong tea he hoped was on the back of the stove. His day was already almost six hours old, and more hours than he wanted to calculate still stretched ahead of him. It seemed like a justifiable opportunity to demonstrate his conviction for reasonable working conditions.

Mr. Penard had other ideas. "Find Sarah," the butler snapped.

Archie looked at him, his eyes seeking more information.

"She's gone missing. If she is not standing in this kitchen in the next ten minutes, I will advise Mrs. Banning to send her back to St. Andrew's."

Frankly, Archie had no idea where the girl would be, and if she were sent back to the orphanage, he would feel no great loss.

"If you have to, take the market carriage out," Mr. Penard said, "and circle the neighborhood."

Once Mr. Penard turned his back, Archie sighed and reached for his jacket again, sliding his arms into the sleeves even as he stepped back into the hall. In the dimness of the hall, he did not see Charlotte step off the bottom step and nearly knocked her over.

"I'm sorry." He reached out to catch the stumble he had caused. Her arms were full of the baby. Taking her elbow, he walked with her back to the kitchen. He had his instructions from the butler, but he was not inclined to save Sarah's skin at the expense of Charlotte.

"What's going on?" He placed a hand gently on the head of the child in her arms.

"I found him screaming in his crib. No one knows where Sarah is, and Miss Brewster has asked to see the child."

"Why does she want to see him in the middle of the morning? Why does she want to see him so much at all?"

Charlotte shook her head. "I can't stand here and try to sort it out. She's waiting. I have to go."

She pushed through the butler's pantry and out of his sight.

Charlotte grew more pale each day, Archie believed. And the grip the child had on her was, well, curious. She was hiding something from him—he had known that for a long time—but Archie had not quite reasoned his way through why the child's presence made her secret so urgent.

13

Charlotte carried the baby through the dining room and across the foyer, pausing under the arched parlor doors to curtsy with him in her arms.

"Oh, Charlotte, you've brought him!" Miss Brewster settled onto the settee and opened her arms to receive the boy.

Charlotte put him in the eager arms, then stepped back an appropriate distance. She would not leave the room—at any moment Miss Brewster might require assistance—but she withdrew to stand against the wall next to the door, allowing the guest to interact freely with the boy.

It did not take long for Henry to wriggle off Miss Brewster's lap and stand independently next to the settee. With one little fist he gathered a handful of blue silk skirt. Charlotte stoically stifled the grimace that came with the vision of the damage he might do to the fabric, but Miss Brewster seemed amused. When he tried to step away from the settee and pointed at a porcelain statue on a table, though, Miss Brewster restrained him.

"Oh no, we mustn't touch Flora's things!" Miss Brewster laughed lightly. She looked up at Charlotte. "I was expecting Sarah would bring him down."

"She was not available," Charlotte responded quietly.

"I hope she'll be ready when it's time to air the baby this afternoon. Of course, I still want to take him out. It's just that I couldn't wait another minute to see him."

"Yes, miss."

"I do believe he's become quite comfortable with me." Miss Brewster laid a hand on the baby's cheek and smiled broadly. "He seems as happy to see me as I am to see him."

Charlotte could not argue. The little boy did seem to accept Miss Brewster's attentions amiably. The words Charlotte had overheard rang in her ears. *Someone with an attachment to the child has come forward.*

Sarah stopped in her tracks. The baby was not there.

She spun around, the air sucked out of her chest, and scanned the day nursery. He could not have climbed out of the crib, she was sure of that. Running over to the hat shop on Michigan Avenue had taken longer than she anticipated. She would not always wear the cap of a nanny. The day would come when she would need a silk hat suitable for the symphony. Why should she not become familiar with the latest fashions during the baby's nap? It had seemed harmless enough, and it was not the first trip she had made to Michigan Avenue.

But now the brat was not in the nursery.

The call button jangled, and she scrambled to answer it. "Yes?"

"Ah, the wandering Miss Cummings has come home." Mr. Penard's voice was steel. "Perhaps you would deign to grace me with your presence in the kitchen."

"Yes, sir. Right away."

Sarah blew out her breath and rolled her eyes, but she had no choice but to present herself to the butler in the kitchen as quickly as she could.

Mrs. Fletcher stood at the butcher block, breading pork chops, but Sarah ignored her and stood beside the table where Mr. Penard sat.

"To be fair, I will give you the opportunity to explain yourself," Mr. Penard said simply, "although I doubt that even you can construe a reasonable justification for this behavior."

"He sleeps soundly," Sarah said bluntly. "I didn't see the harm in taking a bit of air on my own."

"You are young and inexperienced, but I would have thought you understood the parameters of your responsibilities sufficiently to exercise better judgment than this."

Sarah held her silence, refusing to let the butler humiliate her.

"However the child came to this household, he has become important to Mrs. Banning because of her Greenville cousin." Mr. Penard stood and put his face so close to Sarah's that she wanted to back up. "I will not tolerate further neglect. I'm sure other arrangements could be made for the child."

"That won't be necessary, sir," Sarah said through her teeth. His dark eyes were wild this close up, but her feet held firm.

"If Mrs. Edwards did not expect you to be here upon her return, I would send you back to St. Andrew's immediately," Penard said. "At the very least, I propose to assign responsibility for the child to Charlotte, while you return to the kitchen until your judgment has matured."

Mrs. Fletcher let a meat cleaver drop so hard it nearly made Sarah laugh.

Penard turned toward the cook and cleared his throat. "Do you wish to say something, Mrs. Fletcher?"

"Charlotte has become quite capable in the kitchen. I cannot spare her."

The butler's eyes moved from cook to maid. "You have one more chance, Sarah. If I discover that you have infringed in such a manner again, you will find yourself in the scullery without discussion. Is that clear?"

"Yes, sir." Sarah seethed. "Where is the child now?"

"Miss Brewster asked for him. Charlotte has taken him to the parlor."

"Then I'll go and relieve her."

"That would be appropriate."

Sarah stepped sharply across the kitchen, her shoulders back and her hands held proudly in front of her. The kitchen maid was in the parlor with her charge. That must never happen again.

Dinner was a smaller group that evening. Oliver was out with Pamela Troutman, and Emmaline Brewster was dining at Violet's, so it was just Flora, Samuel, Leo, and Richard. The menu was as rich as ever: curry soup and rolls, breaded pork chops, noodles, parsnip fritters, tomato pie, stuffed cucumbers, and German chocolate cake. Because of the relative simplicity of serving a meal for only four, Mr. Penard had taken a rare evening off, leaving Archie and Charlotte to attend the family with quiet efficiency.

Archie ladled the curry soup from the porcelain tureen with a hand-painted floral pattern into the four gold-rimmed china bowls. Its yellow cream swirled into placidity in each basin. When everyone had been served, Flora picked up her spoon, and the others followed her cue.

"I can't understand why I haven't heard from Cousin Louisa," Flora said. "I sent her our telephone number in my last note and encouraged her to call as soon as she had word when they could come. I welcomed them to stay with us while they visit Chicago."

"Perhaps they just haven't made any arrangements yet." Samuel spread butter on his roll. "The fair continues for another six weeks."

"But in her note she sounded most eager to meet the child as soon as possible. She's even excited that he's not a newborn and thinks it will be amusing to have a toddler around the house."

"I'm sure she'll contact you soon enough."

Charlotte stood at the sideboard against the wall, watching for the first possible signal that the diners were finished with their soup.

Someone with an attachment to the child has come forward.

If Charlotte was right about what she suspected, the family entertained no conjecture about Emmaline Brewster. Although the family was not always around when Emmaline took the baby outside, she made no secret of her growing affection for him. Considering the way Emmaline felt about the baby, Charlotte found it implausible that she had meant anyone but herself when she said someone with an attachment had come forward. But how could she justify her attachment? It was not as if she had a real claim any more than Louisa did.

Archie gently nudged her. "The soup bowls," he whispered.

Charlotte moved into action, quickly stacking the four

bowls and making room for Archie to come around with the meat platter.

"If we can believe the girl's reports, the boy has made a comfortable adjustment here," Flora observed. "That makes me hopeful he will make a smooth adjustment to Louisa's home as well."

"I still wish we could find his mother," Leo mused. "I hate the thought that she may be experiencing regret over having abandoned him and be unable to claim him."

A shiver shot up Charlotte's spine, and she reached a hand out to the sideboard for balance.

"Perhaps we could help her," Leo continued, "if only we could find her. Lucy might want that."

"Lucy is on her honeymoon." Flora left no room for argument. "I have not yet forgiven you for sending her a telegram that may cause her distress."

"She doesn't seem to have received it, so no harm done." Leo picked up a knife and cut a bite of pork. "Maybe she didn't mean to give him away. Maybe she was asking for something else when she left him here."

"I'm not a mystery detective," Samuel said. "I'm a lawyer, and you're a mechanical engineer. We do what makes sense for the most advantage."

"The only mystery here is why Louisa has not telephoned or written." Flora tore a roll in half with particular vigor. "I'll give her one more week. Then I'm going to write to her again."

Charlotte dared to put her feet up on a small padded stool as she sat in a chair under the kitchen window.

"You look bone tired." Archie pulled another chair from the table and positioned it next to her. "How many hours have you been up today?"

She yawned. "If I tell you, you won't like it."

"Yet you refuse to see that you deserve better."

"I suppose you have more propaganda."

He nudged the footrest. "I don't need propaganda to know what makes sense."

"This is the only job I have, Archie," Charlotte said. "It's not a bad place to live, and I eat well."

"Yet you're more thin and pale by the day."

"Miss Brewster will be home soon. As soon as I help her out of her gown, I can go to bed myself. You can make sure the carriage gets put away properly and get some rest too."

"I'm going to make sure you sit here with your feet up until you absolutely have to get up." Sitting beside her, Archie weighted one shoulder toward Charlotte.

In the silence, Charlotte thought about closing her eyes. The conversation over dinner reprised relentlessly in her head.

"What are you thinking about?" Archie asked.

Charlotte shrugged and leaned away from him. "Mrs. Banning seemed quite upset at dinner."

Archie nodded.

Charlotte debated. If she told him what was on her mind, it would be harder than ever to resist those brown eyes. Archie cared for her. She knew that.

"Are you concerned about Mrs. Banning?" Archie asked.

She decided to plunge in but looked away. "If someone on the household staff knows a piece of information that someone in the family might want, does that member of the staff have an obligation to disclose it?"

"What are you talking about, Charlotte?" He leaned closer still. "Do you know something?"

"No. Maybe. I don't know. I guess not."

"That clearly resolves the dilemma."

Charlotte shook her head. "Never mind. It's nothing, really. Mr. Banning would call it hearsay and inadmissible in a court of law."

They both lurched off their chairs when the front door thudded closed, the sound echoing through unoccupied rooms.

"There she is," Charlotte said. "I'll meet her in the suite to get her settled, then my day will be over."

Archie reached for her hand, and to her own surprise she let him take it. Hold it. Warm it.

"Charlotte, I'm worried about you."

"Don't be. Miss Brewster won't be here much longer, and things will ease up."

"And the baby?"

What did he mean?

"The baby, Charlotte," he said softly. "I know you found him in the laundry basket, but something about his being here has changed you."

She broke the gaze and his grip. "I have to go."

14

Crisp white linens generously graced the dining room table under delicate blue lace. Charlotte carried the first of the hand-painted blue china from the cabinetry in the butler's pantry, preparing to lay the table for the family's dinner. Completing the daily midafternoon chore meant that she would be free to help in the kitchen as the evening mealtime approached. After nearly a year in the Banning household, Charlotte could set a table with china and crystal in her sleep. Sighing, she stepped to the window and looked out at what was really on her mind.

Emmaline Brewster was settling Henry in the buggy in front of the house, and the little boy grinned with pleasure and reached for her cheery face. Behind Miss Brewster, Sarah stood idle and made no effort to conceal her displeasure at the way the Bannings' houseguest had taken over with the child. Anyone could see that Sarah's presence on these afternoon outings was perfunctory. Miss Brewster was competent and comfortable in handling the baby without assistance. The entire staff had endured repeated grievances from the girl about what she perceived to be unreasonable intrusion. More than once, Charlotte had bitten her tongue and stifled the urge to voice the observation that Miss Brewster seemed to genuinely *like* the baby, which was more than could be said about Sarah.

But he was her baby.

Charlotte's throat thickened at the thought of the choices that lay ahead. Her stomach responded by surging upward, a sensation that had become all too familiar in the last month. More than once in the middle of the night she resolved to claim her son first thing in the morning. She could not bear another day of overhearing plans for him to be adopted or suspecting what Emmaline Brewster planned to do. Then dawn would break, and with it the fear that overwhelmed resolve and produced visions of Henry in a workhouse. No matter how many times she told herself Lucy Banning Edwards would never stand for that, Charlotte could not be sure. By breakfast, she was not willing to take the chance.

And for another day she would endure the tension between two women over the care of her child while she could not even call him by his name.

Forcing breath from her pent-up lungs, Charlotte turned back to the table and began arranging plates. This was not much of a birthday, but it was better than last year.

Archie stuck his head around the corner from the pantry. "Are you ready to do the marketing?"

"I thought Karl was going to take me." Charlotte swiftly laid three crisp linen napkins at three place settings.

Archie grinned. "I have some say with the coachmen now, and I find myself at your disposal for the rest of the afternoon."

Charlotte smiled against her will. "I still have to finish the table first."

Archie cajoled Charlotte into sharing the driver's seat with him. "It will be easier to talk," he reasoned.

"Who said I want to talk to you?"

"I'm an irresistible conversationalist." He leaned toward her and nudged her shoulder slightly with his, a gesture that had become familiar whenever he was beside her. He was determined to make her smile as much as possible this afternoon. Dissolving the gray dusk that seemed to envelop her was no easy feat, but Archie Shepard was no quitter.

He let the horse carry them north along Prairie Avenue, intending to cut over to State Street in a few blocks.

"There they are with the baby." Charlotte sat alert.

Rather than follow her line of sight, Archie chose to watch her face. Her chin twitched to one side and her lips pressed closed, as if she wanted to say something but thought better of it. The expression in her eyes was not that of a detached maid.

"Sarah is more unhappy by the day," Charlotte said.

"She didn't exactly start out happy." Archie finally took his eyes off Charlotte to look at the baby's entourage. Miss Brewster pushed the pram with besotted pride. Sarah trailed a step or two behind and made little effort to disguise her scowl.

The horse trotted past the baby buggy, and Charlotte rotated in the seat to look over her shoulder at Miss Brewster, Sarah, and the child.

He would never know what she was looking for if he did not ask. "Charlotte—"

"Let's go to the post office first." Charlotte cut him off and faced forward once again. She inched away from him.

"We have to get rid of the packages so we have room for the staples and produce."

"Yes, ma'am!" Archie clicked his tongue, and the mare picked up her pace. Whatever had come over Charlotte as they passed the baby was behind them. She was all business now. Perhaps he could still extract a smile. "Would madam prefer to wait in the carriage while I go in the post office?"

Charlotte sat up primly. "Madam is nowhere near that helpless."

"But madam must be exhausted from the effort of digesting her luncheon."

"One might think so, but madam has become quite accomplished at digesting luncheon."

Archie laughed. "See? Even you can see how ridiculous they seem sometimes."

Charlotte shrugged. "It's all they know. They've always lived that way."

"Because of people like us! Have you ever stopped to calculate how many servants it takes to keep them comfortable? The live-in staff is only the beginning. Day workers come in and out of the house all day. I doubt the Bannings can even tell you the name of the woman who scrubs their clothes or the man who trims the hedges along the side of the house."

"Archie, do we have to talk about this now? I thought we were just having a bit of fun, but you sound ready to stand on a corner soapbox and give a speech."

Though he had made her smile, his own mood had shifted. "I want better. For myself. For you. For us."

Charlotte fell silent again as Archie guided the horse to the curb in front of the post office. No matter how many times he hinted at his hope for the future, she never responded in kind. Her silent discouragement was not enough, but she dreaded hurting him with the truth that there could be nothing between them.

A streetcar rattled by.

"Miss Lucy likes to ride the streetcars," Archie said. "I used to pretend I didn't know she was doing that when she was not using a carriage."

"I know." A half smile crossed Charlotte's face. "She's the one who taught me how easy it is to get around that way."

"But now you never go anywhere."

"I don't have anywhere to go." Her smile faded.

"I'm going to fix that," Archie said, "starting today."

In front of the post office, Archie jumped down and reached for the packages tied together on the floor of the cart. He dispensed with the packages, and they proceeded to the dressmaker's shop to pick up fabric samples from New York City. When Charlotte returned to the cart with the swatches, Archie grinned at her and nudged the horse into motion.

"Where are we going?" Charlotte asked. "The grocer is in the other direction."

"I know where the grocer is," Archie assured her. "But I have you to myself, and I'm going to make the most of it."

"Archie, what are you talking about? The vegetables—"

"The vegetables will still be there in an hour. And the rice and the flour and the sugar."

"An hour! Archie, you're making me nervous."

"No need. My intentions are entirely honorable."

"But Archie—"

"You deserve a special day," Archie said, "and I intend to give it to you."

Charlotte gasped. "How did you find out it's my birthday?"

Archie's jaw dropped. "It's your birthday? Today?"

"You mean you didn't know?"

He shook his head, chuckling. "No, I did not know. I just thought you deserved to relax for a while. Your birthday is all the more reason to take a slight detour."

"You could have turned around there." Charlotte swiveled toward the disappearing row of familiar shops.

"One hour, Charlotte. With everything on our list, even Penard is not expecting we'll make it back in time for tea. We have time."

He slowed the carriage at an intersection, and they waited for a train to rumble past.

"I think carriages are becoming old-fashioned." Archie shouted over the roar of the train. "Streetcars and trains are so much faster."

"But it's hard to carry three bushels of vegetables on a streetcar."

"I haven't forgotten about the vegetables." The train passed, and Archie moved the horse through the intersection, then to the curb outside a tea and sandwich shop. He jumped down. "Let's go in."

Charlotte's eyes grew wide. "To a tea shop? In the middle of the afternoon?"

Archie laughed and tied the reins to a post. "Surely you've been to a tea shop before."

She fumbled with her skirts. "A time or two when Miss Lucy insisted. But in general, no, I don't go into tea shops."

"Then today is your lucky day, birthday girl." He offered her a hand. She hesitated but then laid her hand in his. He held it tight.

She used to leave the house regularly on Thursdays and be

gone for hours, and every other Sunday afternoon. Where did she go, he wondered, if she did not even go to tea shops?

Charlotte had to admit that sitting in a shop with Archie Shepard was a pleasurable experience. The shop was not fancy—nothing like the Palmer House Hotel or the restaurants in Marshall Field's department store. It was a world away from the exquisite shops along the lakeshore with their stone fireplaces and crystal chandeliers. This shop had only a half dozen small tables with green and white striped tablecloths hanging down a scant six inches. Archie seemed on friendly terms with the shop's owner, which made Charlotte wonder just how often he managed to stretch an errand with a brief side trip.

"Mickey, your best pot of tea." Archie signaled the man behind the counter. "And a couple of your famous corned beef sandwiches. We have a birthday girl here!"

Mickey came out from behind the counter to serve the tea and sandwiches himself, taking the opportunity to clap Archie on the back and wish Charlotte a hearty happy birthday.

"Have you been up on Mr. Ferris's wheel yet?" Mickey braced his hands on two empty chairs and leaned in jovially. "What a view!"

"I've been up," Archie said, "but I don't believe Miss Farrow has."

"Then she has quite a treat ahead of her."

Charlotte shook her head. "No, I don't. I do not intend to go up in that contraption."

"It's not a contraption," Archie protested. "It's as safe as a carriage on the streets of Chicago, and you do that."

Charlotte shook her head again. "It's *not* the same."

"It's much more exciting!" Mickey slapped the back of his hand against Archie's shoulder. "Keep after 'er. Take 'er up yourself!"

"She went to the fair with the family, but she was on duty." Archie's eyes sparkled. "I'll take her just for fun and she'll go up with me."

"No, I will not!" Resisting his sparkling brown eyes was getting more difficult by the moment. It was one thing to turn away to chop a potato or polish a fork, but here, away from Prairie Avenue, it was not as easy to find a distraction. With both hands she lifted the hefty sandwich toward her mouth and pondered how to bite into it without making a mess.

She would remember this moment forever.

A year ago on her birthday, she had been heavily pregnant and desperately fearful. The next day she gave birth weeks early, and trepidation propelled her rapid choices.

Suddenly she wanted Henry in her arms.

"Archie, I think we should go." She put her sandwich down unbitten.

"But we haven't been here ten minutes." Archie spoke with his mouth full of corned beef. "The tea hasn't even had a chance to get cold."

"Please, Archie. It's a lovely gesture, but it doesn't feel right."

"Charlotte, it's all right to think of yourself for a few minutes."

"I'm sorry," she said. "I'd just like to go to the grocer's and get back to the house. I'll enjoy the sandwich later, I promise. I'll take it with me." She would not look at Archie, sure that in that moment his eyes would melt her resolve and bring her to the brink of truth. And after a year, she could not risk the truth.

At the grocer's, Charlotte quickly filled three bushels with fruit and vegetables, and at the dry goods store, Archie hefted bags of staples into the carriage. Charlotte sat in the back among the groceries before Archie could suggest otherwise. As they turned from State Street onto Eighteenth Street and trotted east toward Lake Michigan, Charlotte welcomed the familiar sight of the spires of the Kimball mansion on Prairie Avenue, marking the prestigious neighborhood from several blocks away. She felt an odd comfort as they approached the house that had sheltered her secret all this time.

When they turned onto Prairie Avenue, Archie had to go around a carriage disgorging tourists for their self-guided exploration of the neighborhood.

"And now, ladies and gentlemen," Archie pronounced dramatically, "I give you the richest of the rich, the lifestyles of the famous and elite. Don't dare to close your eyes for even a second. You won't want to miss the exquisite glamour of Prairie Avenue, which far outweighs the lavish beauty of the Alabaster City known as the world's fair."

"Oh, hush," Charlotte said, but she couldn't help but laugh.

And it felt good to laugh.

But she still wanted Henry in her arms.

15

Out in the courtyard the next morning, well away from the back doors, Charlotte snapped the rug from the servants' hall and released the accumulated dirt of dozens of boots over the last several days. Dust whirled in freedom before landing on the fall breeze and blowing to far-flung settlements. Charlotte then hung the rug over a clothesline and whacked it with a rug beater.

Across the courtyard, the baby played in the grass, rolling and giggling and squealing until even Sarah relented and turned up one side of her mouth in amusement. Charlotte knew her son should have been in the nursery getting ready for his morning nap, but she was glad for a few minutes to witness his delight at the touch of grass on his skin.

"It was a good idea to bring him outside," Charlotte called to Sarah as she folded the rug twice and slung it over an arm.

"I couldn't stand being cooped up in that nursery another minute!" Sarah stood with her arms crossed. "This courtyard could use a bench, though."

"Sit in the grass with the baby."

Sarah scowled. "Hardly."

Suit yourself. "Maybe he'd like to have his bottle out here this morning before he goes down for his nap."

"I suppose that would be all right. Bring it out."

Charlotte set her jaw against the urge to answer Sarah's tone. Instead, she took the rug into the hallway and restored it to its usual place. Then she went into the kitchen to warm the baby's milk, having already decided to add a couple of extra ounces to this feeding. He seemed to gobble down everything in sight these days to fuel the active curiosity that had him toddling around the nursery during all his waking moments.

When Charlotte returned to the courtyard with the bottle, Sarah was sitting on a stone ledge about three feet off the ground, and the baby was next to her, tapping his heels against the brick.

"I don't think that's safe for him, Sarah." Charlotte handed the girl the bottle. What was she thinking, putting the baby up there? "Hold on to him."

"I'm right here. What could happen?"

"Babies move quickly." Surely Sarah had never cared for a toddler before. Charlotte reached for Henry.

Sarah slapped Charlotte's hands away. "He's not your business."

"If he gets hurt, he won't be your business either." Charlotte stepped back. "Just hang on to him."

The baby reached for the bottle, and Sarah surrendered it to him. Tilting his head back, he drank eagerly. A fraction of a second too late, and from a step too far away, Charlotte saw his torso wobble.

"Watch out!" she shouted.

Sarah startled and reached out one arm, but the baby slid

through her grip and down along the bricks to the stone path below.

Charlotte was there in an instant. "Look what you've done now!"

Archie let the old mare take her sweet time sauntering past the overhang that shaded the passage along the side of the house. For the most part, the household staff came and went by the servants' entrances on the other side of the house, where the servants' hall opened into a flow of several interconnected workrooms. However, the narrow courtyard access on this side allowed deliveries to a back door directly off the kitchen. Archie intended to maneuver as close to the door as possible and unload the meat cuts for which Mrs. Fletcher had been too impatient to wait for the butcher's delivery. When he saw Charlotte crouched on the ground, however, he yanked the horse to a halt, jumped out of the cart, and ran toward her.

He grabbed Sarah's elbow and shoved her out of the way. "What happened?"

"He wouldn't sit still," Sarah said.

"You should never have had him up on the ledge with you!" Charlotte screamed. "I told you to hang on to him!"

Archie's eyes widened. He had never heard Charlotte's voice at such volume or so full of passion.

Charlotte's left hand cupped the baby's head against her apron. Her hand reddened steadily. The milky remains of a shattered bottle were splayed around the walkway.

"What have you done, Sarah?" Archie made sure his voice sounded more controlled than Charlotte's, but still insistent. "You'd better go get Mr. Penard."

Sarah quivered, but she finally turned and went in the house. Archie squatted next to Charlotte.

"He's not breathing!" she screamed.

The child's blue eyes were wide open, though, and to Archie's relief, at that moment, he inhaled and let loose with a shriek.

"That's a good sign," Archie said over the baby's screams. "Where is the blood coming from?"

Slowly, Charlotte turned the baby in her arms so they could inspect the wound on the back of his head. "I will never forgive her," she uttered through gritted teeth. "If Mr. Penard had just given me charge of the baby, none of this would have happened."

"It's not your fault," Archie said. "He wasn't your responsibility." He put an arm around her trembling shoulders, feeling the thinness of her form under his hand.

Blood continued to seep onto Charlotte's apron.

"I should not have stepped away. I knew it was unsafe."

"Charlotte, he wasn't your responsibility," Archie repeated. "Don't chastise yourself over a mistake Sarah made."

"The result is the same. He's bleeding in my hand."

"He needs a doctor," Archie said. "Even Mr. Penard will be able to see that." He pulled a handkerchief from a pocket and slipped it between the boy's skull and Charlotte's hand. Then he moved his hand to cradle hers, stilling the shiver he felt there.

The baby wailed and thrashed against Charlotte's grip, but she held him still.

Mr. Penard stormed out the kitchen door, a pale Sarah behind him. "How badly is the child hurt?"

"He needs a doctor," Archie said. "The gash may need to be stitched closed."

"Archie, you will go for the doctor," Mr. Penard said. "Charlotte, you will take the child to the nursery to await the doctor. Sarah, you will sit in the kitchen and not move until I am finished with you. Is that understood?"

"Yes, sir." Sarah wrapped her arms around herself and looked away.

"If the child is seriously harmed in any way, you will face Mrs. Banning yourself." Mr. Penard's face flashed red. "You will take full responsibility for this."

"Yes, sir."

"Charlotte, take the child upstairs. I will bring hot water momentarily."

Archie jumped back in the cart and, mindless of the meat cuts, prodded the mare to move much faster than she was inclined to do.

The baby was breathing normally again at last. Every few minutes, though, he howled with fresh vigor. Charlotte laid him on the table in the nursery and peeled off the blood-soaked shirt. One side of his body, from cheek to heel, bore the scrapes of ragged brick against his tender skin, but the back of his head was the only place actively bleeding, and the flow had slowed.

Mr. Penard entered with a pot of hot water and a stack of fresh rags. Charlotte went right to work, wincing as she got enough of the dirt and blood cleared away to see the trueness of the wound. Mr. Penard looked over her shoulder and sighed heavily.

"Clean it up the best you can," the butler said quietly. "The doctor will decide what is necessary." He closed the nursery door behind him.

Every time Charlotte touched the cut even lightly, the baby wailed. Finally, though, satisfied that the worst of the bleeding was past, she laid him with his head on a clean rag to absorb the seepage while she sponged off the scrapes along the side of his little body. There would be no hiding the marks, she knew. In a few hours, Emmaline Brewster would no doubt call for Henry as usual and be horrified by what she discovered.

Charlotte picked up her son and moved to the rocking chair. Instinct told her not to let him sleep, however, so she refrained from rocking. Instead, she positioned him on her lap in a way that she could see his face and coax him to stay awake and look at her. She kept one hand on the cloth behind his head at all times.

"Oh, Henry," she said softly, "I had my birthday yesterday, and today is yours. This is not fair. This is not what I wanted for your first birthday. I was going to bring you a bakery cake to share with Mrs. Given. Now no one can even know."

Charlotte examined every discolored scrape. Henry's face was still set in a scowl from his injuries, but his eyes were open and focused.

"I can't let you go," she whispered. "I am going to find the right moment—soon—and tell Mrs. Banning the truth. Whatever happens, we'll be together."

A rap on the nursery door startled her.

"Yes?" She expected one of the other maids.

The door opened, and Emmaline Brewster entered, her full burgundy silk skirts rustling with every step.

"Miss Brewster!" Charlotte exclaimed. Emmaline had never been to the nursery before.

"I've just overheard a distressing conversation between the

other maids," Miss Brewster said. "It would appear that the information was accurate. The child is injured!"

She crossed the room quickly as Charlotte struggled to stand without jostling the baby.

"Archie has gone for the doctor," Charlotte explained, "but I think he's all right."

"It's clear Sarah is not to be trusted with the child's welfare," Miss Brewster said firmly. "I will care for him myself."

"I'm sure that's not necessary," Charlotte said quickly. "He's quite calm now. I can manage."

Miss Emmaline stroked one of his legs. "I couldn't bear it if anything happened to him."

Charlotte believed her. Henry turned his head to the familiar form—new to the nursery—and managed a wan smile.

Miss Emmaline sat in the rocker Charlotte had just vacated and put her hands out. "Let me hold him and wait for the doctor."

Charlotte swallowed hard and laid her son in the eager arms of Emmaline Brewster.

16

Henry was fine. It took both Charlotte and Emmaline to hold him still while the doctor put two stitches in the back of his head, but as soon as the fuss was over and he had something to eat, he perked up.

Fortunately—in Charlotte's mind—Mr. Penard banned Sarah from the nursery, at least for the time being. The girl was sternly admonished to move her personal belongings back to the third floor female servants' rooms. Emmaline Brewster prevailed on Flora Banning to designate Charlotte for the baby's care, under Emmaline's personal supervision. Mrs. Fletcher, of course, made it clear to Mr. Penard that she expected Charlotte's continued help in the kitchen. Someone would have to train Sarah, after all, and Mrs. Fletcher was persuasive that dealing with an impudent scullery maid was the last thing she had time for.

Charlotte moved the high chair down to the kitchen so she could corral Henry safely within her sight at least some of the time. Emmaline insisted she did not require assistance for the afternoon airings. Charlotte did not feel one bit sorry for Sarah when Emmaline took the baby out and the girl was left to scrub pots. While Henry slept in the daytime, Charlotte ran up to check on him frequently, never lagging in her efficiency at her other tasks. At night, she slept in the room next to his, and hers was the first face he saw in the mornings.

She counted the coins in her dresser drawer again. Soon she would have her September wages to add.

A week passed, and Charlotte had not spoken to Mrs. Banning yet. It was Emmaline Brewster who worried her. The lady of the house was blissfully unaware of what her houseguest was planning, and Charlotte frankly wondered how anyone could miss the signs. But Emmaline was still weeks away from leaving Chicago and trying to take the child with her. Flora was still hopeful to hear from Louisa, and that process would take weeks as well. Charlotte believed she had time.

Henry was down for his morning nap. With the baby sleeping, Charlotte scurried back to the kitchen to make sure Sarah was cleaning the potatoes Mrs. Fletcher intended to bake for luncheon, then she would lay the table.

She did not speak to Sarah as she went through the kitchen. The two of them had exchanged the fewest possible words in the last week. Satisfied that the potatoes were under control, Charlotte moved through to the dining room, where the table linens needed to be changed. She gathered the tablecloth in her arms and carried it back through the kitchen to the workroom. The laundress would deal with it on Monday morning. In the servants' hall, she met Lina, the parlor maid, coming in the female servants' entrance.

"I have a letter for you." Lina handed Charlotte a crumpled envelope.

Charlotte's eyes widened. Who would be sending her a letter? She inspected the envelope, which bore only her first name in carefully printed letters.

"It didn't come with the regular mail," Lina said. "I left that on the tray in the kitchen the same as I always do. A man asked me if I worked on this street and if I knew Charlotte Landers. I said I knew Charlotte Farrow. He laughed and handed me the envelope."

"He laughed?" Charlotte echoed.

"He asked if you had a baby, and of course I said that was ridiculous. I said he must be looking for another Charlotte, but he insisted I bring the letter."

"Thank you," Charlotte managed to say. "Yes, I'm sure it's a muddle that has nothing to do with me."

"I have to polish the upstairs hall today." Lina's mind was already on her own tasks as she turned away.

Charlotte expelled a breath, and the next one seemed reluctant to come. Only a handful of men in the world would know to ask for Charlotte Landers. And to suspect a baby. The envelope quivered in a grip grown numb with fear. Frantically, Charlotte glanced around, then ducked outside to the courtyard.

She didn't see me, Archie thought as he watched her shoulders heaving. She stumbled away from the house, fumbling with something in her hands, tearing an envelope, unfolding a page, reading the words written on it. He saw the breath go out of her. She did not refill her lungs.

"Charlotte!" He stepped into view.

She sucked air at last as she stuffed the papers into her apron pocket.

"Charlotte, what's wrong?" Archie cradled her elbows and searched her pallid face.

She stared at him blankly, shaking her head.

"Charlotte, talk to me." He laid one hand against an ashen cheek and felt the warmth rising there.

She shuddered under his touch and shook her head.

"I saw you reading something," Archie said. "A letter. It upset you. That much is plain. Whatever it is, you don't have to bear it alone."

Her hand moved to her pocket.

"Charlotte, I can't stand to see you this way. Talk to me. Let me share your load."

Her face stilled and her eyes, spilling tears, locked into his. Archie took her face between his hands and bent to put his forehead against hers.

"You have to know I care for you," he said, "so whatever it is, you can tell me."

He heard the sound her throat made as she swallowed, and he put his lips on hers ever so gently and held them there. Finally she responded. He felt the return pressure he had waited so long for.

Sarah was blessedly alone in the kitchen. Having everyone watching her every move was becoming annoying. Did they seriously think she could not peel a stupid potato without supervision? The whole matter was unfair. She had done a good job with the brat, and one fleeting moment of distraction had undone everything. Nobody gave her a moment's peace now, and she detested the kitchen work. She threw her knife down on the butcher block and slouched into a chair at the table.

A small silver tray sat in the middle of the table with the

day's mail. Sarah had seen Lina leave it there earlier, and now she idly flipped through the envelopes. She had watched Mr. Penard examine the mail on countless mornings, sorting out what related to household accounts and passing on to the Bannings the more personal envelopes. Sarah moved a pink envelope to the bottom of the pile, revealing a cream colored envelope with elaborate writing.

It was addressed to Miss Charlotte Farrow.

Sarah looked at the return address—Mrs. Will Edwards, care of a hotel in Paris, France. She fingered the envelope, curiosity welling.

Charlotte broke away abruptly, putting two fingers to her lips. "What have I done?"

Archie smiled at her. "You let me love you for just a moment. Perhaps you even loved me back."

"I'm sorry, Archie. I made a mistake. I should never have done that." Absently, she wiped her hands on her apron. She turned her back and walked toward the house, hardly letting herself breathe until she was safely within the walls of the day nursery.

Opening Henry's door, she watched her son sleeping. He was the only thing that mattered. For a moment she had let herself forget that. For a moment, she had let herself be a woman responding to the touch of a good man. For a moment, she had let herself forget about the truth of her life and hope for happiness.

But it was a mistake. What Archie wanted was not possible, and it was unfair to let him think it might be.

Especially now.

He knew where she was. He had been on Prairie Avenue, in the right block. He was resourceful enough to determine the right house if he wanted to.

She had been so careful for a year.

Charlotte closed Henry's door and stumbled to the rocking chair. Miss Brewster had sat in this chair several times in the last week during her regular visits to the nursery.

Miss Brewster.

Suddenly what Charlotte suspected made perfect sense. Especially for Henry.

Mrs. Fletcher entered the kitchen with a sigh.

Sarah jumped back to her post at the chopping block and pushed a pile of potato peels into the slop bucket on the floor. The letter slid out of her hand and into the bucket. Sarah grimaced.

"That bucket looks almost full," Mrs. Fletcher said. "You may as well dump it in the bin outside right now."

"I don't think it's quite full." Sarah eyed the letter now coated in glop.

Mrs. Fletcher picked up a wooden spoon and pointed it at Sarah. "I don't think you want to argue with me, Sarah. Dump the bucket."

17

Flora Banning's face was as red as Charlotte had ever seen it.

Charlotte was pouring coffee in the parlor after dinner two days later. The meal had been uneventful as far as Banning dinners went. They hosted no guests, and in fact young Richard was not there, having accepted an invitation to dine with a friend's family. Miss Emmaline had been out all afternoon—leaving Charlotte to walk the baby herself—and remarked more than once how tired she was and that she had a mind to cancel her engagements for the next several days. After dinner, Samuel, Flora, and Emmaline moved to the parlor. Leo and Oliver went about their own business, as they usually did in the evenings. But a routine evening erupted into a spectacle as Flora Banning read the handwritten note on pale pink paper that had come in that day's mail.

Flora waved the paper in the air. "I demand an explanation!"

Samuel raised an eyebrow at his wife's outburst. "What on earth are you going on about?"

"This note! It came in today's mail, and I've only just now had a chance to read it."

"Who is it from?" Samuel accepted the cup and saucer

Charlotte offered, the coffee sweetened heavily the way he liked it.

"Louisa. It's brief, but clearly something has gone amiss, and I want to know what it was."

"My dear, I still don't understand what you're talking about." Samuel set his coffee down, reached across the end table that separated him from his wife, took the note from her hand, adjusted his glasses on his nose, and read aloud. "Dear Flora, You can imagine my disappointment to learn that someone with an attachment to the child has come forward. Of course this may be the best thing for the boy if it is a blood relation. Under the circumstances, though, I believe we will delay our visit to Chicago and the fair until the wound of disappointment is not so fresh as it is just now. Yours truly, Louisa."

"What is she talking about?" Flora demanded. "I know nothing of anyone with a claim on the child. He's been here five weeks in the care of the staff."

Charlotte poured another cup of coffee and handed it to Emmaline Brewster, keeping her eyes from staring at the face of the woman in a copper-colored satin gown with pearl buttons Charlotte herself had buttoned up the back three hours ago.

When Emmaline took the saucer, the cup rattled uncharacteristically.

Emmaline immediately set the coffee down on the table on front of the settee. This situation required all her concentration. She had known this moment would come, but she reasoned that time was on her side. The longer she was in the Banning house spending time with the child, the more sensible her plan would seem when it was discovered.

"Flora," Emmaline said at last, "I am the one with an attachment to the baby."

"You? What attachment? What are you talking about?"

Emmaline folded her hands together and laid them calmly in her lap. "He's an attractive, agreeable child, and he has stolen my heart," she said simply. "As you know, I often take him out in the afternoons, and we are very comfortable together."

Flora's face was no less red. "But what possible claim could you have on an abandoned child? He can't be yours!"

"No, he is not mine—yet. I would like him to be. My claim is simply that I find him enchanting and have formed an attachment. He knows me now and responds well. You know I can give him a good home with many advantages."

"But it was all arranged with Louisa, and you knew that!" Flora was on her feet now. "Why would you interfere without the courtesy of speaking to me?"

Emmaline had been calculating for weeks how she would comport herself in this inevitable moment. "I regret I was silent so long and let Louisa's hopes be raised, but she is young and married and will have many opportunities for family happiness ahead of her."

"How could you take matters into your own hands when you knew I had written to Louisa?" Flora slapped the arm of her chair with the letter.

"I believe I have been brought to Chicago at this time to meet this child," Emmaline said, "and our futures are bound together."

Flora and Samuel stared at her, speechless, so Emmaline continued.

"I will need to have some renovation done on my house, of course, and I'm prepared to begin the arrangements immediately to make ready a proper nursery. My butler can engage a nursemaid. I am unsure of the legalities of adopting an abandoned child, but it can't be difficult. After all, thousands of children every year are put on trains and sent west to find new homes."

"I have already looked into the process," Samuel admitted. "I anticipated that need on Louisa's behalf. The laws are fairly loose."

"Then we're halfway there," Emmaline said. "Of course I would want a legal adoption. He would be my son in every sense."

"It's a matter of due diligence to be sure we cannot locate his mother." Samuel stroked his chin. "It does not seem as if that should be troublesome."

"Samuel!" Flora put one hand on a hip. "You cannot seriously entertain this notion."

Emmaline was prepared for this objection. "I did not expect Samuel to represent my interests in making Teddy mine permanently."

"Teddy?" Flora asked.

"Short for Theodore," Emmaline explained. "The name means 'gift of God,' and I believe this child is a gift from God to me at this point in my life."

"Emmaline, your behavior shocks me." Flora sank back in her chair. "Clearly you have given this a great deal of thought without so much as a word to me."

"I understand you are shocked." Emmaline buried her hands in the folds of her skirt. "I don't mean to hurt anyone. This must seem rash to you, but I promise you it is not. I believe things happen for a reason. I believe God has brought me to this house at the same time as he brought this child to your home because he wants the two of us to be together. My claim to this child is divine providence."

"How do you know divine providence does not intend this child for Louisa?" Flora's pitch rose.

"Because I am here, and she is not. God is answering my prayers in his own way."

"We need not decide anything tonight," Samuel intoned. "Perhaps we should reserve further discussion for a more suitable time."

"Yes, of course." Emmaline gathered her skirts and stood up. "I should retire for the evening and give you some time to think about this." She turned to Charlotte. "Would you please come upstairs as soon as you're finished clearing up in here?"

"Yes, miss," Charlotte said softly.

Was Miss Emmaline right? Did things happen for a reason? Did God orchestrate meetings between lonely women and motherless little boys?

Except he wasn't motherless.

Charlotte fingered the crumpled envelope she always kept in her apron pocket—she could not risk anyone finding it unattended. Lina seemed to have forgotten all about it, and Charlotte had avoided Archie for the last two days. She evaded his glance at the table where the staff shared their meals. If he came into the kitchen for any purpose during the day, she found a reason to step out without speaking to him or even looking in his direction.

Two days after the kiss, she still felt the sensation of his hand against her face, of his lips on hers, of his arms around her, and the warmth of her own response.

It had been a mistake, and she could not afford to make another one.

She had stayed in the parlor long enough to clear away the coffee service. Both the Bannings lost interest in coffee and dessert after Emmaline's revelation. Charlotte returned the service cart to the kitchen and left the washing up for Sarah, turning her focus to what awaited her in Miss Lucy's old suite.

On the second floor, she knocked on the door and entered when Emmaline responded. Emmaline was seated at the vanity, removing pins from her hair. Charlotte moved across the room and took over the task, laying the hairpins in a neat row.

"Would you like to take off your gown now?" Charlotte asked. "Then I'll brush out your hair."

Emmaline stood up and moved away from the vanity, while Charlotte fetched a nightdress and robe from a hook in the closet. After laying them on the chaise lounge, Charlotte set to work on the tedious row of tiny pearl buttons up the back of the gown, pulling each one out of the thin braided loop that held it in place.

"I suppose you have an opinion about what happened in the parlor," Miss Emmaline said.

Charlotte swallowed. "It's not my place, miss."

"No, I suppose not. All you did was find Teddy outside. But I've seen you with him, so I know you're far from heartless when it comes to his best interests."

"A child deserves the best his parents can give him," Charlotte said cautiously.

"And if he has no parents?"

Charlotte fumbled with a stubborn loop but said nothing.

"I don't know Cousin Louisa," Emmaline said. "She may even be a distant relative of mine, since we are both related to Flora somehow. I never meant to hurt her. I am not a cruel person, Charlotte."

"No, of course not, miss."

"Flora likes to manage things," Emmaline said. "She's been that way for as long as I can remember, whether I was visiting Chicago or she came to New Hampshire to see the family there. She has a fixed way of thinking about how things ought to be done."

"Yes, miss." Charlotte's fingers trembled at the top button.

"Sometimes it's not necessary to manage a situation," Emmaline continued. "Sometimes the answer is staring you in the face, and all you have to do is see it. That's all I've done."

Charlotte eased the gown off Emmaline's shoulders and down below her waist, holding it in place while Emmaline stepped out of its fullness. She laid the dress on the bed to hang up later, then turned to undo Emmaline's corset. A few minutes later, Emmaline sat again at the vanity, this time in a nightgown, while Charlotte stood behind her, brushing out thick auburn hair.

"Did they say anything after I left the parlor?" Emmaline asked.

Charlotte hesitated. "It's not my place," she said again.

Emmaline reached up and stopped the brush in midmotion, catching Charlotte's eye in the mirror.

"Did you check on him before you came in here?"

"Yes, miss. He is sleeping well."

"Charlotte, you and I are on the same side when it comes to Teddy. You see him the way I do, as a real little boy who deserves a happy future."

"Yes, miss."

"Why shouldn't that happy future be with me?" Emmaline asked. "He needs a home, and I have a lavish house with everything a child could ever dream of. I don't believe in coincidence."

Charlotte resumed brushing. "Do you really believe things happen for a reason?"

"Don't you?"

"I never thought much about it," Charlotte admitted.

"Teddy is meant to be mine. I just know it."

Charlotte put the brush down. "I'll turn the bed down before I go."

"Thank you, Charlotte."

As soon as she could, Charlotte fled down the servants' stairs and out to the courtyard to lift her face to the night sky. Constellations glittered from unfathomable places, while closer to the ground a breeze cooled Charlotte's flushed face.

"Is anybody even there?" she asked aloud, staring at a far distant point of light.

Her hand was in her apron pocket, fingers wrapped around the folded envelope. She did not need to look at the note again to remember what it said: *Imagine my surprise when I took a tour of Prairie Avenue and saw you. What have you done with it?*

Charlotte let herself fall to the grass where her baby had played only last week, and covered her face with both shaking hands.

18

Charlotte, you haven't left the house in almost two weeks—and I mean that literally. You haven't been to the markets or shops. You barely even go out in the courtyard anymore." Alone in the kitchen with Charlotte, Archie trailed her as she inspected a shelf of staples.

"I'm fine, Archie," Charlotte said. "I have so much to do, with the baby, and Miss Emmaline, and laying the table every time I turn around."

"You should tell Mr. Penard it's too much." He did not believe for a moment that she was fine. "Surely Lina and Elsie can help more than they do. And Sarah."

Charlotte scoffed and shrugged out of Archie's grasp to set a carton of baking powder next to the dwindling supply of sugar. "She seems capable enough in the kitchen, but she's slow. Mrs. Fletcher is apt to go after her with a meat pounder if she doesn't speed up soon."

"You can't bear this load," he insisted. "I've been saying that for weeks. I'm tempted to speak to Mr. Penard myself."

"Please don't do that." She met his gaze finally.

"I can't help feeling there's more than you're telling me.

You're working yourself into exhaustion because you're frightened of something. Tell me what it is."

"I don't know what you're talking about, Archie."

He exhaled. "Charlotte Farrow, you are as stubborn as anyone I've ever met. Fine. Do what you think you must tonight, but tomorrow morning you are going to the World's Columbian Exposition for Chicago Day. Miss Emmaline Brewster wants you to, and the Bannings have put you at her disposal."

"Right now I have to go up to the nursery," she said.

"Don't change the subject." He held his position.

"I really have to go."

Archie glanced at the wall clock. "You put Teddy to bed two hours ago."

"He didn't seem settled to me. I want to check on him."

"Are you afraid for Teddy?"

"Why would I be afraid for the baby?"

Her voice did not carry the determination of her words. "I don't know. You tell me."

She looked him in the eyes. "Archie, it would be better for everyone if you leave me alone."

"I don't agree. It would be better for you if you told me what's going on."

"You would be entirely wrong about the matter."

The pasty color of her face only heightened his resolve to gain her trust, but this moment had yielded all it would.

She turned to go up the servants' stairs. "As you pointed out, tomorrow is going to be a big day. I still have a lot to do tonight so we can be ready in the morning. So do you."

From the bottom of the steps, Archie tracked her swift progress up the stairs. Too swift.

In the morning, the entourage gathered. Charlotte handed Archie a basket to set inside the carriage. The baby buggy already was strapped to the back of the carriage.

"I'm surprised Miss Brewster has not moved out of the house," Archie said, "after the stir she caused. Surely she has resources to stay somewhere else."

"She won't leave without the baby." Charlotte thought that much was obvious.

"Mrs. Banning could insist." Archie stood beside the open carriage door.

Charlotte shook her head. "She can't risk what Miss Brewster might do in a showdown."

"And what might Miss Brewster do?" Archie twirled a button on his jacket. "She has no claim."

"She might bring in the authorities," Charlotte said. "Then the Bannings would have no claim either."

The front door opened and Emmaline Brewster appeared at the top of the steps with the baby in her arms. Behind her was Violet Newcomb, and then Sarah.

Emmaline had decided that Chicago Day was the perfect day for the fair. Such an undertaking required elaborate preparations, however, so Emmaline had conscripted Archie to drive the carriage and lift the baby buggy, and both Charlotte and Sarah to help manage Henry or attend to other needs that she and Violet might have.

"Didn't she go to the fair last week?" Archie asked.

Charlotte nodded. "With one of Miss Newcomb's eligible bachelors. I don't think she much cared for him, but she did like the fair."

"Does Mrs. Banning know she's taking the baby?"

"Mrs. Banning left early this morning and will be out for the whole day."

"She won't be happy."

"Miss Brewster is not going to steal the baby while we're all with her. Nothing will happen."

Archie glanced toward the door. "Is she really bringing Sarah today?"

Charlotte rolled her eyes. "She thinks maybe Sarah has learned her lesson and might be trusted with the baby again. She lets Sarah sit with him while he's asleep at dinnertime."

Emmaline Brewster descended the steps. "What a beautiful day. There's no reason Teddy should not know his Chicago roots."

At the carriage Emmaline handed the boy to Charlotte to hold while she settled in her seat. Charlotte stroked his head before handing him back to Emmaline.

"No one knows exactly how old he is," Emmaline said. "'Chicago Day' at the fair is a perfect day for a birthday. October 9. That will be his birthday."

Archie next offered a hand to Violet Newcomb, who settled herself in the carriage next to Emmaline. Then it was Charlotte's turn. She slid to one end of the bench across from Emmaline, leaving plenty of room for Sarah. The girl smiled warmly at Archie and held his hand longer than necessary, in Charlotte's opinion, before sliding onto the bench herself.

Charlotte turned her gaze out the window on the other side of the carriage. She could not blame Sarah. Archie Shepard had much to commend him, and Charlotte had asked him to leave her alone just the night before. Perhaps Sarah's flirtations would make him reconsider his persistence.

At the last minute, Karl appeared and hoisted himself up on the driver's seat beside Archie. Emmaline had specifically asked for Archie to accompany her for the entire day, but they would need someone to stay with the carriage and horses while they walked the fairgrounds.

Archie got the horses moving. Charlotte thought, *It takes half the household staff to take a woman and child to the fair.* If there were a simpler way, apparently it had not occurred to Emmaline Brewster. A train or streetcar, for instance, would have saved a lot of trouble, in Charlotte's opinion. Lucy Banning Edwards would have taken public transportation. The thought made Charlotte smile. But Emmaline was not Lucy, and no doubt even Sarah was gloating at the poor souls who could not afford to go to the fair by carriage.

Archie headed east on Eighteenth Street and within a few blocks turned south along the drive running along the lakeshore, which would take them down to Jackson Park. Charlotte settled in for the journey, resigned to the crowds and congestion sure to characterize the day. From Emmaline's lap, Henry cooed at Charlotte, and she could not help but smile at him.

"See!" Emmaline said. "Teddy is already having a good time. Happy birthday, Teddy!"

They were inside the fairgrounds at last, entering through the Cottage Grove Avenue entrance on the Midway Plaisance, rather than by boat on the pier or the massive railroad station that served the fair. Archie took the baby's buggy off the back of the carriage before Karl disappeared with the horses, and Sarah took charge of arranging the baby in the buggy.

With Emmaline pushing the buggy and leading the way, the entourage progressed along the Midway.

"They want to break the attendance record for a world's fair today." Emmaline spoke above the clamor of the crowd. "That's why I thought it would be fun to bring Teddy today—the biggest birthday party in the world."

"Yes, miss," Charlotte said. "Someday it will be a wonderful story to tell."

Sarah took this opportunity to push in front of Charlotte and follow more closely behind Emmaline and Violet. She craned to see the baby in the buggy and left Archie and Charlotte to bring up the rear. Charlotte glanced awkwardly at Archie.

"You're going to have a nice day," he said. "Just let yourself."

In the thick crowd, Charlotte could hardly discern the attractions along the Midway Plaisance, the one-mile stretch of parkway incorporated into the fairgrounds and now populated by sideshows, concessions, and games. Merely avoiding collisions with other fairgoers required all the concentration she could muster. When Emmaline stopped briefly to adjust the toys in the buggy, Charlotte took advantage of being stationary to look around.

Even against the din around her, she heard herself gasp.

That muscular form was unmistakable. Or was it? All she saw was a profile, with his head turned the other way. The hair was longer at the collar than he had ever worn it, but it had been more than a year, and a man could change his mind about a haircut. She could not see if the permanent sneer seared into her memory was part of this man's face, or the eyes that never quite believed anything anyone said.

"Charlotte?" Archie said. "What is it?"

She shook her head. "It's nothing."

His note had said he was in Chicago. He had even been on Prairie Avenue. She knew his tone well enough to hear it even in his written words. He could be patient, but he never walked away from what he wanted.

When she looked again, he was gone.

Finally, they approached the Court of Honor, pausing to admire the welcoming statue, *The Republic*, rising in grandeur at the east end of the Grand Basin. Around the water, fourteen massive stately buildings of the fair beckoned, each one covered in the same gleaming white stucco. Dozens of smaller buildings filled out the landscape.

"I hardly know where to start." Emmaline surveyed several directions. "Leo mentioned his fascination with Machinery Hall, but I also heard it's just a collection of steam engines. I don't suppose it's really of any interest."

"We only saw half of the Liberal Arts Building," Violet observed. "There is so much more to see there."

"I wonder what Teddy would like to see," Emmaline mused.

Henry would be happy splashing his hand in the lagoon and rolling in the grass, Charlotte thought.

"Perhaps the Electricity Building," Emmaline said. "I hear they are displaying electric fans and even sewing machines. Little boys like inventions, don't they?"

"I think I read there are farm buildings and animals," Charlotte ventured. "He . . . Teddy . . . might like that." She choked on the name.

"That's a wonderful idea. Let's find the animals."

They did find animals, and Henry was mesmerized. Charlotte knew he had seen the occasional stray mutt or tomcat in Mrs. Given's neighborhood, but the range of farm and exotic animals on display had him pointing and squealing for two hours. Sarah held him up to stroke the cow and the baby lamb, and at the caged wild animal exhibit, Sarah held him and pointed and called each lion and tiger and cougar by name. Charlotte did not take her eyes off the girl. Whatever Emmaline's reasons for thinking Sarah deserved another chance, Charlotte remained skeptical. Finally, the little boy sank into his buggy, exhausted. They slowed their pace to allow him a nap. Now Sarah was walking in front, pushing the buggy, with Violet and Emmaline behind her.

When Charlotte ventured a glance at Archie's face, she found him smiling at her. "What are you looking so silly about?"

"You are at a world's fair," he said, "yet you seem determined not to enjoy yourself! I intend to do something about that."

She sighed, and a hesitant smile emerged. "It's all a bit overwhelming." She was surprised Archie was speaking to her at all, after her rebuff of the evening before.

"Wait until we go on the Ferris wheel." Archie rubbed his palms together in a quick swishing movement.

"I can't possibly go up," she said flatly.

"You must! You'll never experience anything like it."

She shook her head. "I don't care. I don't trust that thing."

"You won't know if you don't try."

She turned away from him then, determined to keep her feet on the ground for the rest of the day.

When it was time for lunch, Emmaline insisted they go into the New England Clam Bake Restaurant near the lakefront, where she could sit down and be served clam chowder, baked beans, and pumpkin pie.

"Teddy's still sleeping," Emmaline said. "Perhaps you can

find a place in the shade to sit with him. Violet and I will send some food out as soon as we're seated."

Violet and Emmaline entered the restaurant. Sarah put on her best nanny face and took charge of the buggy, walking with such resolve to a small outdoor table that Archie and Charlotte had little option but to follow her.

Charlotte was grateful to be sitting down, though the sun's glare made her squint. She allowed herself to sip on a cold iced tea while they waited for their food. Sarah was gently jiggling the buggy in the absence of conversation.

Suddenly Charlotte stood up. Had it been a passing blur, or had she seen him? She took a few quick steps along the walkway toward the lakefront, examining every direction. When she felt the touch on her shoulder, she spun around, breathless.

"Charlotte, what's wrong?" Archie asked, scanning her face.

She looked back over her shoulder. He was gone again—if he had ever been there in the glare. Perhaps she only thought she saw him. Surely it was just someone with a similar appearance passing in the throng.

"Something caught my eye." Charlotte shook her head. "I thought . . . it's nothing. Let's sit down."

"Yes, let's sit," he said, "and discuss how extraordinary it will be to go up in the Ferris wheel."

She laughed nervously. "You're not going to give up, are you?"

And he did not give up. At every opportunity, he expounded on the science and safety of the Ferris wheel. At the end of the day, when they had to walk back through the Midway to meet Karl with the carriage, the moment came. By then they had walked all around the Court of Honor, ducking in and out of the glimmering white buildings. Despite the length of the line for the Ferris wheel, Emmaline insisted they should all go up and sent Archie to purchase the tickets. They stood together in the snaking line. Charlotte inched forward with the others, every moment taking her closer to terror. Clearly Miss Emmaline expected the group to enjoy the attraction together. Even Violet Newcomb seemed eager for the experience. Archie nudged Charlotte's elbow a couple of times, no doubt intending encouragement.

She could not do it. At the last minute, Charlotte stepped out of line with the buggy.

"The baby is sleeping," Charlotte pleaded. It was true that he had dropped off again during the long wait. "We shouldn't wake him to take him. He's had such a stimulating day. If he becomes upset on the Ferris wheel, he'll disturb everyone in the car."

She held her breath while Emmaline considered.

"She has a point," Violet said. "The baby is worn out already."

"I suppose you're right," Emmaline said at last. "Taking him might not be the wisest thing."

"The rest of you go," Charlotte urged. "I'll stay down here with the buggy and wait for you. Wave to me from the top."

"I thought I had you persuaded," Archie whispered.

"I'm sorry, Archie, I just can't." Charlotte took a further step back. "I can't make myself get on that platform."

Sarah pushed forward, fearless. "Come on, Archie."

Charlotte breathed a sigh of relief as Emmaline, Violet, Archie, and Sarah took their places in one of the cars. Emmaline and Violet found seats among the twisted wire chairs while Archie and Sarah drifted to one end of the car and stood together in the crowd. With riders boarding from six separate platforms into cars that held sixty people each, more than two thousand people could brave the wheel at one time. Charlotte simply could not be one of them. She rocked the buggy with gentle rhythm as she observed the process. The car she watched shifted with each turn of the wheel until finally all the cars carried their load. As the wheel began nine minutes of revolution without stopping, Charlotte inspected the machinery supporting the movement. Even if she understood the engineering and physics of the wheel, it would not make any difference. She could never get on such a machine and be lifted so far off the ground, dangling in a box with nothing solid beneath her. Archie could pester all he wanted. She could not do it.

The profile crossed her vision again—the third time today. But this time he turned his face, and she saw the sneer was still there. His eyes caught hers.

Lathan Landers was in Chicago.

19

Brisk air filled her lungs in a welcome sensation, the sun not yet up but its luminous pink promise rising on Prairie Avenue. With the staff breakfast well in hand, Charlotte stole a few minutes to slip outside to the courtyard and wait for the day to overwhelm the shadows. She had perhaps an hour before Henry would awake and clamor for his oatmeal.

The excursion of the day before had left her sleepless and rattled. She passed much of the night sitting on the floor of the little room where her son slept, watching his chest move up and down. In the somber darkness, in the deepest watch of the night, she made up her mind. Now she had to make peace with her decision, and for that she had come outside, wrapping around her shoulders a cloak Lucy Banning Edwards had given her as a brace against the cold bite of predawn October air. She sat on a ledge—the one Henry had fallen from—and closed her eyes, whether in fear or prayer she was not sure.

Warmth beside her made her open her eyes. "Archie, what are you doing out here this early?"

"I might ask you the same thing." He settled in beside her.

"I just wanted some air," she said softly, "before the day gets underway."

He leaned against her and nudged her shoulder in his familiar gesture. "I don't believe you."

She looked at him squarely. "I don't care."

He hoisted himself off the ledge to stand in front of her perch. With an arm on either side of her against the brick, he blocked her in. "Charlotte, you're not telling me something important, and I want to know what it is."

"You know very little about me that is of any importance," she said.

"That's true. But I know *you*. I've been watching you long enough to know that in the last few weeks, something has frightened you. I want you to tell me what it is so I can help you."

She tried to look past his brown eyes to the view over his shoulder, but he ducked and bobbed his head until she had no choice but to let him look into her eyes.

Archie took her chin in one hand and leaned toward her. "You don't have to be alone," he whispered before kissing her.

Her hands moved to his chest to push him away. "Archie, no."

"No one is around to see," he assured her. "We can have this moment." He leaned toward her again.

"No, we can't." She pushed against him. "It's so much more complicated than you imagine."

He stepped back at last but wrapped his fingers around her hands. "Then explain it to me, Charlotte. Just tell me."

She shook her head. "I can't."

"Yes, you can. It's ripping you up—whatever it is. I saw how jumpy you were yesterday at the fair. When we were up on the Ferris wheel, I saw you. Sarah and I looked for you to wave. Something frightened you, and you suddenly picked up a sleeping baby who was perfectly happy where he was. Even Sarah made a comment."

"Archie, please."

He moved not an inch.

"Trust me," she mumbled, "it's better if you don't know."

"Trust *me*," he replied quickly. "Trust me, Charlotte. Tell me why you cannot return my affection."

She lost herself in his steadfast eyes searching and pleading. His grasp felt different this time. He was not about to let go of hand nor eyes. At last she found a whisper. "Because I have a husband."

His eyes clouded. "But—"

"I know," she said, still whispering. "It's unthinkable, and Mr. Penard would never have taken me on if he knew the truth."

He squeezed her hand. "But Miss Lucy knows, doesn't she? Is that what I see between the two of you?"

Charlotte shook her head and wiped a tear from her eye. "She doesn't know about my husband. Not exactly."

"Something else?"

Silence bore down on them.

"I have a baby," she finally said.

Archie drew a deep breath. "Teddy."

Charlotte nodded again. "His name is Henry, not Teddy. His birthday is September 20, not October 9."

"That certainly explains a lot of things," Archie said. "I knew that child had a hold on you. I just never guessed anything like this."

"Miss Lucy discovered him when I first got here. He was

a newborn then. I was ready to go before there was any fuss, but she said she wanted to help."

"I remember. You had just gotten here, and all of a sudden she needed a ladies' maid to sleep in her suite. You had a newborn in the Banning house under Mr. Penard's nose and he never suspected!"

"Henry was very small and never cried. He was no trouble."

Archie chuckled softly.

Charlotte straightened her back. She failed to see what was so amusing.

"It seems to me you've already lived through the worst," Archie said. "That was wildly brave, Charlotte."

"I didn't have a choice. I had to earn some money before I could put him out to board."

"And Lucy?"

"She used her connections at the orphanage and helped me find a woman to board him with."

"When Lucy Banning puts her mind to something, she's thorough," Archie said. "Mr. Leo and I looked through all those records ourselves. We found nothing that remotely resembled your son."

"I never knew what arrangement she made," Charlotte admitted. "She assured me the expense was taken care of, but whenever I could, I left a little extra for Mrs. Given myself."

"Mary Given," Archie muttered, "the woman with the twins."

Charlotte's eyes widened. "Yes, she was taking care of twins until they turned two years old a few months ago."

Archie nodded. "We found that in the record. But there was nothing to trace Teddy—Henry—to Mrs. Given. Miss Lucy must have been taking care of the boarding cost herself."

"Honestly, I had no idea. I don't know how I'll ever repay her."

"I can't imagine she would accept repayment. But how did the baby end up here?"

"Mrs. Given had a family emergency and had to go to Omaha. She just showed up with him two days before the family came home from the lake and said she had to catch a train. Right there." Charlotte pointed to the spot in the courtyard where the sheets had flapped in the wind that day. "Then Sarah found me sitting there with him a minute later. I didn't know what to do!"

"And everyone jumped to conclusions about the baby left for Lucy."

Charlotte lifted her shoulders in a slow shrug. "It seemed like I was being given some time to figure out what to do. If I said he was mine—"

"Penard would have put you out immediately."

She nodded as she squinted into the rising sun. "Even if Miss Lucy were here, I'm not sure she could have influenced him under such extreme circumstances."

"She might take you on at her own home when she sets up housekeeping."

"I hope so, but that's months away. And what am I to do with Henry until then? I can't bear the thought of putting him in the orphanage. They do wonderful work, but he's so little, and it's so big."

Archie exhaled heavily and leaned back against the wall. "They still want to send him to that cousin in Greenville, you know."

"No! He's not going to Greenville."

"Because it is so far? Or because it holds some danger?"

She nodded. "Too close to home. Henry is going as far away from there as possible."

"You're taking him away?" Archie asked. "Where will you go?"

Charlotte shook her head. "I'm not taking him away. I'm *sending* him away. I made up my mind last night. I'm going to help Miss Emmaline take him to New Hampshire."

"What!" Archie's dark eyes flashed. "You can't give your son away."

"It's the best thing for him."

"You're his mother. You're the best thing for him."

She shook her head again, emphatically. "I can't keep him safe. Yesterday proved that."

"You saw something at the fair."

She nodded. "His father."

"Your husband."

Tears began afresh. "He is *nothing* of what a husband should be."

"But you are legally bound to him."

"Not of my own will, but legally, yes." Charlotte nodded. "It seemed as if every time I turned around, there he was. And I received this a few weeks ago." She reached into her pocket for the note she always carried for several weeks now and handed it to Archie.

Archie unfolded the paper and held it up in the brightening sky. He read it quickly, then crunched it in his fist.

"He was here, Archie," Charlotte said, "on Prairie Avenue. He gave that note to Lina and asked after me using my married name. I saw him yesterday, and he saw me."

"Hundreds of thousands of people were at the fair yesterday," Archie said calmly. "Maybe it wasn't him."

"It was him, Archie. He saw me taking care of a baby, and he knows I'm on this street."

"Why has he not come looking for you again, then?"

Charlotte shook her head. "Even he wouldn't just come to the front door and ask for me, and I hardly leave the house."

"That much is true."

"He's a patient man if it means getting what he wants. I can't take the chance that what he wants is Henry."

"Have you absolutely nowhere you could take Henry?"

"No. I never thought he would find me here, and he has."

"It's a fluke. The fair has brought so many people to Chicago."

She shook her head. "I will *not* hand Henry over to him. And I can't keep Henry safe anymore. Even if I thought he were safe somewhere else, I can't provide for him on my own. He has to go with Miss Emmaline."

"Charlotte, no, don't do this," Archie pleaded softly. "You've told me now. You're not alone any longer. Let me help."

"I'm a married woman with another man's child." Charlotte whispered words she hated to speak. "Why should you want to help me?"

"Because I care for you, Charlotte Farrow. And this man does not sound like someone I should encourage you to go back to. If he were, you wouldn't be here."

"He's not." Charlotte blew out breath. "Miss Emmaline thinks it's divine providence that she came to Chicago and met Henry . . . Teddy."

"And what do you think?"

"It's hard to know what's right."

Archie shook his head. "You don't have to believe something just because Miss Emmaline said it."

Charlotte looked at Archie full on. "Don't you believe in God?"

"Yes, I believe in God. I just don't want you to be too quick to believe that he wants you to send your son away. It is possible Emmaline is interpreting difficult circumstances in a way that seems right from her perspective. That doesn't mean it's the will of God."

"But what if it is?" Charlotte choked on a sob.

"What if it's not?"

"I've made up my mind." Charlotte resisted more tears. "It will break my heart to send him away, but at least I'll know he'll have a good life with someone who thinks the sun and moon rise and set on his smile. Even Moses's mother had to let her son go to a life she could not be part of. That's in the Bible."

The kitchen door thumped behind them, and they both startled.

Sarah glanced from Charlotte to Archie. "Shouldn't you be inside with the baby?" she said to Charlotte.

"I just came out to see the sunrise." Charlotte slid down from her seat on the ledge and clutched her cloak around her. "I'll check on the baby now."

"If old Penard knew you were out here, he would have stern words for you."

"Sarah!" Archie's tone held no patience. "Mind your tongue when you don't know what you're speaking of."

Sarah lifted her head. "I know perfectly well what I'm speaking off—a maid and a coachman alone in the courtyard together before the sun is fully risen. I'm sure Mr. Penard would be happy to receive my report."

Charlotte brushed past Sarah without looking back at Archie and disappeared into the kitchen.

Archie strode over to Sarah and spun her to look at him directly. "If you say one word of this to Mr. Penard, I will personally see that you are put out of the house."

"On what grounds?" She stared at him, daring. "I rather think I am to be made nanny again if Miss Emmaline has anything to say about it."

"You were never nanny."

She clamped her teeth together.

He slammed through the kitchen door. Sarah followed slowly. There was something between those two that ought not to be there. She was sure of it. This was not over.

20

Charlotte held the two suits for Emmaline Brewster's inspection.

"The pale pink silk, I think," Emmaline Brewster said. "Yes, the pink, with the pearl necklace and my hair on top of my head."

"Yes, miss." Charlotte laid the pale pink silk on the bed and returned the blue satin to a hook in the closet. Though made of delicate silk, the pink skirt had an elaborate drape with asymmetrical swags at the hips that made Emmaline's waist seem more slender than it was. The suit's jacket featured tiny pleats across the front and buttoned down one side.

Charlotte helped Emmaline out of the ordinary day dress she had worn all morning. Though it was something Emmaline would not leave the house in, the sage green broadcloth print was still far finer than anything Charlotte could ever hope to wear. But in an hour's time, Emmaline would be entering the Henderson household for a luncheon, and an ordinary day dress would not do.

"I do wish this were simply a ladies luncheon," Emmaline moaned as Charlotte held the pink skirt for her to step into.

"Wednesday midday seems like an odd time for the Hendersons to arrange a social event. Flora says Mr. Henderson is more unbalanced than ever. Mrs. Glessner has implied that he does not make any effort to control himself, and Flora has seen for herself the way he behaves. I'm hardly looking forward to this luncheon."

"Perhaps it will not be so bad, ma'am." Charlotte held the jacket open for Miss Emmaline to put her arms in the sleeves.

"I can always hope not to be seated next to him." Emmaline shuffled slowly to the vanity table and fingered the string of pearls. "I'm getting tired of all this socializing. I'm surprised Flora has tolerated me all this time. I don't dare defy her by refusing to go."

"Shall I fasten the pearls, miss?" Charlotte knew she must handle the pearls despite the tremble in her fingers.

Emmaline handed the necklace to Charlotte. "I suppose Flora is still hoping I'll meet someone and lose interest in the baby. But I'm still hoping she'll come around to seeing that Teddy belongs with me. If Cousin Louisa comes to Chicago, I'll lose him."

Charlotte swallowed hard. "Miss, may I speak?"

Emmaline turned and looked at her, wide-eyed. "Of course."

"Maybe you should take Teddy and go," Charlotte said, barely above a whisper. "Maybe it's time."

Emmaline stared at her. "Do you mean I should take him without the blessing of Flora and Samuel?"

Charlotte nodded, pressing her lips together.

Emmaline sank into the chair in front of the vanity table. "Flora is hoping Louisa will come as soon as next week. She's been stubborn about this, even when she knows how much I want the child."

"Anyone can see you adore him," Charlotte said.

Emmaline looked up and beamed. "I do adore him! How can anyone resist him? Surely he would steal Louisa's heart the way he stole mine."

"But if he's gone when Louisa comes," Charlotte said, "perhaps they would not follow."

"They'll be angry."

"Yes, miss. The Bannings do not like to be contradicted."

"They certainly do not. But that does not make them right."

"No, miss." Charlotte's knees wavered, but her resolve did not.

"Teddy knows me now. He's comfortable with me. I'm quite persuaded he's genuinely fond of me."

"It's clear he is." Charlotte's voice caught despite her best effort to remain calm. "Perhaps it's best if you go."

"You're quite serious, aren't you?" Emmaline's face paled as she considered the proposition.

Charlotte nodded, her throat thick to the point of stifling her breath.

"I'm not sure I can manage it on my own," Emmaline said. "I can take care of him, I know that. But getting everything ready, making the arrangements to steal away—I'll need some help."

Charlotte's heart thrust against the walls of her chest. She would shrivel up and die inside, but Henry would be happy and safe. Her heart would never mend, but Henry would never want for anything.

"So you'll help me?" Emmaline asked, her eyes pleading.

Charlotte nodded one last time.

Archie prodded the horses into the coach house, where he unhitched the carriage. He handed the reins to Karl to stable the horses.

"How was the lunch at the Hendersons?" Karl asked. "The usual hoity-toity stuff, I imagine."

Archie snorted softly. "Mrs. Banning has a month's supply of stories about Mr. Henderson, and she complained about the skimpy portions all the way home. Miss Emmaline seemed particularly antsy. The whole affair took too long. I don't think she liked missing her walk with the baby."

"That drama is over—at least until the next time!" Karl laughed and ran his hand through the mane of a gelding before leading him to a stall.

Archie left the coach house and walked along the side of the mansion to the servants' entrance. He had not snatched a moment alone with Charlotte since the previous morning in the courtyard. At least now he understood why she was driving herself to exhaustion every moment of the day. Frenetic activity left her no spare moment to indulge her feelings about the crushing loss she was contemplating.

In the kitchen a few minutes later, Archie found Charlotte alone—at least for the moment—and washing the greens for the dinner's salad.

"They just got home from a lunch party," Archie commented. "Yet here you are, getting ready to feed them again."

Charlotte shrugged but did not speak.

Archie moved across the room to be close to her. "I'm glad to find you alone."

"I'm not alone," she said, gesturing to where the high chair was set up next to the table. Henry slapped the tray in greeting, and Archie smiled at the boy.

Charlotte began tearing the greens into bite-size pieces. "Actually, I've been hoping to talk to you." She did not lift her eyes.

Archie put a hand on Charlotte's shoulder. "You can always talk to me—especially now . . . after what you told me yesterday."

"That's what I want to talk about," Charlotte said. "I want your help."

"You know I want to help you."

"I hope you mean that." She paused her work to look him in the eye. "I'm going to help Miss Emmaline take him. She's going to need a ride to the train station with her trunks. I'm hoping you will take her when the time comes."

Archie froze, his hand sliding off her shoulder. "Charlotte, no. You can't do that."

"I've thought about it constantly for almost two days." Charlotte resumed tearing salad greens. "Letting Miss Emmaline take him is the best thing. He'll be safe and in a good home far away from here. From . . . that man."

Archie moved swiftly across the room and stood beside the high chair. "But Charlotte, he's your baby. You can't give him away."

"If it's the best thing for him, I have to."

He could see her mind was made up. She picked up a carrot and began to peel furiously, as if she could give away her child and continue with the next thing that had to be done.

Archie lifted the boy from the chair and carried him toward his mother.

He shook his head slowly. "I'm sorry, Charlotte, I can't do what you ask."

She looked at him sharply. "But you said you wanted to help."

"That's not what I meant, and you know it." He stroked

the boy's feathery head. Archie spoke again, hardly more than breath. "Look at your son, Charlotte."

"I don't have any option, Archie." She attacked another carrot. "I have nowhere to go, I can't take care of him here, and I can't possibly let the Bannings give him away to someone who lives in Greenville of all places. He's fond of Miss Brewster, and she's devoted to him. She can give him so many things that I can't."

"You're his mother."

She spun and glared. "Don't you think I know that? That's why I have to do this. I have to give him the best I can, and this is it."

He saw a hardness in her face he had never witnessed before. But if she were going to do this, she would have to do it without him.

"I want to help, Charlotte, but not this way. Let's talk more. Tell me more details, and we'll figure something out. Maybe I can find a place for you to stay with Irish friends, at least until Miss Lucy gets back. I might at least find a place for Henry. Give me some time to help."

"Archie, please. I've waffled for weeks. Now I've made up my mind. Help me."

He shook his head. "Even if I thought this were wise, I can't involve a Banning carriage or horse in what they are sure to perceive as an outright kidnapping."

Charlotte whacked a carrot in half, then set the knife down. "I understand. I shouldn't have thought to put you at risk. Never mind, then." She took Henry from Archie's arms.

"Miss Lucy would never want this," Archie said.

Sarah tromped in from the servants' hall with a bushel basket of potatoes, and let its weight thud to the floor. "I don't know why we have to do so many potatoes. They're not going to eat them all. They never do."

Archie stepped away from Charlotte, who simultaneously moved in the other direction and put Henry back in the chair.

"Mrs. Fletcher works out the menu with Mrs. Banning," Charlotte said. "It's not our place to question it."

"It's never our place to have an independent thought," Sarah muttered.

Charlotte thwacked a yellow sweet onion.

Archie moved toward the hall. "I'd better see that the carriage gets wiped down properly." In the doorway, he turned to look back at Charlotte one more time and did not like the hunch that had invaded her posture.

Sarah considered Archie's reluctant steps out of the kitchen. *I may be the scullery maid, but I'm not blind.*

Sarah picked up the basket of potatoes once again and lugged it closer to the working area of the kitchen. "Shouldn't the baby be upstairs? It's nap time."

"He's getting too old for so many naps," Charlotte said. "He didn't want to sleep." She wiped her hands on her apron, then picked up a slice of bread on the counter, carried it to the high chair, and broke off bits for the baby to pick up from the tray.

"Why did Archie say that?" Sarah asked.

"Say what?"

"He said, 'Miss Lucy would never want this.'"

Charlotte shrugged.

"Am I supposed to peel all of these?" Sarah picked out a potato. "I am acquainted with Miss Lucy, you know. All the children at the orphanage know who she is."

"Yes, I suppose they do."

"She took a special interest in me." Sarah pressed on. "That's why I've come to the Banning house in the first place. Although I don't know why she could not have found me a proper job in Mr. Field's store."

"I'm sure she would want you to make the most advantage of the opportunity you have."

"So why did Archie say, 'Miss Lucy would never want this'? Is it about Teddy?"

"Yes, you are supposed to peel all those potatoes," Charlotte said.

Sarah persisted. "Does Archie think Miss Lucy wouldn't want Teddy to go to Greenville? Is that it? Or is it all the attention Miss Emmaline gives him?"

Charlotte returned to her vegetables. "It was a private conversation that does not concern you."

Sarah thumped the potato down on the cutting block and wheeled out of the room.

Upstairs, in her own narrow room, Sarah removed a small bamboo box from the wobbly shelf in her closet and extracted the envelope she had saved from its demise in the slop bucket, the one addressed to Charlotte Farrow from Mrs. Will Edwards. Obviously she could not give it to Charlotte now, covered in grime no one could blame on the postal system and delayed for so long.

There was something in that letter, and Sarah was going to make it her business. She began to pick at the sealed flap.

Charlotte sat with Henry in the nursery a few minutes later. Mrs. Fletcher had returned to take over the meal preparation, and Henry had begun to protest his confinement to the high chair in the kitchen when he would rather have room to walk about in the nursery. As Charlotte sat in the rocking chair watching him, he toddled around the room, banging his hands on various surfaces as if to see whether one of them might behave differently than the others.

She had to make up her mind about the quilt—whether to send it with him or to keep it because it had been hers and then his.

Charlotte did not even know how much more time they would have together. Was it days? Hours?

Henry bumped against her knee. When she smiled at him, he grinned back.

"Ma-ma-ma-ma-ma," he said.

Her heart leaped and her eyes widened. "Yes! Mama," she whispered back.

"Ma-ma-ma-ma-ma," he repeated.

"Did Teddy just say 'mama'?"

Charlotte looked up to see Miss Emmaline standing in the doorway to the nursery. Fumbling for her voice, she answered, "It sounded like it."

"I've been trying to teach him to say that." Emmaline was clearly pleased at his accomplishment. She squatted, her wide skirt melting into a broad circle around her, and opened her arms. "Teddy, come to Mama."

Henry walked into Emmaline's arms.

21

Are you sure?" Anxiety flushed Emmaline Brewster's face.

"The family is out of the house," Charlotte said, "but they'll be back for dinner." She handed Emmaline the hat that would complete her traveling ensemble.

"I never thought it would happen in just two days." Emmaline glanced around Lucy's suite. "It feels odd to just walk out and leave my things behind."

"I've packed a small bag with the things you'll need for Teddy," Charlotte said. With enough practice in the last few days, she could now call her son by his new name without choking over the word. "I'm sure Mrs. Banning will instruct me to pack up your belongings once . . ."

"Once they discover the ghastly thing I've done," Emmaline supplied. "I don't care about any of it. Gowns and jewelry are easy enough to come by, but a child!"

Charlotte's pulse pounded in her head. "The baby should be waking up soon, so you might want to go to the nursery, miss, to get him. I'll run over to Michigan Avenue and hail a cab."

Without waiting for a response, Charlotte scurried from the room, down the back stairs, and out the back door off the kitchen. She cut through the courtyard and under the narrow covered passageway to the street, emerging on Prairie Avenue beyond the sight of the front door. A quick glance around confirmed she had found the afternoon lull when there was little activity on the street. Charlotte hastened her steps north along Prairie Avenue to Eighteenth Street, where she turned west and darted toward Michigan Avenue. She hardly felt the tears when they first began. As they streamed more freely, she surrendered to hot grief. By the time she reached Indiana Avenue, she tasted salt dribbling down both cheeks, and when she halted at the corner of Eighteenth and Michigan, she could barely see clearly enough to determine whether the hansom cab she saw there was empty.

She paused to gasp for breath and wipe her eyes with the heels of her hands. Four days had passed since the unsettling sights of the fair. Three days since she had made up her mind. Two days since she had first spoken to Miss Emmaline of the plan.

Four days. The start of eternity.

Eternity without Henry.

"Miss, are you looking for a cab?"

The voice startled Charlotte and reinvigorated her resolve. "Yes."

The cabbie held open the door for her, and Charlotte entered the cab. Softly she gave instructions. Park on Eighteenth Street east of Prairie Avenue, behind the Kimball mansion. Wait for a woman with a baby buggy. Take her to the train station. It would have been so much easier if Archie had simply agreed to help. They could have packed Emmaline's things in her trunks and had them waiting for the right moment. Perhaps Emmaline could even have left directly from the house under the guise of an outing. But Archie had refused, and this plan was the best Charlotte could manage.

When she got out of the cab behind the Kimball mansion, Charlotte gave the driver one of her precious coins to assure him he would be compensated for following these peculiar instructions and not left waiting for a mysterious fare.

"Wait right here," she said firmly. "It will be only a few minutes." She turned and walked toward the house, her heels clicking rapidly against the sidewalk.

The scene was just as she had hoped. The timing was perfect. Karl had brought the baby buggy around to the front of the house, where he was waiting for Miss Emmaline. Charlotte retraced her steps through the courtyard, into the house, and up the back stairs. In the nursery, she found Emmaline holding the boy in her lap and coaxing him to put his arms into the sleeves of a tiny blue jacket. She wore a light woolen cape over her own traveling clothes.

"Ready, miss?" Charlotte asked.

"Ready."

Emmaline stood up, Henry in her arms. He reached for Charlotte, and she stroked a couple of his fingers.

"He'll miss you, Charlotte. You're so gentle and understanding with him."

"Yes, miss," Charlotte said. "Karl has the buggy waiting, and the cab is around the corner."

"Then let's go."

Charlotte picked up the small bag she had packed for her son.

"What about his quilt?" Emmaline asked. "I know it's old and threadbare, but he's attached to it."

"Yes, miss."

Charlotte's throat knotted as she stepped into the little room with the crib and lifted the quilt. She had wrestled for two nights about whether to send it with him and come to no conclusion. Her grandmother had made that quilt. If she sent it with Henry, the only thing she would have left of her grandmother was the old Bible. And Emmaline would no doubt intend to replace the quilt in the baby's affections with something finer. But Emmaline was right. Henry was attached to the quilt, and the train journey would be smoother for them both if he had it. Perhaps Emmaline would even save the quilt for him and someday tell him he had been found with it.

In front of the house, they settled the baby into the spacious buggy. The bag was tucked away under the quilt. As soon as they appeared on the front steps, Karl left them to their routine. Any onlooker would see an ordinary scene, one that anyone in the neighborhood expected to see at this time every afternoon.

Emmaline pushed the buggy herself. "I don't know how I can repay you, Charlotte," she said. "I don't even know why you would help me do this, but I am deeply grateful that you have."

Charlotte groped for words. "It's the right thing for Teddy, and that's all that matters."

"Still, I fear the repercussions for you if your part in this is discovered."

"Pay it no mind, miss. I'll wait for a while, then take the buggy back like we always do." Surely Archie would not say anything. Charlotte had not spoken a word to Archie since his refusal to help. He knew nothing of the particular plan being executed that day.

The cab was there right where it was supposed to be. When

the driver saw the buggy, he jumped down from his seat and held open the door. Charlotte leaned over the buggy and picked up her son.

My son.

He gave her a face-splitting grin, oblivious to the gravity of the moment. She forced herself to smile back as Emmaline settled in the cab. Charlotte stroked her son's cheek and ran a hand down his small back.

"I'm ready for him now." Emmaline held her arms open.

"Yes, miss." Charlotte leaned into the cab and handed the boy to his new life. "Good-bye, Miss Emmaline. Good-bye, Teddy."

"Ma-ma-ma-ma-ma," the little boy said.

Emmaline glowed with pleasure. "Mama's right here. We're going to have such a happy life together."

The driver secured the door and took his seat. A moment later, the slow clip-clop began, leaving Charlotte alone on the street with an empty baby buggy.

Sarah pushed the broom around the kitchen briskly. It seemed to her that Mrs. Fletcher was far too fastidious about the cleanliness of a kitchen that was never empty enough to stay clean. The cook was at the stove, tending to the dishes that would feed the servants in a few minutes before making final preparations to serve the family dinner.

Mr. Penard came through from his pantry. "Where is Archie?"

Mrs. Fletcher shrugged without bothering to turn around. "I thought you sent him out on an errand."

"I did. He should have been back long ago."

Sarah thwacked at the crumbs under the high chair. "He always does that, you know."

"You hush and get that mess picked up," Mrs. Fletcher said.

"It's true." Sarah persisted in her argument as well as her sweeping. Mr. Penard chastised her for taking liberties with her time. Why should Archie do so without consequence? "Archie has been disappearing a lot. Everything takes him twice as long as it should."

"He's taking advantage," Mr. Penard said. "He has too much freedom. Perhaps it was a mistake to make him coachman."

Mrs. Fletcher dipped a ladle in the mushroom soup and inspected the creamy liquid as it fell back into the pot. "I'm sure he has his reasons."

"His reasons are irrelevant," the butler said. "It's time for him to fetch Mrs. Banning."

"I'm sure he knows that," Mrs. Fletcher said. "He's probably there now."

"I shall speak to him sharply as soon as he comes in. The future of his employment is at stake."

"Have you used up all your mercy on that one?" Mrs. Fletcher waved the ladle in Sarah's direction.

Sarah seethed.

"Mrs. Fletcher," Mr. Penard said, "perhaps you would like simply to speak your mind."

She shrugged. "You've had plenty of reason to dismiss the girl, yet she is still here. And now you're talking about dismissing Archie because his work takes longer than you think it should. Have you no mercy for him?"

"Mrs. Fletcher, I'll thank you to hold your tongue after all. I am ready for my supper."

"Sarah, come get the serving dishes," Mrs. Fletcher said. "Then call the other maids."

Sarah propped her broom in the corner she had been sweeping and strutted across the kitchen.

"Wash up first," Mrs. Fletcher said sharply. "You'll not come to my table with dirt smeared on your face."

It's not your table! Sarah wanted to scream as she plunged her hands under water and dabbed at her face. Mrs. Fletcher was a servant just as she was. The only difference was that Sarah did not intend to still be sweeping this stupid kitchen floor in fifteen years.

Sarah turned when she heard steps on the back stairs. "Where's the baby?" Sarah picked up a basket of bread and set it on the table. "Are you bringing him down to eat with us?"

"I don't think so," Charlotte said.

"Why not?"

"He's had enough excitement today."

"Why? Did you change his routine?"

"Sarah, leave her alone," Mrs. Fletcher said. "The child is no longer your concern. Fix Charlotte a tray to take upstairs. Later, you can sit with the boy while he sleeps when she comes down to serve."

Sarah snatched a tray off the counter and loaded it roughly, then shoved it at Charlotte.

Something about this was not right. Sarah intended to find out what.

"I don't understand where Emmaline is," Flora Banning mused as Archie ladled creamy mushroom soup into the gold-rimmed china bowl in front of her. "I was not aware of any obligations she had this evening. Charlotte, are you sure she is not dawdling in the nursery?"

"No, Mrs. Banning. She's not in the nursery." Charlotte had not thought her heart could pound any faster, but it did.

"When is the last time any of the staff saw her?"

"We took the baby for his airing this afternoon as usual, ma'am."

"And she hasn't called for you since then?"

"No, ma'am. I have not heard from her." Every word Charlotte spoke was truth.

"What if she has become ill?" Flora asked. "Someone should check on her. I'll do it myself." She pushed her own chair back from the table.

"Eat your dinner, Flora," Samuel urged. "Emmaline is a grown woman, not a child for you to look after."

"But this is most unlike her. I won't be satisfied unless I check on her."

Archie finished serving the soup to Samuel, Leo, and Richard and now stood stiffly in his white formal wear beside Charlotte at the sideboard. Penard stood at the butler's pantry door as Flora swept out of the dining room, into the foyer, and up the marble stairs. The rest of the family spooned their soup and had little to say. Charlotte's knees quaked under her black dress and starched white apron. She had hoped for more time. Samuel signaled he was finished with his soup, and his sons soon followed. Charlotte stepped forward to remove the dishes as Mr. Penard carried in the trout. He set it on the sideboard to wait for the mistress of the house.

Flora Banning's skirt swished in warning of her rapid step. She paused between the pocket doors that separated the foyer from the dining room. With the flip of a switch, the electric lights overwhelmed the candles on the table.

"She gone," Flora announced.

"What do you mean, gone?" Samuel blinked mildly in the sudden brightness. "Perhaps she had a dinner invitation?"

"When I did not find her in Lucy's suite, I decided to check the nursery."

"You went to the nursery?" Leo asked. "You haven't been in the nursery since Richard outgrew it."

"It's still my nursery," Flora said adamantly, "and I see no reason not to inspect it if I choose to."

"Penard," Samuel said, "serve the fish, please."

"How can you eat at a moment like this?" Flora's face flushed in a mix of confusion and impatience. "Sarah was sitting in the day nursery. She told me the child was already asleep for the night, but I asked to see him."

The vise tightened on Charlotte's stomach.

"Why would you wake a sleeping baby just to look at him?" Samuel asked, signaling Penard once again.

"Samuel, for a lawyer who has argued before the Supreme Court of the State of Illinois, you're not following very well."

"Then perhaps you'd better just state your point plainly, Flora."

"Sarah went to get the child, and he was not there."

Samuel looked up at last. "Not there?"

"It's clear as day, Samuel. Emmaline has taken the child."

Penard's eyes flashed at Charlotte.

"What about the quilt?" Leo asked. "The baby had a quilt when he arrived."

"Sarah said it was gone," Flora answered.

Leo's shoulders sagged. "Then I have to agree with you, Mother. The child is gone."

Samuel cleared his throat. "Charlotte, you indicated you had aired the baby with Emmaline as usual this afternoon."

"Yes, sir," she whispered.

"Did she indicate to you her intentions in any way?"

"No, sir." Charlotte was the one full of intentions, and she was aware of each one.

"It was my understanding that you were caring for the child now."

"Yes, sir." Charlotte heard the quiver in her own voice.

"Then how is it that he seems to have disappeared?"

"Samuel!" Flora said. "For goodness sake, stop interrogating the poor girl. And don't blame Sarah either. They are not responsible. Everyone thought the baby was asleep in his crib, but Emmaline has taken him. Most of her things are untouched, but her handbag and cape are missing."

"Father has a point," Leo said. "Could Emmaline really have done this without help?"

"You underestimate her determination," Flora said. "Emmaline has been freely coming and going from the nursery. She would only have to walk out the front door with a sleeping baby and find a cab. She could be on a train to Boston within minutes of leaving Prairie Avenue."

Charlotte hoped that was exactly what had happened.

Samuel stiffly straightened his lapels but said nothing.

"Louisa is due to arrive on Tuesday," Flora said. "What am I supposed to tell her?"

22

The sharp rap on her bedroom door woke Charlotte, but she did not move. She could not.

"Charlotte!" Mrs. Fletcher called from the hallway.

Charlotte intended to respond, but her lungs would not draw sufficient breath.

The rap became urgent. "Charlotte, answer me!"

Charlotte managed to turn her head toward the door, her eyes mere slits.

"I'm coming in," Mrs. Fletcher announced. As the door opened, she continued, "Do you have any idea what time it is? You should have heated the griddle thirty minutes ago."

Can't you see my heart is broken? The words clanged in Charlotte's head mercilessly, ricocheting from one side of her skull to the other.

"I'm sorry."

"Are you ill?" Mrs. Fletcher pressed.

Charlotte thought perhaps she had moved her head a quarter of an inch. She hoped it looked like a nod.

The steps required to cross the room were few. Mrs. Fletcher laid her hand on Charlotte's forehead. "No fever. But I grant that you look ghostly."

"Yes, ma'am." Charlotte's whisper was nearly mute.

"It's to your credit that you have only missed breakfast once before, but even Penard seems to have forgotten about that."

I never gave away my son before.

"I suppose I'll have to do without you in the kitchen today," Mrs. Fletcher said in resignation. "Mr. Penard will have to ask Lina to help serve. You may have the day in bed, but if I discover you are lollygagging, you will regret it."

"Yes, ma'am."

"Do you require a doctor?"

Charlotte closed her eyes and shook her head slightly.

"I'll send the girl up to check on you later and see if you need anything."

"Thank you."

At last the cook left.

Charlotte had sobbed half the night, her fist stuffed in her mouth to stifle her lament. That she had done what she believed best for Henry did not mitigate the wrench of every conscious thought, the ripping that left her lying on her narrow bed unable to speak, much less stumble down to the kitchen to flip griddle cakes. She had nothing left of him. She had never even written his name in the family tree in the front of her grandmother's Bible for fear it would prove his existence to the wrong person.

She turned and gazed at the Bible sitting on the table next to the bed, where she had placed it months ago in a moment of belief that it was possible to find solace in its words once again.

Charlotte had once loved that Bible. As soon as she could hold it and walk at the same time, she had carried it on Sunday mornings into the white clapboard church her grandparents had helped to build. "Remember, Charlotte, God is always with us," her grandmother used to say.

Where is he now? Charlotte wanted to know.

Her own parents rarely went to church, but Charlotte had loved the singing and the reading and the shared meals of the church that brought together farm families from miles around. As she grew, however, she heard a tone in the preacher's words that made her feel as if she had been a bad girl even though she knew she hadn't and her grandmother knew she hadn't. Charlotte tried to keep going after her grandmother died, because not going would surely make her more naughty. But by then the scolding became shouting condemnation in every sermon. Soon Charlotte no longer resisted her parents' expectations that she perform her morning chores on Sunday just like any other day.

What was the point?

Charlotte closed her eyes again, seeking the oblivion of sleep.

In the tack room of the coach house, Archie Shepard wiped dry the bits and reins he had used that day, then hung them on the wall. He was fairly certain the Bannings were in for the evening now. Their usual Sunday morning outing to Second Presbyterian Church had been followed by dinner at the home of the Meekers on Calumet Avenue, an outing that relieved the kitchen staff of preparing luncheon and gave most of the household staff several hours of welcome respite. Because it was only five blocks away, Archie had dropped the family at the Meekers' and returned to the coach house to await word from Penard that Samuel Banning had telephoned and was ready to be picked up. The family was home now. All that remained of his workday was to serve the soup at the evening meal, which he only continued to do so he could see Charlotte.

He wondered now if it would be better not to see Charlotte in the dining room anymore. He didn't know what to say. Perhaps it was time to give up the pretense of being footman as well as coachman.

Karl came through the door that separated the carriages from the stables.

"Have the horses got enough hay?" Archie asked.

Karl nodded. "I threw it down myself not an hour ago."

"Good. The carriage is polished. We should be able to put our feet up for a few minutes."

"You missed the servants' lunch," Karl observed.

"I was busy transporting the family to theirs."

"Mrs. Fletcher kept a plate for you."

Archie sat in a wicker chair and pulled a stool over for his feet. "I'll wait for supper."

"If I didn't know better," Karl said, "I'd say you're avoiding the kitchen."

"Why would I do that?"

"You tell me. I suspect it has something to do with that maid you never take your eyes off of."

"Mind your own business, Karl."

"If you paid any attention, you would know she hasn't been out of bed for almost two days."

"I pay enough attention to know that," Archie snapped. Charlotte had missed every meal since Friday's supper. While he hated the thought that she might be ill, he had been relieved not to have to face her. She had not even given him a chance to help, to see if there might be a solution to keep both Charlotte and Henry safe.

"Mrs. Fletcher is losing patience," Karl said. "Mr. Penard too. They can't trust the new girl the way they trust Charlotte."

If only Charlotte could trust someone. Anyone.

"I suppose whatever's ailing her will pass soon enough," Karl said. "For her own good, she'd better make it to breakfast tomorrow."

Sarah sat next to the kitchen window, where the best light was. The needle between her slender fingers was one of the smallest she had ever seen, but its slight touch was required for the satin fabric she was mending. Mrs. Banning had asked for someone to repair the fraying seam behind the fringe on the gold pillow that adorned the settee in the parlor. Sarah smiled as she remembered the shocked look on Mrs. Fletcher's face when she volunteered to do the stitching. Sarah was skilled with a needle, and even Mrs. Fletcher would have to admit it.

Sarah bent over the fabric, making tiny stitches along the seam and pulling them snug but not tight to the point of stress. The thread was a good color match. The miniscule stitches were visible only on close inspection. She glanced at the clock, aware that soon Mrs. Fletcher would appear to put the roast in the oven and dinner preparations would be underway. What Sarah wanted to know was whether Charlotte was going to get out of bed and come down to help cook and serve.

Sarah was increasingly convinced of a link between Charlotte's supposed illness and Emmaline Brewster's departure with the child. She just was not sure what the connection was. The letter had something to do with it. That was the only thing that made sense. Five days had passed since Sarah had torn open the envelope and read the letter for herself. In fact, she had read it so many times she had it memorized—and she still did not understand it.

Dear Charlotte,

It seems my family is mired in a mystery. Leo's telegram gave only the sketchiest details, but I found myself wondering what your impression is of the situation. I genuinely hope you are not caught in the middle somehow, but if you are, do send me a note at the hotel in Paris.

When I get home, I'll have so much to tell you. I hope to find you well in every way. Don't lose your joy.

Lucy

So far, however, no matter how many times Sarah repeated the words of the letter in her head, she did not understand them. The mystery had to be the baby who showed up. Everyone under the Banning roof knew that Leo had written to his sister about it. But why would Miss Lucy care what Charlotte thought about the situation? Why would she think Charlotte might be caught in the middle? In the middle of what? What did she mean by "Don't lose your joy"?

And why was Lucy Banning Edwards writing to a kitchen maid in the first place?

Just as Sarah expected, Mrs. Fletcher clomped down the back stairs.

"I'm glad you're here, Sarah," the cook said. "I was going over the dinner menu in my head and realized I don't have enough barley. I'm sure the cook at the Glessners' would spare us some. I want you to go over and ask."

"Two more stitches," Sarah murmured.

Mrs. Fletcher approached and peered over Sarah's shoulder. "You're doing nice work," she admitted. "I'm not sure I could have done better myself."

Sarah pulled the final stitch snug. At least Mrs. Fletcher could see the plain truth under her nose.

Mrs. Fletcher took the pillow from Sarah's lap. "I'll give it to Mr. Penard to return to the parlor. You go fetch the barley. Four cups should be sufficient."

Wrapped in a light cloak, Sarah sauntered up the street to Eighteenth, then crossed and followed the side of the house to the female servants' entrance. A few minutes later, she had more than enough barley in the ceramic bowl she carried from the Glessners'.

Was that Archie she saw at the corner? He had not been there a few minutes earlier. And who was the man he was talking to? Sarah had never seen him before, and he was not dressed as if he were in service in the neighborhood. Even in the dimness of late afternoon light, Sarah could see the man's black suit was ill-fitting and overly worn in the back, but it was definitely not the garb of a servant. He gestured broadly as he spoke, a bundle of papers in one hand.

Sarah made her way back to the Banning kitchen and delivered the barley. Mrs. Fletcher was at work at the stove, and Mr. Penard sat at the table with paper and pen. Sarah supposed he was making one of his infernal lists.

"I just saw Archie talking in the street," Sarah said casually.

Mr. Penard lifted an eyebrow. "He should be in the coach house."

Sarah shrugged. "He's not. He's up at the corner talking to someone."

"Who?"

"I don't know. One of those anarchists, I suppose."

Penard slammed a hand down on the table. "If he has any thought of his position, he will not talk to those people. The audacity of doing it right on Prairie Avenue!"

Mrs. Fletcher turned and stared at Sarah. "Perhaps it is just somebody he knows."

"He'd better not know any of those anarchists. I will not have my staff's heads filled with their labor nonsense."

"Sarah, go to the cellar and bring me some turnips," Mrs. Fletcher snapped.

Sarah huffed, but she went.

23

As Monday morning dawned, Charlotte swung her feet over the side of the bed and pushed herself upright. Her parched throat ached. For the last two days, she had been out of bed for only moments at a time and had not been dressed and downstairs at all. The cook sent Sarah up with trays periodically, but Charlotte left them untouched. Mrs. Fletcher's tone the night before had been clear. Either Charlotte was ill enough to require a doctor to get better, or she must get out of bed.

A doctor could not cure what ailed Charlotte any more than food would. She had to get up. The day awaited.

Charlotte sponged off with the tepid water in her washbowl and pulled on a black dress. Taking her white apron with her, she descended the stairs to see what the breakfast menu was. Mrs. Fletcher was already at the griddle frying French toast while Sarah chopped fruit.

"You're up," Mrs. Fletcher said flatly.

"Yes, ma'am."

"Put your apron on and lay the table in the dining room."

Charlotte was relieved to have a few minutes of solitude

in the dining room, even though she knew it would be short-lived. She was upright but far from steady on her feet as she set the table with glazed ceramic plates and folded starched napkins. Logically, she knew nourishment would be a wise choice, but the thought of food repulsed her.

It was not long before she heard the muffled sounds of increased activity in the kitchen. The staff was gathering for their breakfast. Charlotte's stomach burned with nerves. Archie would be at breakfast, and she was not sure she could look him in the eye.

Archie's spot at the kitchen table remained vacant. Charlotte hardly heard any of the breakfast conversation over the din his absence created in her head. Was he staying away because of her? Why was no one commenting on where he was? She ate next to nothing but forced down a cup of tea.

As the clatter of utensils slowed and the staff pushed back from the table, satisfied, Mr. Penard stood and pressed his hands together. "It's time. Mr. Banning will be down any moment now."

Charlotte nodded and stood, then moved into the dining room to await the family. To her surprise, Flora Banning, in a sky-blue silk robe, trailed immediately behind her husband. Most mornings, she called for a tray in her bedroom long after her husband left the house.

"Where's Richard?" Samuel Banning asked. "I told him to be ready to leave early today."

"Samuel, you're not listening to me," Flora lamented. "Louisa was due to arrive tomorrow. I had to telephone her and tell her Emmaline has kidnapped the child. Do you have any idea how difficult that was for me to do?"

"I'm sure it was a thorny conversation, Flora dear, but it

does not change the fact that I have an early morning meeting with an important client. In case you haven't noticed, we're in the middle of a depression. If I'm to keep you in circumstances you consider comfortable, I must cater to this client." Samuel pulled the chair out for his wife and she flounced into it.

"I haven't slept since we discovered the child was gone. Charlotte, coffee please."

Charlotte stepped forward with the sterling silver pot and poured coffee into the ceramic cup. "Would madam like something to eat?"

Flora sighed dramatically and gazed at the choices on the sideboard. "I suppose I must keep up my strength. Just once piece, though."

"Yes, ma'am."

"I will never forgive Emmaline for what she did. Never!"

Leo and Richard entered together.

"Are you still talking about that baby?" Richard slumped into his chair.

"Sit up straight, Richard," Flora said. "Samuel, you are an attorney. Surely you can propose some legal action."

"I'm not sure what grounds there would be," Samuel said as Charlotte set a plate in front of him. "The child was abandoned. We had no particular claim on him."

"He was left on our property. We took him into our home for several weeks. We provided his food and care. That must give us some claim," Flora insisted.

Leo spoke up. "Mother, are you sure Louisa would want to pursue adopting the child under these circumstances?"

"If we could get the boy back with a clear legal claim, I don't see why we should not give him to Louisa."

"Perhaps the child is happy with Emmaline. They seemed to get on well."

"He's a baby," Flora retorted. "He would get on well with anyone who paid him attention, and Louisa would give him a great deal of attention."

Charlotte dropped a serving spoon, and it thumped softly on the rug beneath the sideboard.

Charlotte caught Leo's glance as she stooped and snatched up the spoon, setting it aside and taking another from the drawer. The pieces clinked against each other in her quivering clasp.

"Charlotte, we were given to understand you've been ill," Leo said.

"Yes, sir, but I'm better now." Charlotte turned to the platter of French toast. "What would you like for breakfast?"

"Do we have sausage to go with that French toast?"

"Yes, sir."

"I don't know how you can be so interested in food when we have been betrayed," Flora said. "Samuel, you must do something."

"I'm not sure there's much that can be done."

"You must promise me to try."

Samuel sighed. "Very well. I will consult with the partners at my firm. Charlotte, let Archie know to have the carriage ready in ten minutes."

"Yes, sir."

Charlotte pushed through the butler's pantry and into the kitchen. The sight of Archie sitting at the table startled her.

"There's my cue," he said simply. "I'll get the coach."

And he was gone, without turning his brown eyes toward her. Charlotte had steeled herself twice already this morning to face him, and twice he had evaded her. He left behind a plate he had barely touched, clearly anxious to avoid an encounter.

"He's missing a lot of meals these days," Mrs. Fletcher observed. "He just doesn't show up, and sometimes no one knows where he is. Mr. Penard is losing patience."

He's leaving. The thought stabbed Charlotte, and she wondered if he would even say good-bye to her before he left the Bannings' domestic staff.

Archie dispatched with the morning drive uneventfully, dropping Richard at school and Mr. Banning at his office downtown. On the way back to Prairie Avenue, he let the horses set their own unhurried rhythm. Mr. Banning was having luncheon at the Palmer House, which would ease Archie's day, and he was already planning to send Karl to fetch Richard from school.

He had to admit he was hungry, having eaten little since discovering Friday evening what Charlotte had done and plunging into a dark mood of deliberating what he might have done differently. At noon, Archie sat at the servants' lunch table, eating the beef stew and biscuits placed in front of him but saying nothing and dodging Charlotte's glance—as he was sure she was avoiding his. His plan took form.

Mrs. Banning ate her luncheon alone that day, and the meal was not drawn out. Charlotte cleaned up as usual. Then the maids would have their customary afternoon lull—not time off, but a few hours when they might put their feet up on a footstool and mend linens or write shopping lists. Archie made sure Karl would be ready to bring Richard home and then proceed to the University of Chicago to carry Leo home for dinner. Archie would have to go downtown for Samuel himself, but if he hurried, his scheme would work.

This business of avoiding each other was getting them nowhere. Someone had to take the first step so they could look into each other's eyes again. He was not going to give up on Charlotte.

Archie bided his time, monitoring the movements of the female staff carefully and expecting that, if they followed their routines, Charlotte would be alone in the kitchen for a brief interval.

Finally, it happened. Charlotte was sitting in the chair under the kitchen window. She did not pick up any stitching but simply let her head fall against the back of the chair and closed her eyes.

"Charlotte," Archie said softly.

Her eyes startled open and stared at him.

"Come with me," he said.

She looked around the room. "Where?"

"Trust me. I want to show you something. We'll come back in plenty of time for dinner preparation."

"But Mrs. Fletcher—"

He reached for her hand. "Charlotte, please, just come with me. Trust me." He fastened on her eyes, pleading.

"I'm already in hot water for being . . . ill."

"Take a risk."

She was silent, her face twitching in consideration. At last she spoke. "All right."

They walked briskly up to Eighteenth and Prairie, then turned west.

"Where are we going, Archie?" Charlotte asked.

"Michigan Avenue, to catch a streetcar."

"And then?"

"You'll see."

He could not predict how she would respond. He only knew he had to show her.

Archie helped her onto the streetcar and paid their fares, then led her to a seat. They rode silently north to Jackson, then changed streetcars to ride west. At Jefferson, they got off and walked north two blocks. Archie took Charlotte's elbow and steered her toward a rising block of red brick and glass windows. They stood across the street from the structure.

"There," he said, "is my future, and I hope *our* future."

Charlotte raised her shoulders and shook her head. "I don't know what I'm looking at—or why."

"This building belongs to Warder, Bushnell & Glessner," Archie explained. "Look at it. The factory where they make the farm equipment is in Ohio, but this is the reason Mr. Glessner came to Chicago. This is the headquarters, the heart of the company. I want to work here."

"I don't understand, Archie."

"I told you that if I ever left service I would want to take you with me."

"I remember," she murmured.

"I want to work for Mr. Glessner, and I don't mean as his butler."

Charlotte laughed nervously. "It is a position that seems to open up frequently."

Archie shook his head emphatically. "That's not enough

for me. I know you came to Chicago with Henry and went into service. But I don't know what happened that made you so afraid. I brought you here to see this"—he gestured toward the long, multi-storied building—"and to show you that it's possible to dream of a better life. It's out there. We just have to grab hold."

Archie gripped both of Charlotte's shoulders and looked her straight in the eye.

Her lip trembled. "But . . . you were so disappointed at what I did . . . for Henry."

He nodded. "I admit I wish you had made another decision. But I'm not going to give up even on that."

"I still have a husband, Archie," she whispered. "What future can we have?"

"If you truly believe you are in danger because of your husband, then I want to help you find a way to break the legal bond. And once you're safe, I want to get your baby back."

"It's too late!"

"I refuse to believe that."

"Archie, I have a husband. I gave away my child. Even if it were possible for him to be safe with me, how could I break Miss Brewster's heart?"

"I don't know how it will work out. I just know it's not over."

"But things happen for a reason," Charlotte said. "Miss Brewster did not think it was coincidence that she came to Chicago when she did. She thought it was God's plan for her to meet the baby."

"She came with certain wishes for a husband and family," Archie said, "just as you came with certain fears. That's not the same as trusting God."

"I'm a little disappointed with God," Charlotte admitted softly.

"I know," Archie said, "but that can change too."

Sarah put aside the linen napkins Mrs. Fletcher had given her to hem. She had only finished three, and the set was eighteen, but it was time to start on the soup for dinner. Charlotte did not seem to be anywhere in sight. In fact, Sarah had not seen her for nearly two hours.

Mrs. Fletcher came down the back stairs as Sarah tucked the sewing basket in the bottom shelf of a cupboard. At the same moment, Mr. Penard entered the kitchen through the butler's pantry. He went directly to the annunciator board and pushed the button for the coach house. Karl answered.

"Send Archie in, please."

"He's gone out," Karl responded.

"Out? Where? Did Mr. Banning call for a coach?"

"No, sir. The carriages are all here."

"But Archie is not?"

"No, sir."

"When he comes in, send him to me immediately."

"Yes, sir."

Sarah crossed to the sink to fill a pot with water. "I'll wager he's out talking to those anarchists again."

"He'd better not be." Mr. Penard looked around the kitchen. "Where is Charlotte? The child is gone. Shouldn't she be back in the kitchen?"

Sarah chuckled. "Maybe if you find Archie, you'll find Charlotte too. They seem overly friendly, if you ask me."

Mrs. Fletcher raised a meat cleaver higher than necessary

and whacked it through a pork roast. Sarah jumped when the blade struck wood.

"Mind your own business, Sarah," the cook said.

"Archie is testing my patience," Mr. Penard said. "If I discover there is truth to either of Sarah's suggestions, he will find himself seeking another position, and it will not be on Prairie Avenue."

24

"I want everything cleared out before lunch." Flora Banning stood in the middle of her daughter's suite. "Everything must look exactly as it did when Lucy left. Every book, every picture frame, every pillow. Charlotte, I'm sure you know the details of how Lucy arranged the room."

"Yes, ma'am." The three maids lined up against one wall of the anteroom to the suite. Flora's hostility had seemed to fester throughout Monday so that on Tuesday morning, she was on a rampage to rid the mansion of any hint that Emmaline Brewster had ever walked its halls.

"Lina and Sarah, you do exactly as Charlotte says." Flora crossed the suite to the closet and opened the door. A long line of hooks held gowns in a spectrum of colors and fabrics. She reached in and took a green silk off a hook. "Sarah, why don't you take this one and see if you can make it over to suit you."

"Yes, ma'am," Sarah answered. Charlotte could see the light go on in the girl's eyes.

"In fact," Flora said, still rummaging among the gowns, "take the brown day dress and the ivory suit as well." She threw all three garments on the bed. "Mrs. Fletcher tells me you have a talent with the needle. You might as well get some experience. Perhaps someday I'll ask you to alter one of my gowns. You can practice on these."

"Yes, ma'am."

Charlotte followed Sarah's salivating gaze to the haphazard mound of expensive fabric on the bed.

Flora swept back toward the door, her lavender satin skirts with navy blue braid rustling furiously. "When you're finished in here, you can close up the nursery again. Just pack everything back the way it was in the attic. Archie or Karl can help you with the heavy things. And if you find that Miss Brewster took anything that does not belong to her, let me know immediately."

Charlotte had been careful not to pack anything for the baby that belonged to the Bannings. Henry had left only with his beloved quilt and the few items of clothing Emmaline had indulged in during a visit to Marshall Field's store downtown.

Flora stood in the doorway, hands on hips, and surveyed the room one last time. "Perhaps it's time to redecorate in here. Some new William Morris carpets and some fresh swags for the windows. I don't care what Samuel says about the economic depression."

She pivoted and marched down the hall. The maids listened to her footsteps and looked at one another with eyes wide.

"She truly wants to wipe out Miss Brewster," Lina said. "I've never seen her like this."

"She doesn't like to be crossed," Charlotte said. At that moment, she was grateful she had not disclosed her own secrets to Flora Banning, no matter what Archie said. The severity in Flora's voice confirmed she would not have tolerated a maid with a child even long enough to consider the question.

Sarah scurried across the suite to the bed and lifted the

ivory suit to her face. "These are beautiful! And she gave them to me!"

Charlotte winced. "She's just angry with Miss Brewster. I don't think you should keep the dresses."

"Of course I'll keep them!"

"But they belong to Miss Brewster."

"Mrs. Banning said I was to have them. You heard her yourself."

Charlotte shrugged, refusing to expend further energy on a pointless conversation. Sarah would not change her mind and do the right thing.

"Where shall we begin?" Lina asked.

Charlotte moved to a corner where two steamer trunks sat side by side. "I suppose we will fill the trunks as neatly as we can with the gowns."

"What about the jewelry?" Lina picked up a pair of earrings and held them to her own ears in front of the mirror.

"I'll wrap everything in velvet, and we'll tuck it in among the gowns."

"It might be stolen," Lina said.

"It's probably paste anyway," Sarah said.

Charlotte exhaled. "It's not paste. The trunks must have keys. We can inquire about mailing the keys to Miss Brewster directly so she will have them when the trunks arrive."

Sarah scoffed. "Mrs. Banning did not seem in a frame of mind to make things easier for Miss Brewster."

"Mr. Penard will have the address," Charlotte said. "We don't have to trouble Mrs. Banning. Lina, help me with this trunk."

Together they scooted a Chinese hardwood trunk out to the middle of the room and unfastened the leather straps and silver buckles to open it wide.

"Let's start with the full-skirted gowns first," Charlotte suggested, "and arrange them in the bottom."

"How in the world did she ever get all these gowns in two trunks?" Lina took a blue silk gown with gold beaded trim and held it in front of herself before the mirror. "I can't even imagine wearing something so beautiful."

"I won't have to imagine much longer," Sarah gloated. "Even the brown day dress is exquisite. Look how exact the pleats are, and the fabric is so sturdy without being heavy."

Lina chuckled. "Where will you wear a dress like that?"

"On my days out."

"These are too fancy. I like the dresses Miss Lucy wears," Lina said. "They're practical without being frumpy, stylish but you can still move in them."

"She likes to be able to move freely at the orphanage," Charlotte said. "She is not one to have nine yards of fabric getting in the way of every step."

Lina folded in the wide skirts of the blue silk and laid it in the bottom of the open trunk. "Do you ever wonder what it would be like to visit Paris and see the fashions for yourself?"

"Paris?" Charlotte wrapped a set of earrings.

"I love the fashions from Paris." Sarah put down the ivory gown and picked up both the green dress and the brown one. "I'll certainly visit someday."

"Sarah, start helping," Charlotte said. "You haven't done a thing to pack the dresses."

Sarah grunted but released the day dress.

"At least Charlotte has her letter." Lina leaned into the trunk and smoothed the copper dress.

Charlotte froze with a strand of pearls in one hand and a velvet cloth in the other. "What letter?"

"It was weeks ago. I left it on the tray in the kitchen with the other mail."

Charlotte forced herself to swallow. "You gave me a letter you said did not come in the mail."

"I remember—the man in the street who had your name wrong. This was the same day, but it was a real letter. It had a foreign postmark and everything. It was from Paris."

Charlotte's chest tightened.

Sarah turned her back to the other maids and clutched the green silk against her form in clenched fists. It had not occurred to her that of course someone else would have seen that letter—someone must have placed the mail on the silver tray on the table. Her eyes darted around the room as she listened to the exchange between Charlotte and Lina. No one knew she had seen the letter. No one could prove anything. Sarah put the gown down and turned to the closet, choosing a pale yellow chiffon to fold and place in the trunk.

"Think, Lina," Charlotte said, "did you see what happened to the mail that day?"

Lina shook her head. "I put it on the tray as usual. I only remember because I thought how odd it was that you got two letters in one day, and I don't ever remember you getting even one letter before."

Curiosity about the second letter almost did Sarah in, but she pulled herself from the brink of asking. She had to divert attention. "Perhaps you're confused. Anyway, it can't have been important. That was weeks ago."

"It was clearly addressed to Miss Charlotte Farrow," Lina said. "No one could mistake it."

Charlotte slowly wrapped the pearls in the blue velvet cloth. "The only other explanation is that someone took my letter."

"Who would do that?" Lina asked. "Mr. Penard fancies himself in charge of everything, but even he would not take a letter addressed to someone else."

Sarah stuffed the yellow gown in the trunk and retreated to the closet for another. She took both pieces of a peach-colored broadcloth walking suit off their hooks.

"Are you sure all of these dresses came out of just two trunks?" Sarah said. "I don't see how there will be room for the hats." She plucked a peach velvet hat off the closet shelf and waved it.

"What happened to my letter?" Charlotte pressed Lina.

"Misplaced in the kitchen, perhaps?" Lina suggested.

"Did Miss Brewster bring any hatboxes?" Sarah held the suit in one hand and with the other cocked the peach hat on her head. In her peripheral vision, Charlotte sat on the edge of the open trunk. Sarah's pulse pounded.

"We clean that kitchen from top to bottom every day," Charlotte said. "Someone would have found a letter long before now. Are you sure you didn't notice anyone else looking at the mail that day?"

"I don't pay attention after I collect the mail." Lina folded a linen jacket and nudged Charlotte off the trunk. "I just put it on the tray for Mr. Penard."

"Maybe it was thrown away by mistake." Sarah pressed her lips together. That was almost the truth.

Lina gasped at the suggestion. "Mr. Penard would never make such a mistake!"

"Then the letter must be in the house somewhere." Charlotte raised her fingers to her temples.

"Perhaps if we let the rest of the staff know it's missing," Lina said, "someone will remember."

"I could ask Mr. Penard to inquire," Charlotte mused. "If a mistake has happened, he would want to know in order to prevent it in the future."

Sarah's hands went slippery with sweat. "I hardly think that's necessary."

"It wouldn't do for me to be asking questions." Charlotte fingered the edge of her apron.

"Then don't," Sarah said.

"But suppose a piece of the Bannings' mail went missing."

"If it's important, Lucy will write you another letter from that fancy hotel." As soon as she spoke the words, Sarah winced.

Charlotte marched across the room and spun Sarah around. "You saw the letter!"

"You're right," Lina said. "I remember now. The return address was a hotel."

Sarah shrank from Charlotte's face.

"Sarah Cummings," Charlotte said through gritted teeth, "you tell me this instant what you know about that letter."

Sarah bent at the waist and ducked past Charlotte. She cast the broadcloth suit and its hat into the trunk. "All right. I admit it. I saw it!"

Charlotte and Lina stared at her wide-eyed.

"You looked at a letter addressed to me?" Charlotte could not believe she had heard correctly. Surely even Sarah would recognize the impudence of the transgression.

"I didn't mean anything by it." Sarah shuffled three steps back. "I can't help it if I'm curious."

"But it was my letter." Charlotte followed Sarah across the room.

"I just wondered why Lucy Banning would be writing to a kitchen maid."

"That's none of your business, Sarah. What do you know about what became of my letter?"

"I . . . had a bit of . . . an accident with it," Sarah confessed.

Charlotte crossed her arms and clamped her lips together. Sarah Cummings had tried her patience one time too many.

"I dropped it in the slop pail accidentally, and then I couldn't just put it back on the tray."

"So you stole my letter?" Charlotte seethed, every muscle in her body itching to slap the girl. "Where is it now?"

Sarah looked at her feet. "In my room."

"Go get it."

"We're supposed to be packing the gowns."

Charlotte set her teeth. "Sarah, go get my letter right now."

Lina added, "Mrs. Banning did say we should do what Charlotte says."

Sarah turned her eyes to Lina, but Charlotte did not release her own stare.

"Fine," Sarah said finally, "but it was an accident, so you have no right to be angry."

Charlotte rapidly wrapped jewelry while Sarah was out of the room, keeping her head cocked for the sound of Sarah's step on the back stairs near Lucy's suite and ignoring Lina's attempts at conversation. Finally Sarah reappeared.

Charlotte snatched the soiled and crumpled envelope out of Sarah's hand. Lucy's familiar flowery handwriting peeked out from the dried smudges and smears of the slop pail.

"This has been opened," Charlotte said.

Sarah shrugged slightly.

"Have you read my personal mail?"

"I told you, I can't help it if I'm curious."

"You don't have an ounce of self-control in your scrawny little body." Heat flashed through Charlotte.

"I didn't understand it anyway. It's as if she was writing in code."

"Perhaps that's because it was none of your business."

"Or maybe it's because you have a secret. Why would you suddenly get two letters in one day? One of them was not even in the real mail, just a man in the street. Maybe Mr. Penard would be interested in that!"

Charlotte exhaled, lowered her shoulders, and turned calmly toward the stunned parlor maid. "Lina, I would appreciate it if you would continue putting the gowns away. I will be back in a few minutes."

Charlotte took the back stairs down to the half level where the nursery was situated and entered. Instinctively she moved to the rocker and with trembling hands extracted the letter from the envelope. Sarah was right. It was like a code.

Lucy had guessed.

Whatever Leo had said about the child was enough for Lucy to discern his true identity.

Don't lose your joy, the note said.

"It's too late," Charlotte murmured. "I gave my joy away."

25

Two days later, Charlotte tucked her chair under the kitchen table after the staff lunch and took the back stairs to her room.

Thursday was the one day each week she could count on a few hours off duty, so she could leave the cleaning up to Sarah. In the old days, she went every Thursday to Mrs. Given's house and spent the afternoon and evening with Henry. And then for a few weeks she was afraid to leave the house for more than a few minutes, because Henry was there and she wanted to know he was being well cared for.

Henry was gone.

And she had nowhere to go.

Charlotte sat on her bed, her knees tucked against her chest, and pulled the cotton blanket up around her. She leaned her head back against the wall and closed her eyes, hoping to dream of a brown-haired smiling toddler with radiant blue eyes.

She woke when she heard scuffling across the hall and realized Sarah had come upstairs. If Sarah was finished cleaning up after luncheon for the Bannings, that meant the time was midafternoon. Tears seeped from Charlotte's eyes again, as they had so often in the last week, and she wiped them away with the backs of her hands. In her mind, she heard Archie chiding her about not taking the precious few hours she was entitled to away from the house.

He was right, she decided. Henry was gone, and it was her own doing. What was there to gain by secluding herself in her room, swimming in self-pity at every opportunity? Charlotte swung her feet over the side of the bed, stood up, and crossed to her closet to lift a gray suit off a hook. Lucy Banning had given her the suit, along with a hat. Charlotte had not worn anything but maid's garb since the day of Lucy's wedding in June, when she had helped Lucy into her gown then lingered in the balcony at Second Presbyterian Church to observe the wedding.

Lucy and Will were so happy together. Charlotte mourned that she would never experience that gift.

Charlotte laid the gray suit on her bed and opened the top drawer of the rickety dresser. She took out the letter from Lucy to read for the twentieth time, then sighed heavily, not sure she would have done anything differently if she had received the letter when it arrived. Henry was still safer in New Hampshire.

She pushed closed the drawer with the letter inside and quickly changed her clothes. It was time to go out—somewhere. Wearing the gray suit, she stepped into the hall. Sarah's door was open, and the girl was wearing the green silk dress Flora Banning had bestowed on her two days ago. She had put the time to good use already. The waist was more tapered and the shoulders less broad.

Their eyes met. Not a word had passed between them since Tuesday morning.

Charlotte straightened her back. "The gown looks nice. Clearly you have real talent."

Sarah's jaw fell slack and for once she had nothing to say.

"I mean it," Charlotte said. "You've done a beautiful job. I hope you get to wear the dress someplace special."

Charlotte slipped out the servants' entrance and began wandering south down Prairie Avenue. She had no destination, but she could not simply walk for the next seven or eight hours. A gaggle of gawkers moved north toward her, abuzz with wonder at the size of the mansions on the street and the intricate architecture and gilded carriages parked at the curb.

The fair.

I gave away my baby because he *was at the fair. But was it really him?*

Charlotte hurried her steps and turned toward Wabash Avenue and the nearest streetcar at the next opportunity. The answer was at the fairgrounds.

Archie hung his jacket on the back of a kitchen chair.

"Is there tea?" he asked. The afternoon driving schedule would not permit him to slip over to Mickey's shop today. Coffee would do in a pinch, but a good pot of strong Irish tea would hit the spot.

Mrs. Fletcher pointed with a wooden spoon. "On the stove. Just made it. Plenty strong."

Archie took a cup down from the cupboard and opened the icebox for the cream. "Where's Charlotte today?"

"I haven't seen her since lunch." Mrs. Fletcher dumped a bowl of bread dough onto a layer of flour and leaned into it with the heels of her hands. "I don't know why Mr. Penard agreed to give her the day off when she just spent an entire weekend in bed, but he saw fit. It's the other one I'm looking for."

"Sarah?"

Mrs. Fletcher eyed the clock. "She has three minutes to present herself or she'll be sorry."

Archie poured his tea and stirred in the cream. "So do you think Charlotte is up in her room?"

She studied him. "I don't see how that's any of your business. You'll not be going there."

"No, of course not. It's just . . . I know she was ill. She may be relapsing." He carried his tea to the table and sat down. Steps on the back stairs made him turn his head hopefully toward the door.

Not Charlotte. Sarah.

"Just in time," Archie said, glancing at the clock.

Sarah sneered.

"We don't have Charlotte tonight," Mrs. Fletcher said, "so don't dillydally."

"Sarah, have you seen Charlotte?" Archie sipped his tea casually.

"She left a while ago," Sarah answered. "She had on that gray suit Miss Lucy used to wear, acting as if she had someplace important to go."

Where would she go? Archie wondered. He had spent weeks trying to convince her to take her days off, and today of all days she decided to go out. Where? From what little she had told him, he gathered she did not have a friend in the city.

He filled his lungs at the realization of what would pull her away from the house after losing her child. The tea was hot, but he gulped it.

"I have to go out," he announced, "and I might not be back before dinner."

Mrs. Fletcher looked up sharply. "You'll need to take that up with Mr. Penard."

Archie thrust his arms into his jacket. "No, I have to go right now. Karl will have to pick up Richard and Mr. Banning. Let the footman serve the soup."

"You're going to be in serious trouble." Sarah said.

"Mind your own business." Archie wasted no time getting out of the house and over to the streetcar.

Charlotte stood at the entrance to the Midway. She could never know if he was in there unless she paid the fare and went through the gates.

This was absurd, she told herself. Millions of people had come from all over the country for the fair—even from around the world. Why should she think he was still there?

She stepped to the side of the throng crawling toward the gates and leaned against a lamppost, her eyes closed and the image of him turning in recognition ten days earlier dangling before her. Fear had cut through her, the pain blinding her from the details of that moment. She had seen only his face—that sneer—and instinctively lifted their son from the buggy and evaporated into the passing crowd. When she glanced back, he was gone.

But now she saw it clearly. Every detail. The shirt he was wearing with a red stripe across the shoulders. A uniform. And in his hands, the tool he held. A wrench.

"He was working," she said aloud. "He works here. That's why he would still be here."

Charlotte stepped toward the gate.

26

In his blue and yellow livery, Archie stuck out on the cable car full of worn browns and muted grays, but he did not care. People looking at him could concoct their own explanations for why a man in a coachman's uniform was riding the cable car. The only thing on his mind was Charlotte, who must have passed these same blocks earlier in the afternoon. Taking the Cottage Grove cable car down to the Exposition made the most sense, and Archie was confident he was following the path she had chosen to the Midway. The question was, how much of a head start did she have? And what would she do when she got there?

The mile-long stretch of exhibits and sideshows was overwhelming in itself with noise and attractions. If she considered venturing into the fair proper, the chance of finding a man who might or might not have been there ten days earlier was next to nothing, and Archie's hope of finding a slender young woman in a gray suit was just as absurd.

If only she would let him be with her. She should not have to go through this alone.

Every time the cable car lurched to a stop at a corner for passengers to board and disgorge, frustration roiled in

Archie's belly. Just because a cable car made the most sense as a mode of transportation did not mean it was fast enough when he was in a hurry. Archie gave up his seat to a weary-looking shop girl and stood in the aisle, considering the benefits of moving toward the door even though the cable car was a long way from where he planned to get off.

The last place Charlotte had seen her husband—or thought she saw him—was at the Ferris wheel. Expecting to find him there made little sense, but it was the only starting point Charlotte had.

The cable car pitched to a stop once more.

Charlotte put one foot in front of the other and stepped from Cottage Grove Avenue through the entrance to the Midway Plaisance. She did not have to look for the Ferris wheel. It rose two hundred and fifty feet into the air, towering over everything around it and dominating the view of anyone who dared lift eyes from the crowded displays of foreign cultures, sideshows, and games.

Walking slowly, Charlotte concentrated on trying to remember precisely what she had seen that day. His trousers were black, and the white shirt with the red stripe had a round neckline. Charlotte remembered seeing a lot of other men dressed that way on both occasions when she visited the fair. While millions of people came to Chicago to visit the fair, thousands found employment on the fairgrounds, at least for the duration of the Exposition. Charlotte had no trouble believing that someone like Lathan Landers would have come in search of some easy money. The fact that he seemed to be wearing some sort of uniform—and a menial one—did not dissuade her. Lathan ran an elaborate network of bootleg stills and was not afraid to gamble even against long odds. He would have come to Chicago looking to relieve some of the millions of visitors of the cash that weighed them down, and working on the Midway was the perfect opportunity.

Charlotte stopped in front of the Brazilian Music Hall, barely hearing the throbbing pulse emanating from within.

I am out of my mind. If I find him, then what?

She was tempted to turn around and jump back on the Cottage Grove Avenue cable car and ride it as far away as she could get.

The brakes screeched as the cable car made an unscheduled stop. Archie nearly lost his balance. Standing at the back of the crowded car, Archie could not see the cause of the sudden halt. A few passengers took advantage of the opportunity to shove past the people in the aisle and get off the back of the car to saunter on their ways.

Archie pushed in the opposite direction, toward the front of the car. Around him, others craned their necks as well, hoping for a glimpse of what had caused the car to stop.

"It's a horse!" someone exclaimed. "It fell and tipped over a carriage in the intersection."

Archie groaned audibly.

"It probably stepped in a hole and snapped its leg," someone else speculated.

"Who was in the carriage?"

"They can't leave it in the middle of the street."

"What if someone is hurt?"

"The coachman might be trapped under the carriage."

On any other day, Archie might have been interested in this conversation. He was not heartless. He sincerely hoped no one was injured, not even the horse. But on this day, he had only one thing on his mind.

When the cable car driver descended the steps to investigate, Archie jostled through and did the same. Traffic from every direction had come to a halt. A quick assessment revealed no one was injured, but the horse's leg might indeed be broken. No one could estimate how long it would take to clear the intersection.

Archie was not going to wait. Every moment of delay put him farther behind Charlotte and whatever she was getting herself into. He glanced back at the hapless cable car, then moved out of the intersection and began to trot along the sidewalk. He could catch another cable car already farther south on Cottage Grove and still head for the Midway.

Charlotte's nerves would not allow her to hurry. Her mind played out every scenario she could think of. She would find Lathan but be too frightened to reveal herself to him. She would not see him, but he would accost her and put her at an immediate disadvantage. She might look all day and never find him. Maybe he was gone and she would never know the truth of why he came to Chicago. She might find him, approach him, and—then what?

Her feet dragged, but she continued forward motion, past the Chinese Village, past the white shining arches of Old Vienna, past the French cider press. At the Vienna Café, however, she stopped. The small structure was the closest attraction to the Ferris wheel. Charlotte persuaded herself she suddenly wanted a cup of coffee, though in reality she simply needed to relieve her shaking knees, and the small Vienna Café was staring her in the face.

Charlotte settled at a table next to the open wall that looked out on the enormous display of the Ferris wheel. People lined up at the six loading platforms. It took one full revolution to load all twenty-one cars from the six platforms, then the riders would enjoy one nine-minute revolution without any stops. Charlotte had heard enough accounts in the last few months to know that the view from the top of the wheel was breathtaking. Passengers more courageous than she was enjoyed vistas of Lake Michigan along with surrounding states of Wisconsin, Indiana, and Michigan. Even on a cloudy day, much of the excitement was simply in the ride itself.

Yet it terrified her. The thought of stepping into one of the cars, with plate glass windows all around, made Charlotte queasy—even without imagining the sensation of lifting off the ground and swaying in the air.

She drank her coffee slowly, peering out at the ever-shifting flow of visitors enjoying the Midway exhibits. Beyond the Ferris wheel, she saw the Egyptian camels—something else she had no wish to ride—used in the reenacted wedding procession that repeated itself multiple times a day.

She saw dozens—no, hundreds—of people in the minutes that she sat and sipped her coffee.

But she did not see him.

Archie was finally at the entrance, merging into the crowd that went through the gates to the Midway. His eyes darted around the crowded scene before him. How many more visitors had decided this was the day to see the fair before it closed in less than two weeks?

Taking a deep breath, Archie forced himself to be less random in his search. He knew her gray suit would allow her to melt into the background hues. He had to focus, examine every form, look behind every pillar, under every sign, at every movement that caught his eye. He stood in front of the Brazilian Music Hall, the Ferris wheel breaking up the sky when he lifted his eyes, and purposely slowed his breath while he moved his eyes from one form to another. Jugglers and musicians wandered up and down the street, complicating the process of sorting which movements mattered and which did not.

Then, out of the corner of his left eye, he saw a sliver of gray duck into the Chinese Village. Archie increased his stride and was there less than two minutes later.

Charlotte decided to walk a wide loop around the Ferris wheel as she continued thinking. Her musings had persuaded her she wanted to get close enough that if he were there, she would see him. But she did not want him to see her first. When she found him, she would decide how to approach him—she still did not know what she would say. Would she tell him the truth—that she had given Henry away? Would she shriek at him to leave her alone? Would she calmly and sternly demand he disappear from her life? Would she demand a legal divorce?

She sauntered over to the French cider press and pretended to look interested as mounds of whole apples were transformed under pressure into liquid. Then she ambled along

Sixtieth Street toward the Turkish exhibit, its Middle Eastern music wafting and colliding with the sounds of the German Village on the other side of the Midway. Every few minutes, Charlotte would find a post to lean against or a railing to casually support her balance as she turned once again to face the Ferris wheel and scrutinize the forms and faces of the people scurrying around.

The Bedouin, a performer from the Syrian exhibit, brushed passed her with his red and yellow silken robes flapping over his boots of sheepskin. His turban looked slightly askew to Charlotte, and his step seemed weary. She wondered about him only fleetingly, however. She was not watching the exotic performers, nor the fairgoers. Rather, she was interested in the people working to keep the Midway Plaisance in action. They were in constant motion themselves. So far Charlotte had identified three different styles of uniforms worn by people clearly toiling on the Midway, rather than feasting on the concessions and enjoying the sideshows. They were hawking souvenirs and novelties, selling tickets to the individual attractions, collecting trash, giving directions, moving wares.

They were like servants, she thought. People didn't really see them unless they needed something.

Charlotte just needed to see one in particular. He was here. She could feel it.

Archie emerged from the Chinese Village, regretting that he lost both valuable time and the cost of admission chasing the wrong woman. He was within reach of grasping her elbow when she turned her head to look at a display, and he saw her face. And it was not Charlotte. The suit was identical—probably off the rack at Marshall Field's, he realized—but it was not Charlotte.

He stood in the middle of the Midway, contemplating his options. The Ferris wheel was in plain sight before him. As he approached it, he shielded his eyes from the sun's glare and peered at the car lifting off the platform. Quickly he scanned the crowd assembled on the next platform. As frightened as Charlotte was by the Ferris wheel, however, Archie could not imagine she would get on it. At the same time, he imagined she would not stray far—if she had come to do what he suspected. His gaze turned to Cairo Street nearby, just on the other side of the wheel. While Archie doubted Charlotte would go into Cairo Street for her own amusement, she might go if she thought she had seen her husband. As he walked toward the camel at the entrance to Cairo Street, Archie played with the coins in his pocket, wondering if the risk was worth the price of admission.

Charlotte paused her wide loop at the base of the model of the Eiffel Tower, and she could not help but think of Lucy Banning Edwards, who conceivably could be standing at the base of the real Eiffel Tower at that very moment. She was wearing the suit Lucy had given her last Christmas Eve so she would have something to wear to church, and in that church service Archie had held her hand for the first time.

Archie knew the truth now, all these months later, and he still wanted to hold her hand.

She wanted to let him.

But she couldn't, not as long as *he* was out there.

A mock wedding procession emerged from Cairo Street

into the Midway, the camels ornamented brightly and elaborately. On the back of the first animal rode a half-stripped Egyptian who danced with his bronzed, muscular shoulders. The tom-tom beaters followed, and behind them the camel with the canopied howdah bearing the bride. More drums and a procession of priests completed the entourage.

Charlotte's wedding had not had a single festive moment. Although this Egyptian wedding procession was meant for entertainment only, it convinced Charlotte of what she wanted.

She wanted to be free of him. Henry was safe. Nothing bound her to the man any longer.

27

He was there.

When the commotion of the Egyptian wedding procession cleared the street, Charlotte saw Lathan Landers. His back was to her, but the slope of his muscular shoulders and the solid stance of his booted feet were unmistakable. He wore the same black trousers and starched white shirt he had worn ten days ago, and standing with him at the base of the Ferris wheel were two other men in similar garb. If they were supposed to be working, they did not seem too concerned about it. When he threw his head back and laughed, he made a quarter turn. His face crinkled with familiarity that soured her stomach.

Charlotte's first impulse was to spin around, run down the Midway, and lose herself in the Irish Village or some other attraction safely away from the Ferris wheel.

She reminded herself she had not come this far for nothing.

At the edge of Cairo Street, she hovered, veiled—she hoped—by the horde swarming the camels, daring to stroke their necks or contemplating an exotic ride of a lifetime. Lathan and his companions drifted slowly toward one of the loading platforms of the Ferris wheel. He had not seen her yet. She was sure of it.

Laden with brave and nervous passengers, the camels swayed down the street, curious followers trailing after them. Only a gaggle of mesmerized children stood between Charlotte and Lathan Landers, and Charlotte at last found her feet moving.

Toward Lathan. Not away from him.

Still he had not spotted her. She would know from his expression if he had. And then she was close enough that he would hear her.

"Lathan," she said. He turned his head slightly, and she said again, "Lathan."

His form turned and faced her, his bright blue eyes—Henry's eyes—sweeping up and down to take in her appearance. His two friends turned as well, their low whistles stirring up her unsettled lunch.

Lathan glanced at his friends, and a sneer crossed his face. "Forget it. The goods are not as sweet as they look."

As he stepped toward her, Charlotte forced her feet to stay put and swallowed the bit of her noon meal that had worked its way up to her throat.

"You should not have left the way you did," he said flatly.

The weight of breathing pressed on Charlotte's chest. "Why did you send me that note? Why didn't you just leave me alone after all this time?"

"You took something that belongs to me, and I want it."

"I only took what was mine."

He came closer and in one swift motion clasped her wrist. "You're nothing to me, but you helped yourself to something that matters."

"I helped myself to a life where I did not have to dread the sound of you coming back into the house."

"You know what I'm talking about." He tightened his grasp.

Charlotte refused to display pain. "Let go of me, Lathan. You never wanted to be a husband."

He laughed. "Then it worked out nicely that I never had a wife."

A woman in a blue dress and an out-of-style hat approached. "Lathan Landers, get your hands off that girl or you'll be sorry."

Lathan released his grip and turned toward the woman, who took his arm and leaned against him, raising her face for a kiss. He obliged by holding her chin and kissing her hard. The woman giggled under his mouth and wantonly returned the kiss.

A shiver ran through Charlotte as she remembered his touch in the early days. She had always hated it, had never wanted Lathan Landers.

Lathan's hands went to the woman's waist, and at last she pushed him away playfully. "Lathan, we're in public!" But clearly she was pleased with the attention. Lathan laid an arm lazily across her shoulders and turned back toward Charlotte.

"We're off for the day and going up on the wheel," he said to her, glowering. "You'll come with us and we'll finish this conversation."

"I'd rather finish here." She resisted even lifting her eyes to the wheel.

The woman tugged on Lathan's arm. "I've been waiting all day. I insist you come up with me."

"I'm going up," he said again, an arm around the woman but his eyes on Charlotte. "You wouldn't have come looking for me if you didn't want to talk to me."

"Surely we can talk right here. It doesn't have to take long."

Lathan laughed. "You'll look silly talking to yourself, because I'm going on the wheel."

"I'll wait for you, then."

He shook his head. "No. You're coming."

The woman in the blue dress pulled away from Lathan. "Who is this girl?" she demanded to know. "Why does she have to go with us?"

"She's nobody that matters," Lathan answered, "just someone with whom I have some unfinished business."

"I don't like my fiancé dallying with other women."

Lathan laughed loudly. "Believe me, this is the last woman on earth I would want to dally with."

Charlotte felt the flush rise. "I feel obliged to tell you Lathan and I were married two years ago."

The woman slapped his chest. "You swore you weren't married."

"Are you going to believe me or a stranger you just met?" Lathan leaned in and kissed the woman again.

The woman eyed Charlotte, tilted her chin up, and put a possessive arm through Lathan's elbow.

"I see I was wrong to disturb you." Charlotte turned to go, barely keeping herself from running down the Midway.

"Oh no you don't." Lathan reached for Charlotte's wrist. "We still have some things to clear up, and since you've taken the trouble to find me, we might as well do it."

"But you promised we would go on the wheel," the woman in the blue dress whined. "I've been looking forward to it all day."

"And we shall go," Lathan assured her. "She'll come with us. I'll even buy her ticket."

Charlotte's heart pounded, but she did not resist further. If this was what it would take to be finished with Lathan Landers once and for all, then somehow she would muster the resolve. They stood on the platform together—Lathan, the woman, his two friends, and Charlotte. The line inched forward at a steady pace as sixty people at a time filled a car before it lifted off the ground. Lathan had his hand low on the woman's hip and kissed her passionately several times while they waited, each time sneering in Charlotte's direction. She simply turned her head. The truth was plain that Lathan had not sent her that note with any intention of reclaiming her as his wife. He went so far as to deny he ever had a wife. And not once had he asked directly about the welfare of the baby. He spoke of his own child as if Henry were something he owned.

One of Lathan's friends put a hand on her shoulder. "Would you like a little attention yourself?"

"No, thank you." Charlotte shrank back and wondered if she could get out of line after all.

No. Finish with Lathan and be done with it.

They were at the front of the line now. The next car that swung down onto the platform would be theirs. As Charlotte tilted her head back to look at the towering wheel, dizziness overcame her, and she was not certain her legs would support her when the moment came to step into the car. Silently she hoped to lurch toward one of the chairs.

Finally the car swung into place. Lathan, with his arm around the woman's shoulders, sauntered aboard, followed by his two friends. Charlotte tentatively stepped off the solid platform and onto the car, falling almost immediately into one of the twisted wire chairs and not caring that she heard Lathan laughing at her as he positioned himself in front of one of the plate glass windows. The car filled with people, and Lathan drifted to the far end of the car.

Once the car was loaded, it swung up the arc of the wheel and dangled in the air while another loaded beneath it. Gripping the sides of her chair, Charlotte peered between the passengers in her own car and got a glimpse of the Midway exhibits on the ground. She was grateful, though, not to be nearer the plate glass where she might see for herself the distance to the ground.

Fully loaded now, the wheel began to turn.

Nine minutes, Charlotte thought, *and this can all be over. He can be gone for good.*

So far, after insisting she come with him, Lathan was ignoring her. Charlotte was glad for the crowd. Lathan would not take extreme action with so many people around. But she only had nine minutes. She could not afford to waste them letting him watch her grip her chair in fear while he sneered from the other end of the car. Blowing out her breath, Charlotte forced herself to her feet, refused to look down, and moved one uncertain step at a time to where Lathan was once again kissing the woman in the blue dress.

"Ah, so you have decided to join us." He stepped away from the woman and moved uncomfortably close to Charlotte.

"You said yourself we had unfinished business." Charlotte refused to step back from his glare.

"And so we do. Where is it?" He leaned in and gripped her shoulder in one large hand.

It. He sounded just like Sarah, not even able to acknowledge that his son was a living, breathing human being. Charlotte said nothing.

"Where is it?" he repeated, this time through gritted teeth. "No one else knew about that hiding place."

Hiding place? He's not talking about Henry. "I don't know what you're talking about, Lathan."

"There was a lot of money in that jar," Lathan said, "and I want it back."

Charlotte gasped. "This is about money? You want money?"

"What else would I want from you?" he said. "I took what I wanted from you a long time ago, but that doesn't mean I'll let you steal from me. Give me the money, or I swear I'll never let you have a moment's peace."

Now it was Charlotte's turn to laugh. "I haven't got any money! If I had any of your bootleg stash, do you think I would be working as a domestic on Prairie Avenue?"

"I know you found that jar while you were expecting," he insisted. "It can't be coincidence that it disappeared the same day you did—while I was conveniently away. I came home and you and the jar were both gone."

"I don't know what you're talking about," Charlotte said again. "It must have been that girl you brought in to help with the work around the house when I was close to my time."

He still had not asked about the baby. Was it possible he did not care?

"We both know that girl was useless."

"Did you ask her?" Charlotte asked.

"She told me she didn't know where you went."

"I mean, did you ask her about the missing money?"

"You took it."

"No, Lathan, I did not take your money. I took a quilt, my grandmother's Bible, and the baby."

"Yes, the girl told me you gave birth. What was it?"

"Do you even care?"

He shrugged. "Not really. Your parents might like to know."

It was a boy and his name is Henry! she wanted to scream. But she did not. Lathan didn't care about his own child. He didn't deserve to know his name.

"Let me go, Lathan. I don't have your money," Charlotte said evenly. "It looks like that girl was not as stupid as you thought."

"Look, we're at the top!" The woman in the blue dress tugged on Lathan's arm, and he released Charlotte.

Lathan's eyes were ice. "Don't miss the view. It's spectacular."

"Are you finished talking business?" the woman asked.

Charlotte willed herself not to blink as she searched Lathan's face for the answer.

"Yes," he finally said. "We're done."

"Are you sure there's nothing between you and this girl?" the woman asked.

Lathan smiled. "No, nothing between us."

He did not look over his shoulder as he walked away from Charlotte.

The seats were full. Charlotte had no recourse but to grip a railing and remain upright. The car was making its descent now. Charlotte focused on breathing evenly and awaiting the sensation of solid ground.

Lathan's words echoed in her head.

Then it worked out nicely that I never had a wife.

No, nothing between us.

The woman had called him her fiancé. Was he really planning to marry her—and was he free to do so?

One by one the cars unloaded and reloaded. At the platform, Lathan and his friends got off and walked across the platform. He never looked back.

Had she been afraid all this time for nothing? Was he ever her husband?

Had she given away her son needlessly?

28

When Archie emerged from Cairo Street—kicking himself for once again guessing wrong—he determined he needed a new plan. He would stay on the Midway, visible and vigilant. His livery would make him easy to spot, and he prayed Charlotte would welcome the sight, not turn from his help if she saw him. As urgent as the impulse was to find her, he could not chase after every random swish of gray. Charlotte could be anywhere on the Midway—if she was even there at all—so Archie resolved to walk at a pace that would allow him both to cover ground quickly and to examine the pedestrian traffic thoroughly.

Archie strode past German Village while at the same time scrutinizing the entrances and exits to Turkish Village across the way. He continued on toward the Japanese and Irish exhibits. At the Hagenbeck Animal Show, he remembered Henry's glee at the sight. At the Libby Glass Company display he wished he could take Charlotte inside and buy her whatever she considered most beautiful. He paced the entire length of the Midway until finally he was at the entrance to the grand Court of Honor and the fair itself—and there he halted. If he had not been able to find Charlotte in the one-mile stretch of the Midway Plaisance, he had little hope of stumbling upon her somewhere in the six hundred acres of the exhibition. Intuitively he did not believe she had entered the fair. The Midway had been the focus of her anxiety when she confessed to him she had seen her husband.

Archie paused to pull out a watch and examine the time. This was Charlotte's day off, but it was not his. No one on Prairie Avenue would be looking for Charlotte for several more hours, but no doubt Mr. Penard was already pacing the kitchen, awaiting his coachman. By now Archie had missed the staff supper, and Mr. Penard would have discovered that Archie dispatched Karl to pick up Richard from school and Mr. Banning from his office rather than making the late afternoon rounds himself. With the slow progress of congested streetcars at this time of day, it seemed doubtful Archie would return to Prairie Avenue in time to help serve the family dinner.

He stood in the middle of the Midway and sighed. The Ferris wheel beckoned, as it always did, but from this distance, the passengers were specks.

Charlotte, where are you? I want to help you.

Archie resumed his slow round of the Midway exhibits, working his way back toward the wheel and the Cottage Grove Avenue entrance. He searched to the point of staring into the face of every young man on the Midway, lamenting that he did not have even a general description of the husband Charlotte might be searching for. He could be walking right past the man and never know it.

By now the electric lights illuminating the fair and the Midway had come on, casting a counterfeit gladness over the scene.

Archie had to admit he had failed in his quest.

Archie slipped into the kitchen, ready to endure Penard's verbal thrashing. Dinner was over, and Sarah was scrubbing pots. The door from the kitchen to the butler's pantry was propped open, and Mr. Penard was carefully washing china and replacing the pieces in the cabinets.

Mr. Penard looked up when he saw Archie and immediately withdrew his hands from the soapy water and dried them. Archie planted himself in the middle of the kitchen and awaited the inevitable barrage.

"You have a lot of explaining to do, Archie," Penard said.

"He went chasing after Charlotte," Sarah said from the kitchen sink.

"This has nothing to do with you." In Mr. Penard's chastisement of Sarah, Archie heard the prelude to the stiff scolding no doubt coming his way.

Sarah rolled her eyes. "Just trying to help."

"Is what the girl says true?" Mr. Penard probed.

Archie could hardly tell him the whole story. He chose his words carefully. "I was concerned Charlotte might require assistance."

"Charlotte has the day off. If she requires assistance, she has to find it on her own. Your responsibility was here." Penard was unmoving.

"Yes, sir. I'm sorry, sir." Archie hoped that appearing contrite would diffuse the tension. He kept his eyes lowered. Penard would rail for a few minutes, then it would be over.

"You blatantly abandoned your post without permission and without justification," Penard continued.

"Yes, sir."

"Your recent absences have not gone unnoticed, Archie.

You have developed a pattern of being away from the house for lengths of time for which you cannot account, and this is the last straw."

"Yes, sir. It won't happen again, sir."

"No, it won't, because you are no longer in the employ of the Bannings."

Archie's eyes widened and he looked the butler full in the face. "Has Mr. Banning dismissed me?"

"*I* am dismissing you," Penard bellowed. "Your anarchist associations are a threat to the order of the household."

"I have no anarchist associations—"

Penard waved him off. "Do not try to justify your actions. I had hoped that promoting you to coachman would make you more serious about your service in this household, but it's clear I was mistaken. Instead you have chosen to associate yourself with the likes of men who threw a bomb into Haymarket Square."

"I have done no such thing!" Archie protested. "Besides, nothing was ever proven. The governor himself pardoned those men."

"The governor has anarchist leanings as well," Penard countered. "I will not have anyone in my employ perpetuating these misconceptions and influencing the rest of the staff."

"Mr. Penard, I assure you—"

"Pack your things and go, Archie. You will leave the Banning house tonight. Your final wages are on the table."

Archie pulled the heavy coach house door closed behind him and put the latch down. Karl sprang from the stool where he sat polishing his boots, his eyebrows lifted in question.

"I'm out," Archie said, "immediately."

"What possessed you to—"

Archie lifted one hand, palm out. "Don't, Karl. I can't explain it to you, but I would do the same thing again."

"Where will you go?" Karl asked.

Archie shrugged. "I don't know, but he's determined that I go tonight. I wouldn't put it past him to come out here and make sure I'm gone." He shuffled toward the tightly spiraled iron stairs that rose to the loft where the coachmen slept. "I have to gather my things."

He did not have much. Three years of service at the Banning residence had yielded a secure place to sleep, regular nourishment, uniforms he would have to leave behind, and little else. Archie owned one pair of thin-soled boots that were not part of a uniform, one set of clothes, and a jacket that might be passed off as a suit coat in poor light. He had a handful of books that bore witness to how he was inclined to spend what little extra cash he acquired. The coins that jingled in his pocket would not take him far.

From the loft, as he gathered his things into a gunnysack, Archie looked down at the gleaming carriages he had driven for the last three years. For part of that time, his duties as footman included general maintenance tasks inside the house, but for the last year, the coach house had been his domain. The Bannings had two enclosed four-wheel carriages, one larger than the other. Archie had spent countless hours shivering in an exposed driver's seat as the family sat under the warmth of rugs inside the carriages. Two open carriages were used only in the summer. The comings and goings of the family required careful coordination to ensure a carriage was available at every appointed hour. Archie and Karl spent evenings polishing carriages and oiling reins so that equipment was ready at any moment of the day or night. Since he had become head coachman, Archie also inspected the stable of horses every night to be sure at least one pair was always ready for service, and scrutinized reins and harnesses to ensure safety at all times.

He would not miss this. He would get a real job, one that gave him something to show for himself.

But he would miss seeing Charlotte every day. And now he would not even have a chance to say good-bye. He hated to consider what she would think when she found him gone.

Sarah hovered at the female servants' entrance, knowing Archie would have to emerge from the coach house eventually. She almost did not recognize him out of uniform. Instead of the blue and yellow livery he wore for driving or the white formal wear he donned for dinner service, he moved in the shadows, wearing brown trousers, a shirt of indistinguishable color—perhaps once white—and a brown jacket. He carried a gunnysack over his shoulder, but the bulge was small.

She stepped into his path. He slowed his steps and looked at her but did not speak.

"Archie," Sarah said. "I . . . well, I . . ."

"You what?" Archie said harshly. "I heard you tell Mr. Penard I went chasing after Charlotte. That was none of your business."

She nodded. "I know."

"You're always sticking your nose in where it doesn't belong without thought to the consequences."

Sarah straightened her shoulders. "I was going to say I'm sorry, but I don't appreciate your tone."

"You? Say you're sorry?" Archie laughed. "You don't care about another living thing but yourself. You've never been sorry in your life."

"You've only known me a couple of months. You don't know what you're talking about."

Archie shifted his sack to the other shoulder. "Look, I have to find a place to stay tonight. I don't have time to stand here and argue with you." He tried to step past her, but she moved into his path again.

"I don't want to argue, either," Sarah said. "I . . . may have said some things that led Mr. Penard to think . . ."

"This anarchist business—that came from you?" Archie said.

"It may have."

"And now you want me to believe you're sorry."

She shrugged. "Believe what you want. I never meant for this to happen, but if you ask me, it's a good thing."

"Losing my position and having nowhere to live is a good thing?"

She nodded. "This is your chance, Archie. Charlotte may be perfectly happy in service, but you don't want that life any more than I do. I see it in your eyes every day."

"That hardly makes me an anarchist."

"You may not have chosen this, but you're getting out."

In the shadows she could barely see his features, but his presence reminded her of the young man her father had once been. She had been a little girl in those days, and her memories were as gray and drab as the night around her now, but her father had aspired to a better life. He had not settled, and neither would she.

"I have to go," Archie said.

Sarah stepped out of his way.

29

Charlotte's feet clicked along beneath the streetlights of Prairie Avenue, then she cut alongside the Banning house to the coach house. She did not want to encounter anyone else. She only wanted Archie.

The door was latched from the inside, but she paused only briefly before rapping her fingers against the wood. The dinner hour was over, but it was not so late that Archie would have gone to bed.

"Archie!" She did not dare use full voice. "I need to talk to you!"

When she heard no answer, she knocked again. Finally she heard movement from within. Karl pulled open the door and beckoned her in.

"Where's Archie?" she asked. "I was hoping to speak to him before he turned in."

Karl raised an eyebrow. "You haven't been in the house yet, have you?"

"No, I came here first," Charlotte said. "What's wrong?"

"Mr. Penard dismissed Archie tonight and insisted he take his things and leave immediately."

Charlotte's stomach sank. "Why would Mr. Penard do that?"

"Archie went missing one time too many. He was gone most of the afternoon and missed the family's dinner."

"Where did he go?" Archie had been stretching his errands, she knew. But for him to disappear for so many hours—and miss his duties—was unusual.

"Sarah says he went looking for you," Karl said.

Charlotte's eyes widened as the breath went out of her. "He put his position at risk because of me?"

"He never actually said where he went. You know Sarah. She jumps to conclusions."

Charlotte groped for words. "Did Archie say where he would go when he left here?"

Karl shrugged. "No. As a matter of fact, he said he had no place to go. But he knows a few of the Irish crowd. My guess is he'll end up with one of them."

Charlotte lifted her eyes to the loft where Archie had slept for three years, unable to imagine him gone. She had rebuffed his advances over the last year. Now she needed him—wanted him—and he was gone.

"I have to find him," Charlotte said. "Will you help me? We can take the marketing carriage out. He can't have gone far yet."

Karl shook his head emphatically. "I may only be an under-coachman, but I need this position. Mr. Penard could find a dozen men who would rather work for the Bannings than the other families on Prairie Avenue. I can't put my position at risk to chase after Archie and have Mr. Penard discover I'm gone."

"No one is going to call for a carriage at this hour," Charlotte argued.

"Mr. Leo isn't home yet," Karl said. "He went to dinner on Calumet Avenue. He may telephone."

Charlotte sighed heavily. "Then I'll go myself."

"You know you're supposed to be in by eleven even on your day off."

"Maybe I will be and maybe I won't." Charlotte lifted the latch and let herself out of the coach house. Henry was gone. Archie was gone. What did she have to lose if she missed a curfew?

Streetcars were still running, though less frequently than during the peak hours when the city bustled relentlessly. Charlotte scurried to Michigan Avenue and climbed aboard a car going north. The first place that came to mind to look for Archie was the tea and sandwich shop he had taken her to last month without realizing it was her birthday.

She got off the car and hustled toward the shop, whispering, "Be open, be open, be open."

The door was locked.

A light beamed from the back of the shop, and Charlotte was sure she detected movement. With the palm of one hand she banged on the door while jiggling the handle with the other hand. Finally Mickey appeared in the shadows and moved toward the door. He peered out the window at her, his eyes narrowed in suspicion.

"I'm closed," Mickey said.

"I'm Archie Shepard's friend," Charlotte said loudly. "He brought me here a few weeks ago."

Mickey examined her face. "You're the one who left without drinking your tea."

"Yes!" Charlotte exclaimed with relief. "You remember me!"

Mickey fumbled with a key and opened the door. "Archie was none too happy with you," he said.

Charlotte nodded. "I know. But now he understands my reasons."

"You'd better come inside." Mickey glanced around the street.

Charlotte stepped inside gratefully. "I'm looking for Archie. Have you seen him?"

Mickey shook his head. "Not in days. Those Bannings must be keeping him busy."

Charlotte could barely hold back the sob that had been welling for hours now. "Archie's in trouble," she managed to say. "He was dismissed this evening. I thought perhaps he had come here."

Mickey shook his head again. "I haven't heard from him. If he comes in, I'll tell him you were looking for him."

"I have to find him tonight!"

Mickey shrugged. "I don't know where he is. Archie comes in here a lot—though he never brought a young lady before you—but I don't know what else he does with his time. He's a dreamer, that one."

Charlotte inhaled sharply. Archie was a dreamer. "I think I know," she said. "Thank you for talking to me." She spun around and was out the door, ignoring the trailing voice of the Irish shop owner.

From across the street, where he leaned against a smaller structure, Archie studied the red brick building. Even in darkness it was imposing, as if making a pronouncement of fortitude. Archie imagined it would easily stand for a hundred years or more. The edifice would be there when Archie's own future had long become history. He had no doubt that the business John Glessner had helped to forge would be just as enduring.

Maybe it was just as well Penard had sacked him.

Archie had actually been inside the building of Warder, Bushnell & Glessner. One time. On an afternoon off, he had brushed his tired-looking brown jacket and made sure his shirt was clean and starched before entering the doors of the company and inquiring about an application for employment. Carefully, he had filled it out in Mickey's shop—with no tea on the table lest it spill on the form—and returned it later the same day.

Archie was fairly certain John Glessner would recognize him by sight if not by name. The Bannings had loaned him to the Glessners on several occasions to drive an extra coach for a family affair. If his application ever appeared on the desk of John Glessner, the record of his service on Prairie Avenue was clear to see, and Archie could only hope the Prairie Avenue connection would be helpful despite his having been in service. Now he was grateful he had returned the application while still employed on Prairie Avenue and did not have to explain on the form the circumstances of his departure.

First thing in the morning, he resolved, he would march into Warder, Bushnell & Glessner and inquire about the status of his application and any change in current openings. He was not hoping to run the company. A simple clerk's position would be a triumph. His mother had insisted he learn to read and do figures, and Archie had never been more thankful. He sighed and rubbed his eyes with both hands. He still had the night to get through, and if he loitered on this corner much longer, a local police officer was likely to urge him on his way.

On his way to where? That was the question.

"Archie!" a voice whispered behind him. He pivoted to see Charlotte, still in her gray suit, melting into shades of charcoal around her.

Immediately, he lurched toward her and wrapped her in his arms. "I was so worried for you," he whispered. "I spent hours looking for you on the Midway before I had to admit you might not even be there."

"But I was," Charlotte answered. "How did you know?"

He shrugged. "It made sense at the time I left the house."

"I'm sorry about your position. I feel terrible that you've lost it because you were worried for me."

Archie shook his head and kissed her forehead. "Don't be." With an arm around her shoulders he turned back to gaze at the building across the street. "How did you know I would be here?"

She smiled. "It made sense at the time."

He felt her shoulders trembling under his hand. "Charlotte, what happened on the Midway?"

Her tears came freely now as she recounted in detail her encounter with Lathan Landers. Archie held both her hands. At the end of her story, she tightened her own grip on his fingers.

"What did he mean, Archie? Why did he say he never had a wife? How can he think he's free to marry that woman?"

Archie let his breath out slowly. "Because perhaps he really is. You said once you were legally bound to him, but against your will. What if you were not legally bound to him after all?"

"We had a wedding," Charlotte protested. "My parents were there, the minister was there. We signed papers."

Archie cocked his head. "But you didn't want to marry him?"

She shook her head. "My parents arranged it with Lathan without ever saying anything to me. I thought we were going into Greenville to talk to the banker about the grain loan. My mother said we could go into the mercantile and look at new calicos. For some strange reason, though, she insisted I had to wear my best dress. Then instead of going to the bank, we went to the church, and Lathan was there in his black suit. It was all arranged." She sucked in a sob.

What had those monsters done to her? Fury surged through Archie's chest.

Charlotte forced air out and continued. "Apparently my father had interfered with Lathan's stills, tapping them and selling the bootleg behind Lathan's back for quite some time."

"And his daughter was the price of saving his own skin," Archie said.

Charlotte nodded. "Everyone knew Lathan Landers. He had flirted with me in town, but I was never comfortable around him. He was too . . . slick. When he asked if he could take me for a carriage ride, I gave him a polite no thank you. The next thing I knew, I was married to a man I barely knew."

"And you had no choice at all?"

"My mother stood right there with her elbow in my rib, and my father looked so terrified. I didn't know what would happen to him if I refused."

"And the minister?"

Charlotte shrugged. "He was new. I didn't know him well."

Archie exhaled. "My guess is Lathan got his hands on the paperwork. If he's denying your marriage, perhaps he made sure it was never filed."

Charlotte sucked in a gasp.

"The state keeps records of valid marriages," Archie said. "We'll be able to find out the truth."

"But . . . we were . . . together. I had his baby. If we weren't married—"

Archie pulled her to him. "Shhh. Don't."

"Even if the State of Illinois does not recognize our marriage, in the eyes of God—"

Archie shook his head. "That was no true marriage. What that man did to you does not make a marriage. God is not fooled."

Charlotte shuddered in his embrace. Archie tightened his hold on her.

"What have I done, Archie?" she asked hoarsely. "I gave away my son."

"You were frightened." He stroked her back. "You were protecting him from a monster."

"A monster who has no interest in him, a monster who cared more about a lost jar of money than his own child."

"We'll get Henry back," Archie said.

"It's too late." Charlotte's lips barely moved. "It's too late."

Archie released her, then took her hand and began walking. "The only thing that's too late is the hour. I won't be responsible for Mr. Penard unleashing his wrath on you. I'm taking you home. We'll figure out what to do about Henry in the daylight."

Charlotte wiped her face with the back of her free hand. "I'll take the streetcar."

"It's too late for you to be out alone. I'll ride with you to Prairie Avenue."

"And then? Where will you go, Archie?"

He tilted his head and scratched it. He had been thinking about that question for hours without an answer. "I'll find somewhere."

"When will I see you again?"

"As soon as possible."

"But you can't be seen on Prairie Avenue. How will we communicate?"

"I'll figure out something," he said. "Just be watching."

They walked along Eighteenth Street from the streetcar stop on Michigan Avenue to Prairie Avenue. At the corner, standing in front of the Glessner house and across the street from the Kimball mansion, Charlotte stopped, turning toward Archie with a hand on his arm.

"You shouldn't go any farther," she cautioned. "I'll be all right from here."

"I'll watch until you're safely in the house."

She stood close enough to feel his breath and the warmth of his presence, with her face upturned, wishing he could kiss her.

Archie kissed only her forehead, then said, "Good night, Charlotte." He nudged her elbow in the direction of the Banning house.

30

Charlotte minded her own business on Monday afternoon when Mr. Penard interviewed a new coachman at the kitchen table. She had already laid the ornate dining room table for the Bannings' dinner, with three extra places for Pamela Troutman and her parents. Miss Troutman and Oliver Banning had announced their engagement over the weekend, so the evening's meal was even more elaborate than usual. Mrs. Fletcher had been harshly specific in her instructions about the width and angle of the carrot slices for the salad. Charlotte tried three different knives before she found one sharp enough to slice with sufficient precision.

This potential coachman might be a perfectly nice person, she realized, but he was not Archie.

The coachman Mr. Penard was interrogating was older than Archie and came with an impressive list of references. The butler seemed intent on securing a coachman who understood his role in the household and would restore dignity to the position. The man sat painfully erect with the glummest expression Charlotte had ever seen, but he seemed to please Mr. Penard with his answers. By the time Charlotte moved on to producing paper-thin celery slices, Mr. Penard was shaking the man's hand and promising to recommend him to the Bannings.

Charlotte had heard nothing from Archie since Thursday night. She was grateful to be madly busy so she could not entertain thoughts of him wandering the streets. She preferred to think instead that by now he had turned up at Mickey's shop or in the Irish neighborhood where he had grown up and found both a bed and encouragement. Charlotte availed herself of every opportunity to step outside to shake a rug or put the milk bottles out, or even to stand in darkness and look at the stars, hoping Archie might slip into the courtyard—even though she knew he should not take such a risk.

When she thought of Henry, Charlotte could only envision him in Emmaline's arms on the day she had put them both in the cab to the train station. She had no mental image of her son's new surroundings except those she imagined—a bright, airy nursery with a painted red and yellow rocking horse, a sloping yard where he would tumble in winter snow and spring grass, a library full of books he would someday read voraciously under the guidance of a private tutor. Emmaline had no doubt filled his closet with crisp new clothes that made him look less like a baby and more like a little boy.

And what about my quilt? Charlotte wondered as she stopped the knife mid-slice. Had Emmaline already replaced that? Would she even keep it? What would she tell Henry about how he came to be her son?

She roused and resumed slicing. Allowing herself to drift into speculation about Henry's new life accomplished nothing. He was gone. She had done what she believed best at the time. And despite Archie's promises of help, the fact remained that if she had not sent Henry away, if she had claimed him, she would be wandering the streets right alongside Archie, and what good would that do? Certainly it would not have helped Henry.

Archie wished the moon was not nearly full. The last thing he needed was a bath of light poured over his movements while he slowly turned the corner at Twentieth Street and moved north along Prairie Avenue. He paused briefly, shaking his head, in front of the mansion belonging to Marshall Field Jr. and his young bride. The enormous home had been a gift from the senior Marshall Field when the young couple married three years earlier, about the time Archie first came to Prairie Avenue. Indignation gurgled in Archie's throat at the privilege young men like Marshall Field Jr. took for granted. The entire neighborhood screamed injustice. Archie was not sorry to leave. He only wished to find a way to take Charlotte with him.

And Henry.

No matter what Charlotte said, Archie would not accept that it was too late to reclaim her son. That one injustice he intended to rectify. Somehow.

Archie moved along, pausing again in front of the senior Field home to scan the area around the Banning house. He recognized the Troutmans' carriage at the curb in front, a groomsman stroking the neck of one of the mares for want of anything better to do while he waited. Knowing well the man could be out there for hours, Archie was inclined to invite the man into the coach house, and he had to remind himself he had no right to do so any longer.

He expelled his breath with aggravation. He had come all this way, much of it on foot, to see Charlotte, but of course he had no way to communicate with her. He had hoped to catch one of the servants outside, even if briefly, just long enough to send Charlotte a message. With female guests, however, Elsie would be busy attending to all the ladies, and Archie knew from experience that Mrs. Troutman could be unusually demanding. If Charlotte was serving, Lina had probably been conscripted to help in the kitchen. Karl would be the best bet, Archie decided. If the Bannings were dining in, he would be in the coach house making sure the horses were cooled and fed and the carriages spit-shined above reproach. Archie did not dare approach the coach house. He would have to wait to see if Karl would wander outside at some point in the evening.

He kept walking, past the Ream house, the Doane house, and finally to Judge Dent's home next door to the Bannings—though why everyone used the title, Archie did not know. Thomas Dent had never been a judge. Turning his collar up and tipping his hat down, Archie leaned against a light post. He couldn't stay there long. Without a uniform, clearly he was out of place on Prairie Avenue and would be spotted quickly.

And then he saw her. Sarah.

Why couldn't it be Charlotte who needed to step outside?

She had spotted him, he was sure, and now turned her steps toward him in determination. Momentarily he would have to decide whether to trust her.

Sarah tucked the silver tray she carried under her arm. The cook at the Keith house had prepared some specialty pastries for Mrs. Fletcher to serve for the engagement dinner. Sarah had not expected to run into the likes of Archie Shepard when she ducked across the street to return the tray.

"Archie Shepard, what are you doing here?" Sarah demanded to know. "If Mr. Penard sees you—"

He put up both hands to stop her barrage. "He already dismissed me. What more can he do?"

"He could have you arrested for trespassing."

"I'm on a public sidewalk."

Sarah rolled her eyes. She seemed unable to rile him tonight. "I still want to know what you're doing here. You can't possibly have any business on Prairie Avenue, especially at this time of night."

"My business is my business," Archie said, "and I'll thank you not to presume you know anything about it."

Sarah decided to change tactics. "Where are you staying now?" She smiled. "I hope you've found a warm place to sleep and perhaps a new position already."

"I need to see Charlotte," Archie said.

"I'm sure she'll ask you the same questions. Besides, she's busy. The Bannings have dinner guests."

"I can see that. The Troutmans. No doubt Oliver has finally decided to marry."

Sarah smiled quite deliberately again. "Both families are excited. It's sure to be the social event of the year."

"I know Charlotte is busy," Archie said, "but I need you to tell her I'm out here."

"Mr. Penard won't let her come see you."

"It's Charlotte's decision," Archie responded. "All I'm asking you to do is tell her I'm out here. I'll wait for her around the corner, outside the Glessners' coach house."

Sarah nodded thoughtfully. "Yes, you'll be out of sight from the Bannings' house there."

"So you'll tell her?"

"What if she can't get away?" Sarah's lips twisted to one side. "She would want me to tell her everything I know, so perhaps you should tell me how you're situated."

"I'll wait as long as it takes." His tone did not waver. "Please just tell her I'll be there."

Sarah sighed. He was impossible. What he saw in Charlotte she would never know.

"All right. But you could be out there all night, you know. The dinner party will go late, and Mr. Penard will lock up the house."

Charlotte had cleared away the vegetable dishes, and Mr. Penard was serving the salad now. After this final course, only dessert and coffee remained. Charlotte heard movement in the servants' hall and looked up to see Sarah coming through the back door with a strange look on her face.

"Is everything all right?" Charlotte could barely stand to look at Sarah, and every time she did, she thought of Lucy's letter. But something about Sarah's expression seemed suspicious. What had the girl done now?

"Everything's fine," Sarah answered. "I suppose I should start washing up."

"I'm sure Mrs. Fletcher would appreciate it if you did."

"Where is she?"

"Her gout is giving her trouble tonight. The meal is almost over. There was no need for her to stay down here in pain."

"How thoughtful of you," Sarah said.

Charlotte tossed a dishrag on the butcher block. "Sarah, if you have something to say, just say it."

The girl pressed her lips together as if to consider her options. Charlotte sighed and turned to begin cleaning up the butcher block.

"I spoke with Archie," Sarah said casually.

Charlotte spun around. "Archie is here?"

Sarah nodded nonchalantly as she moved toward the sink. "He said he would wait for you around the corner outside the Glessners' coach house."

Charlotte wanted to run out of the house and find Archie that instant, but of course Mr. Penard would be looking for her at any moment to come and clear the salad plates.

Everyone seemed to dawdle interminably over the salad. When at last the dishes were cleared and the coffee served, Charlotte had seen every tick of the clock's hand for the last hour. The Bannings and their guests moved to the parlor for the rest of the evening. Mr. Penard would attend them.

Charlotte's opportunity came at last, and she found Archie right where he said he would be. Glancing around to be sure none of the neighborhood servants who might recognize her were in view, she let him squeeze her hand.

"I found a boardinghouse," he said before she even voiced the question. "The woman who runs it used to be a friend of my mother's, so she's not asking for the rent in advance."

"I'm so glad to hear you found a place," Charlotte said. "I have a few coins saved—"

He was shaking his head. "I can't take your money."

"But I want you to have it. You lost your position because of me, after all."

"You're going to need it," Archie said. "We're going to

figure out how to get Henry back, and you'll be glad for every penny you've saved."

"Henry is gone, Archie," Charlotte said. "I have to believe he's happy and will have a good life. Even if I got him back, a few coins would not make any difference. I'll still lose my position, and then what?"

"Maybe you won't," Archie said. "Lucy's letter shows that she has an idea what's going on. She wouldn't want you to let your son grow up in New Hampshire never knowing his real mother."

"But what can I do? I can't go to New Hampshire and demand Emmaline return my child. No one even knows he's mine. How can I prove it? I never even got a birth certificate for him."

"Lucy could prove it."

"Lucy's not here."

Archie's brown eyes pierced her moonlit gaze. "You can decide to trust someone, Charlotte. You can trust me. And I think you can trust the Bannings."

"After what happened to you? How can you say that?"

"What happened was between me and Mr. Penard. The Bannings had nothing to do with that. Show them Lucy's letter, and they might understand."

"*Might*. It's so risky."

"You've been afraid for so long," Archie said. "It's time for that to change. You don't have to worry about your husband anymore. If you can't trust me or the Bannings, then what about the God your grandmother believed in?"

"She always said God had his way with everything."

"But you're not sure."

Charlotte shook her head. She could not claim to believe if she did not.

Archie pulled her into an embrace, and Charlotte gratefully soaked up the strength of his arms around her. Suddenly, she felt they were not alone. But she buried her head in his chest and when they separated, she saw no one else on the sidewalk.

Archie was right. She was too afraid of every little thing.

Sarah had heard enough. She did not have to stay and watch them slobber over each other. She hurried back down Prairie Avenue to the Banning kitchen and the pots waiting to be scrubbed.

It all made sense now.

Why Charlotte cared so much about that baby that she would run herself ragged taking care of him on top of her other duties.

Why she seemed so secretive, so aloof.

Why the other servants said they did not know what she did on her days off.

Why she had become so "ill" when the baby went away.

What Miss Lucy had to do with it—clearly she knew the truth and had kept the secret from her own parents.

The only mystery was why Archie Shepard cared so much for Charlotte Farrow. But even their affection for each other could be useful, considering the way they were carrying on.

I could have her dismissed ten times over, Sarah thought.

31

Archie slapped the rump of one of the blackest horses he'd ever seen. "A fine animal."

"He'll do to pull a small brougham," Archie's friend Finn affirmed. "He might not have the breeding of your Prairie Avenue horses, but he'll do for Ashland Avenue. Our claim to fame is the mayor—right across the street."

The coach house door stood wide open, giving a view of the street. Across the street, in front of the home of Mayor Carter Harrison, a gas streetlight glowed.

"He's a good man. He believes in the eight-hour workday," Archie said. "But never mind Prairie Avenue. I'm through with that."

"You're not going back?" Finn asked.

"Not even if they'd take me—which they wouldn't."

Finn took hold of the horse's muzzle and began to lead him toward a stall. "The Chalmers might take you on here. We could run the coach house together."

"I suspect Mr. Penard will do his best to make sure I never find another position in service anywhere in Chicago."

"He can't know everyone. The Chalmers have never been to dinner on Prairie Avenue."

"It doesn't matter," Archie said. "I'm looking for a different line of work." And then he would get Charlotte out of service too.

"You could be a lamp lighter. The fellow who lights them on this street is getting too old to go up and down the ladder. He can hardly lift it."

Archie shook his head. "These gas streetlights won't be here much longer. The city will change to electric lights soon enough."

"Who's that chap at the mayor's house?" Finn asked. He let go of the muzzle and patted the horse's face before stepping over to the open coach house door, leather reins in his hands.

"A dinner guest?" Archie speculated. "It's ten minutes to eight. The Bannings always eat at eight."

"You can't get them off your mind!" Finn laughed, then shook his head. "No, he doesn't look like a dinner guest to me."

Archie strolled to the edge of the Chalmerses' lot and let the streetlight bring clarity to what he saw.

The doorbell rang at ten minutes to eight. Wearing her best black dress and crispest white apron, Charlotte stepped across the foyer to welcome the Bannings' Saturday night dinner guests. Elsie was right behind her to take the ladies' wraps and inquire whether they needed any assistance with their gowns or hair. At the parlor's arched double doors, Charlotte announced the arrival of Mr. and Mrs. George Moulton and Mr. and Mrs. John Walsh of Calumet Avenue.

"Is dinner on time?" Flora Banning asked.

"Yes, ma'am," Charlotte answered. "I'll just see if Mrs. Fletcher needs anything."

With a slight curtsy, Charlotte backed out of the room.

"What did everyone think of the mayor's speech today on the fairgrounds?" Leo Banning was already plunging into conversation.

"He always gives a good speech," John Walsh said.

"I can hardly believe the fair is ending in two days," Flora Banning said. "One more round of parades and bands and fireworks on Monday, and it will all be over."

Charlotte turned to stride across the foyer and through the dining room.

At the mayor's house, the front door opened, and light framed the maid.

"That's Mary." Finn joined Archie under the streetlight. "She pretends she doesn't like me, but I know she does."

Archie elbowed Finn. "That man—he looks in worse straits than I do. What can he want at the mayor's door?"

The two of them stood watching the Harrison home, where the maid had left the door ajar. The visitor stepped across the threshold.

"Why is she letting him in?" Archie asked.

"That's the mayor's policy." Finn fingered the reins he still held in his hands. "Anyone can come to his house, and the staff is instructed to admit all visitors."

"I don't like the looks of this," Archie said. He stepped into the street.

A moment later, Mayor Carter Harrison came into view in the hall that ran through the center of the house. At the sound of a shot, the mayor doubled over, and the caller bolted across the lawn.

"He shot the mayor!" Archie started sprinting across the mayor's lawn. Finn was on his heels.

Two more shots sounded before Archie and Finn bounded up the walk toward the Harrison front entry. The commotion instantly unbolted doors around the neighborhood. The Chalmerses themselves sprang out the front door of their home and dashed across the street behind their coachman and Archie.

The mayor's son met them on the sidewalk. "He shot my father!" Preston Harrison said. "I'm not going to let him get away."

Mr. Chalmers was already tearing off his overcoat and rolling it into a pillow. "Go, Preston. Finn, you go with him. I'll look after Carter."

Archie could see nothing from the street but the empty hall. The mayor apparently had stumbled back into one of the main rooms. "Is he still alive?"

"Yes, but just barely," Preston answered. "Let's go."

Mr. Penard was serving the soup himself these days, not bothering to enlist the assistance of the footman or another male servant. Charlotte lingered in the butler's pantry as usual, waiting for his subtle signal that it was time to clear the soup bowls and bring out the baked trout and seasoned oysters. When the time came, Charlotte carried the tray of fish to the sideboard in the dining room, then moved deftly among the diners to remove their soup bowls and spoons. Mr. Penard began to serve the fish.

The telephone jangled in the foyer, and Mr. Penard's eyes told Charlotte she should answer it. It was understood she would tell the caller the Bannings were at dinner and would return the call at the earliest convenience.

A moment later, though, Charlotte stood between the open pocket doors of the dining room. Penard, still holding the fish tray, flashed her a look of appalled exasperation.

"Mr. Banning, sir," Charlotte finally said.

Movement around the table stopped.

"Charlotte, what is it?" Flora asked. "You know we don't take telephone calls during dinner."

"It's an urgent matter," Charlotte said. "I rather think Mr. Banning will want to take this one."

"You'd better be right." Samuel Banning sighed, threw his napkin on the table, and stood up.

Charlotte waited between the pocket doors and watched as Samuel Banning picked up the telephone in the foyer. A moment later he turned back to his dinner guests.

"The mayor has been shot," he announced somberly. "He died ten minutes ago, at 8:27. The news is all over the city."

The three young men pursued the shooter north along Ashland Avenue until he turned onto Monroe and moved east.

"He's heading toward downtown," Archie said.

"He's fast!" Finn was running out of breath.

"We're gaining on him," Archie insisted.

A police officer and several other individuals had joined in the chase. The band passed Racine and Aberdeen and a collection of smaller streets. Archie was close enough to see the man's features whenever he glanced over his shoulder at the crowd pursuing him.

He can't hope to escape, Archie thought and pushed to run faster. They crossed Halsted, dodging and darting between the carriages and streetcars whose riders were oblivious to the event that had just changed Chicago's history. Finn got new wind and surged to the front of the pursuers.

When the man turned again, this time left on Desplaines Avenue, Archie realized his intention.

"He's heading to the police station," he called out to his fellow pursuers.

The pursuers burst through the doors of the Desplaines Street Police Station right behind the shooter, who had approached the sergeant at the desk.

"Lock that man up," Finn said. "He shot Mayor Harrison."

In an instant, the sergeant was out from behind the desk to grab the shooter and pull him into a wire enclosure. The crowd around Archie thickened by the moment.

"My name is Eugene Patrick Prendergast," the prisoner said.

"Do you know that you have killed Mayor Harrison?" the sergeant asked.

"Yes, and I am glad of it. He promised to give me the corporation counselship, and he has not kept his word."

Archie turned to Finn. "He shot the mayor over a job?"

Finn turned his palms up and shook his head.

"Get these people out of here," the sergeant barked.

Officers began insisting that onlookers clear the station and wait outside. In a matter of minutes, hundreds of people had gathered, looking for information on the fate of the man who had murdered the mayor of Chicago.

Around the Banning table, forks clinked to plates and fell silent. Charlotte shuffled slowly to her position at the sideboard, where Mr. Penard had calmly set the tray of fish.

"Do you have any details, Father?" Leo asked.

"Very few. It happened at his home. He was shot three times at point-blank range with a .38-caliber revolver, wounded in the abdomen and the heart."

"Did they see who the shooter was?" Flora asked.

Samuel nodded. "He was some ragged character demanding a city job for which he was not qualified."

"Does this have something to do with all the anarchist nonsense?" George Moulton speculated.

Samuel shook his head thoughtfully. "No, Mayor Harrison was known to have sympathies with the labor groups. This just seems to be a man who was disturbed."

"But the anarchists encourage crime as the way to right what they perceive as wrongs," John Walsh argued. "Perhaps the shooter thought he was getting justice he was entitled to."

"Either way, this is going to shake up the city," Leo observed. "Chicago governance has no clear plan for succession in a situation like this."

"Surely the city council will appoint a mayor pro tem," George Moulton suggested, "probably first thing Monday."

Samuel shook his head. "Any decisions such a person makes will have no legal standing. Leo's right. We could be in for some chaos until a special election is held."

Charlotte glanced from Samuel Banning to his wife and back again, wondering if they were even going to want the roasted wild turkey and trimmings.

Every muscle in Charlotte's body ached by the time the guests had left—much of the dinner untouched—and the kitchen had been put back in order, but she knew she would not be able to sleep yet. At the end of October, the nights carried a threat of frost, so she took her cloak with her when she slipped into the courtyard to raise her face to the stars and ponder the distance of the night sky and its maker. She hoisted herself up on a ledge, gathered the edges of her cloak in her fists, and wrapped herself in warmth.

A better warmth spilled through her as she turned to see Archie moving toward her in the shadows.

He kissed her cheek. "I suppose you heard about the mayor."

"Everyone in Chicago must know by now." Charlotte examined him more closely. "Archie, you look like you've been in a train wreck."

"Something close to that." He leaned against the wall supporting her ledge. "As it happens, I was in the mayor's neighborhood when the shots were fired."

Charlotte gasped. "Are you all right?"

He nodded. "I'm fine. We chased the shooter."

"We?"

"My friend Finn and I. He's a coachman on Ashland Avenue. We almost caught him too, but it turned out he was turning himself in to the police. By the time they booked him, five hundred people were there."

Charlotte laid her head on Archie's shoulder. "He might have decided to shoot at you. I don't know what I'd do if something had happened to you. I've already lost . . ."

Archie stood up straight and turned to face her. "We're

going to get him back, and we're going to figure out a way to be together. I promise you."

Charlotte tore herself away from his brown eyes. "I want to believe that."

"Have you said anything to the Bannings yet?"

She shook her head. "I just can't. If Lucy didn't think it was safe to tell them the truth when she was here, why would it be safe now?"

"Nothing is ever 100 percent safe," Archie said softly. "Sometimes you have to take a risk you're not sure of because it's the right thing."

"My grandmother would call that faith."

"She'd be right. She'd want you to have faith, wouldn't she?"

Charlotte sighed and nodded. "She would have approved of you and the influence you have on me."

Another shadow moved toward them, and Charlotte instinctively jumped down off the ledge.

"Sarah, what do you want?" Archie asked.

"I want to talk to you. Both of you."

Archie sighed. "We're listening."

"I don't know how to say this." Sarah spoke so softly that Charlotte could barely hear her. "I know about the baby."

"What do you know about the baby?" Archie asked cautiously.

Sarah choked on her words. "I know he's Charlotte's baby. I heard you talking the last time."

"You eavesdropped on a private conversation," Archie said, his jaw set.

"You were right there on the public sidewalk," Sarah said in her own defense. "Anyone could have come by."

"But you were the only one who knew we would be there. We trusted you."

"Sarah," Charlotte said, "if you tell anyone, I'll lose my position."

Sarah put her head in her hands. "Please. None of that matters. I know you don't like me, and I know I've given you plenty of reason to feel that way. But this is different." A sob escaped.

"Sarah, why are you crying?" Charlotte had never seen Sarah show an emotion not fed by arrogance.

"It was different when I thought he was an orphan and we didn't know who his mother was. We couldn't do anything about that, and I thought he would be better off with someone like Mrs. Banning's Cousin Louisa. But now I know who his mother is, and I've been thinking about this for days."

"Sarah, what is it you want to say?" Charlotte's chest squeezed in on her breath.

Sarah swallowed hard. "You probably think I'm going to tattle to the Bannings. I've thought about it, I assure you."

"Sarah, please . . ." *I can't believe I have to beg Sarah, of all people,* Charlotte thought, panic welling.

Sarah shook her head. "No. I'm not going to say anything. But I think *you* should."

Archie crossed his arms. "I can't believe that Sarah and I agree on something."

"I lost my parents," Sarah said. "I was a lot older than your son, but I don't think that matters. They abandoned me."

"I thought your parents were killed in an accident," Archie said.

"They were. But that doesn't mean I don't feel they abandoned me. They were gone and I was all alone in that place and could never go home again." She turned and looked Charlotte in the eye. "I don't want your little boy to feel that way someday. Miss Emmaline isn't even married. Everyone in New Hampshire will know she's not really his mother. He's going to wonder someday who his mother is and why she abandoned him. I don't think that should happen. I think *you* have to stop it from happening."

Archie put an arm around Charlotte's shaking shoulders as Sarah retreated into the house.

32

Carter Harrison may have been sympathetic to the labor movement, a position of which the Bannings did not always approve, but he was still the mayor of Chicago—and a popular one elected several times. When the chilly first day of November descended on the city, instead of celebrating the triumphant conclusion of the World's Columbian Exposition, the Bannings were preparing for the mayor's funeral.

Charlotte could hardly wait to get them all out of the house. She had already volunteered to stay behind and ensure that preparations began on schedule for the evening meal.

The coachmen and groomsmen would be occupied all day shuttling the Bannings around the city—first to City Hall downtown, where the mayor was lying in state, and then to the Church of the Epiphany on Ashland Avenue. They would be among the privileged few to be seated in the church for the funeral service because of Samuel's participation in the National Committee of the World's Fair. Even young Richard would stay out of school for the day to pay his respects to Mayor Harrison alongside his parents and older brothers.

Charlotte poured coffee and carried the cup to the dining room table to set in front of Flora Banning.

"Lucy is supposed to be back in the country by now, isn't she?" Flora mused as she lifted the cup to her lips. "I'm sure she would have wanted to attend the funeral if she were home."

Leo nodded and corralled a runaway over-easy egg. "Their original schedule called for them to dock in New York by the end of October."

Samuel lifted a fork full of fried potatoes. "The closing ceremonies were replaced by a prayer service for Mayor Harrison. It's just as well she didn't make a special trip back to Chicago. No bands, no fireworks. Just a twenty-one gun salute to the mayor."

"The whole city loved him," Flora said. "How could they throw a party when the man who brought the fair to Chicago is dead?"

"I'm surprised Lucy hasn't telephoned," Leo pondered. "She never answered my telegram, you know."

Flora set her cup down slightly too hard. "I don't want to talk about that baby. It's too upsetting, and today has enough distress already."

"I'm sorry, Mother."

"Louisa never even came to see the fair. She couldn't bear to come to Chicago after she learned what Emmaline had done. Knowing the child had been in this very house would have brought too much anguish."

"I am sorry, Mother," Leo repeated, "both for you and Louisa. We don't have to discuss it. I'm sure Lucy has her reasons for not responding to my telegram."

Charlotte turned her back to the family, pretending to

busy herself at the sideboard, though all she really did was rearrange the serving dishes. In her apron pocket, Lucy's letter had softened to fragility with all the unfolding and refolding.

"I suppose it's over and done with now." Flora bit into a fresh croissant.

At the other end of the table, Samuel signaled to Charlotte that he was ready for coffee as well. "I'm afraid we don't have sufficient legal standing to take the matter to court. The only circumstance that would prevail is if the child's mother suddenly turned up."

Charlotte's hand trembled as she poured the steaming brown liquid.

"That would hardly do Louisa any good, now would it," Flora said. "It doesn't matter. Whatever vagrant left that child here would not have the gall to approach us now for assistance."

"Mother, you sound a bit heartless," Leo observed softly.

"I said I didn't want to talk about it." Flora pushed her chair back from the table. "I must call Elsie to do my hair in some fashion that will stand up to the elements."

Archie leaned his head back and surveyed the canopy of black trailing from the chandelier in the Council Chamber at City Hall and offering a somber highlight above the heavy cedar casket on the decorated raised platform. The mayor's chair and desk were also draped in black. Archie had joined the line early in the morning and waited with thousands of others for the opportunity to pay his last respects. Behind him, deep in the crowd, anonymous mourners began singing hymns, softly at first then swelling with energy as more voices joined. As Archie shuffled past the casket and the cascades of flowers from police, city workers, and councilmen, he glanced across the chamber to the gallery of reserved seats.

The Bannings, with their familiar profiles and posture, were easy to spot. Mr. and Mrs. Banning and their three sons sat in dark attire, heads lowered respectfully. Immediately Archie began to scan the crowd and saw what he hoped to find—nearly every servant from the Banning house was in the mass snaking around the casket, even Mr. Penard. Everyone but Charlotte. He picked up his pace as much as would be tolerated under the solemn circumstances.

Outside City Hall, Archie pressed through the throng, grateful he was not trying to drive a rig through the curb-to-curb pedestrian congestion. Fleetingly he wondered where Karl might have let the family off and would be waiting with the carriage. Regardless of what the planned schedule was for the funeral service that afternoon, it would be hours before the pallbearers could transport the casket. Thousands still stood in line to walk past. The police no doubt would have to cut off the stream of mourners entering the building, then forge an opening through the crowd for miles to allow the hearse to pass to the church. The massive swarm already pressed in on the four coal-black horses that would strain against the weight of the hearse.

The Bannings were sure to be among those privileged to be seated in the church as thousands stood outside.

The event would take hours.

Hours.

Hours that the family would be away from the house.

Going against the direction of the crowd, Archie nudged people out of his way as politely as he could—but firmly.

Thousands of marchers already were lining up for the procession from City Hall to the church—postal workers, city clerks, police, representatives of ethnic groups to whom the mayor had been kind. Tens of thousands—hundreds of thousands—were staking out their positions along the route west and north. Fortunately for Archie, he needed to go the opposite direction—south to Prairie Avenue.

Charlotte had the bread rising and the fish cleaned. The roast did not have to go into the oven for hours, and the vegetables would be simple and quick.

And the silence was bliss.

The knock on the back door made her close her eyes and exhale, but she strode across the kitchen and answered the knock.

"Archie!" She stepped into his open arms without hesitation.

"I thought you might like a little company," he said, "considering that everyone else who works here is at City Hall."

"Someone had to stay home," Charlotte said, "and I didn't feel up to the crowds."

"Half the city is in the street today." Archie guided her to take a seat at the kitchen table. "That's no exaggeration."

"The shooting is all anyone talks about."

Archie nodded. "Every preacher in the city talked about it on Sunday. At the inquest, though, Prendergast told the family he was sorry for the pain he caused."

"They'll say he was imbalanced," Charlotte said, "and he'll get off."

"A crazy man does not have regrets," Archie pointed out. "But that's not what I came to talk about."

Charlotte's raised her eyebrows.

"While most of the city was busy shutting down the world's fair the last two days or making arrangements for the mayor, I was busy scheming on our future."

"Our future?"

He nodded. "John Glessner has offered me a position as a clerk at Warder, Bushnell & Glessner. I start on Monday."

Charlotte leaped up. "A position! With John Glessner! I always liked that man!"

"He had some questions about why I wanted to leave the employ of the Bannings, since he has known them for years, but he seemed satisfied with my answers."

"Lucy has always thought well of Mr. Glessner."

"This is our ticket, Charlotte." Archie stood up and took both her hands. "You can tell the Bannings the truth about Henry and we'll get him back. We'll get married. Clerks at Glessner's company are allowed to have families."

"I don't know, Archie," Charlotte responded cautiously. "Everything is happening so fast."

"I don't want you to have to spend one more day than necessary separated from your son."

"But my husband—"

"Who might not be your husband. I'm making inquiries. We'll find out the truth. And we'll face the truth together, whatever it is—even if that means finding a way to release you legally."

"But what if—"

Archie shook his head. "No what-ifs, Charlotte. What-ifs have been scaring you half to death for a long time." He leaned his forehead against hers. "It's time for you to choose a happy ending."

The back door squeaked, and Mr. Penard scowled at them as they jumped apart.

"You both know better than this," Penard pronounced without raising his voice. "You will leave the property, Mr. Shepard."

Charlotte nudged Archie toward the door as Mr. Penard disappeared into his pantry.

"He must have seen you leave City Hall," Charlotte speculated in a whisper at the back door. "Why else would he show up so soon after you arrived?"

Archie sighed. "I confess I was hoping for more time, even the whole afternoon."

Charlotte smiled. "I'm so pleased for you about the new position."

"It's the first step," he said. "Now I just need you to promise to take your first step."

She shrugged, barely putting breath behind her words. "I'll try. But Mrs. Banning is still quite flustered about Miss Emmaline snatching Henry. I don't honestly know if she would help me. When she finds out I've kept a secret—well, it's all so frightening."

Penard cleared his throat loudly from across the room.

"Tomorrow is your day off," Archie whispered. "Meet me at Mickey's shop at six o'clock. No one there can object to our being together."

She nodded.

"I love you, Charlotte," he said.

"I love you too," she whispered in response.

He squeezed her hand and was gone.

33

"Do you ever think about the baby?"

Flora Banning's question astonished Charlotte as she sliced into the cinnamon coffee cake she was serving in the parlor. No one else was home in the late afternoon on Saturday, but Flora had asked for the usual tea service. Charlotte calmly slid the slice of cake onto a china plate, laid a fork next to it, and handed it to Mrs. Banning, who was sitting in her favorite side chair.

"Yes." Charlotte answered the direct question.

"I know Emmaline will take good care of him." Flora picked up the fork. "I'm just unsettled about how it all came to be."

"Yes, ma'am."

"You looked after him. You must have developed some degree of sentiment."

"Yes, ma'am. I was fond of him." How could she deny her feelings?

Charlotte wanted to meld into the floral pattern of the rug under her feet, to slip into one of the crimson blossoms and feel it close around her, to be lost in the intricately woven colors. At the same time, she could almost feel Archie's palpable nudge. The door was wide open. All she had to do was walk through it.

Tell the truth.

Open your mouth and say, "I love the baby because he's mine."

Charlotte turned back to the cart and poured Mrs. Banning's tea, adding two spoons of sugar just the way she liked it and stirring thoroughly. She set the tea on the round table next to Mrs. Banning's chair and stepped back to the cart to tidy up.

Flora put down her cake plate and picked up the matching teacup and saucer. "Every time I think of it, my blood boils. Emmaline took advantage of my hospitality and went against my direct wishes. He's a charming child, so it's no mystery that she should become enamored of him, but she's a single woman. He could be in a home where he has both a mother and a father."

Charlotte moved the sugar bowl over a quarter of an inch, shirking off the sense of Archie's presence in a room he had rarely entered while he served on Prairie Avenue.

Flora sipped her tea. "Samuel has given up his legal investigation, but something tells me this is not over. If I think about it long enough, surely I will come up with some legal ground he could use to recover the child."

Charlotte swallowed and forced herself to say, "Yes, ma'am."

"I'm sure Louisa would still take him," Flora said.

Unexpected courage swelled through Charlotte. "What if his mother turned up?"

"She would have some explaining to do."

"And what if she had a good reason?"

Flora put her teacup down and stared at Charlotte. "I

would be very interested to hear what would make a mother abandon her child. If you had a child, you would understand how monstrous that is."

"Yes, ma'am." The knot in Charlotte's throat enlarged instantaneously.

"I certainly could not imagine walking off and leaving any of my four children."

"No, ma'am." Charlotte suppressed a shiver—nearly.

Flora squeezed her eyebrows toward each other. "Charlotte, do you wish to say something?"

Charlotte shook her head.

"You may speak freely with me."

"I'm sorry, Mrs. Banning. I don't mean to upset you further."

"Does this have something to do with the child? I do wish I knew his name. I can't bring myself to call him 'Teddy.' That just reminds me of what Emmaline has done."

"I . . . I suppose I miss him," Charlotte finally said. That much was true.

"That's understandable. After the scullery maid proved unreliable as a nanny, his care was left to you."

"Yes, ma'am."

Flora put the last of her coffee cake in her mouth and chewed, as if waiting for Charlotte to say more.

Sarah's presence joined Archie's, both of them urging Charlotte forward.

"Mrs. Banning, if I may—"

The front door opened and Leo hastened to close it behind him. He strode immediately across the foyer to the parlor and slid out of his overcoat. "Oh good. Is the tea still hot?"

Charlotte dipped her head respectfully. "Yes, sir. I'll just get another cup from the dining room." She scurried out of the room, trembling.

"I couldn't do it!" Charlotte told Archie on Sunday afternoon at Mickey's shop. "I just kept thinking how angry she'll be if she knows I've had a child for more than a year and she didn't know."

"Surely since she knows the child, she would have compassion for the baby's mother," Archie responded.

Charlotte shook her head. "I'm not sure. She thinks any woman who would walk away from her child is a horrible monster."

"You didn't walk away from him."

"No. I did worse. I gave him away as if he were an expensive toy. I knew Emmaline could afford him and I couldn't."

"You don't mean that."

Charlotte put her elbows on the table and hung her head between her hands.

"You thought he was in danger," Archie reminded her, "and you as well. Someone like Mrs. Banning cannot imagine how difficult that choice was for you."

"Even you thought it was the wrong thing to do. You didn't speak to me for days."

Archie took her left hand and forced her to lift her head. "It's only been a few weeks, Charlotte. We can still fix this. Actually, I have good news."

Charlotte met his brown eyes.

"I've had an official response to my inquiries," he said. "The State of Illinois has no record of you ever being married. You're perfectly free."

"But . . . my name. Are you sure you checked under the right name?"

Archie nodded. "You told me Farrow is your grandmother's name. Your maiden name is Charlotte Mae Freeman, and according to the State of Illinois, you have never been married."

Charlotte put a hand to her mouth.

"You could probably press charges of fraud against Lathan Landers. Clearly he intended to deceive you from the beginning."

Charlotte shook her head vehemently. "I just want him out of my life."

"He *is* out of your life, and I am *in* your life. Nothing is holding you back from telling the truth about your son."

"They'll be so angry," Charlotte said. "The Bannings, Mr. Penard—everyone. They'll throw me out."

Archie lifted his shoulders, then dropped them. "So? I have a secure position with a steady salary. I don't care how angry you make them as long as you agree to become my lawfully wedded wife as soon as possible."

Charlotte laughed and cried at the same time. "You seem awfully sure of yourself."

Archie lifted the fingers of her left hand to his lips. "I can't give you a diamond—yet—but I can give you my heart, and my promise that you can never make me angry enough to throw you out."

"I never imagined I could feel this way—not after Lathan."

"Is that a yes?"

"Yes!"

Archie leaned in and pressed his lips to Charlotte's, and she put both her arms around him to freely return the kiss.

34

Charlotte was surprised to find the kitchen in an unusually ordered condition when she returned home Sunday evening after her half day off. Judging from the state of readiness for the morning routine, she thought the family must have eaten dinner away from home and the staff supper had been simple. The staff seemed to have scattered to their own diversions, no doubt welcoming the unexpected free hours. Not quite ready to be confined to her narrow room on the third floor, Charlotte took off her cloak and laid it on the back of a kitchen chair. Out of curiosity, she stuck her head in the butler's pantry, where she could see through to the dining room and ascertain that a few electric lights had been left on. She heard no movement or conversation, however. The Bannings were definitely out for the evening. Charlotte returned to the kitchen and sat in the chair under the window where she could put her feet up on a stool.

I'm an engaged woman!

Of course she couldn't tell anyone. At least not yet. And she didn't want to tell anyone. Love was a sensation to savor. Two years ago, when her parents surprised her with a forced wedding, Charlotte had surrendered girlish dreams of love.

He loves me.

And I adore him.

The clanging telephone disturbed her reverie, and Charlotte stood up promptly. Even if technically she was still on her half day off, it seemed sensible to answer the telephone since not another soul was in hearing distance. Mindful of the incessant clatter of the little bell, Charlotte hastened to the foyer and picked up the telephone.

"Good evening. This is the Banning residence."

"Charlotte? Is that you?"

Charlotte gasped and glanced around to again ensure no one else had responded to the phone's ringing. "Miss Lucy! I'm so glad to hear your voice."

"I've missed you so much, Charlotte."

"Where are you, Miss Lucy?"

"New Jersey. We were in a hotel temporarily, but Will has found us some lovely furnished accommodations. Nothing fancy, which is a relief."

"The house isn't the same without you. I suppose you know Miss Emmaline Brewster was here and stayed in your suite."

"Mother told me before I left that she had invited Emmaline. When I was little and we visited New Hampshire, I used to follow her around as if she were the Queen of England. But never mind about that. Charlotte, I've tried calling a couple of times, but when Penard answered, I hung up."

"Why? Your family has been wondering about you. Leo remarked only the other day at breakfast that you never answered his telegram."

Lucy was silent for a moment. "How could I? I had so many questions for you first, but I couldn't just ask for you on the phone without raising eyebrows."

"No, I suppose not." No one would believe that the Bannings' only daughter urgently needed to speak to a maid.

"That's why I sent a letter. Did you get it?" Lucy asked.

"No. Yes. It's a long story, I received it, but it was delayed."

"You didn't write back. Was I right about what I suspected?"

Charlotte's breath caught. By the time she had gotten the letter, it was too late. "Yes, the child was Henry."

"Leo's telegram was vague. I couldn't be sure what they intended to do. He said something about Mother's cousin Louisa. I don't believe I've ever met her."

Charlotte battled for breath, unable to form words.

"Charlotte?" Lucy asked. "What happened? Did they try to give your baby to Cousin Louisa?"

Charlotte's chest tightened.

"Charlotte, say something," Lucy urged.

"I . . . it's so complicated," Charlotte finally said. "I don't . . . I can't explain everything that has happened."

"Charlotte, where is Henry now?"

Charlotte swallowed and moistened her lips. "In New Hampshire."

"They gave him to Emmaline!"

"No. I did."

"Oh my goodness, Charlotte. Oh my."

"I thought it was the best thing," Charlotte said. "My husband—I saw him here, and Louisa lives in Greenville. That's too close, or I thought it was. New Hampshire . . . well, it seemed . . ."

"Your husband? Are you from Greenville?"

The dam of tears broke free.

Lucy kept saying "Oh Charlotte" over and over, until

finally Charlotte found composure and explained why she had thought she could never send Henry to Greenville.

"We'll get him back," Lucy said emphatically.

"That's what Archie says," Charlotte said.

"Archie knows?"

"He didn't want me to do it. He didn't understand. I was so frightened."

"You must have been. But I'm glad you have someone to talk to, and Archie's right. We will get Henry back. I will deal with Emmaline myself, but you have to tell my parents the truth."

"But—"

"Don't worry about a position," Lucy said. "If they have the gall to dismiss you over this, Will and I will take you on the minute we get home. I'd like to, anyway."

Tears flowed afresh.

"I will deal with Emmaline," Lucy repeated. "I want you to get a piece of paper and take down this telephone number. After you talk to my parents, they can call me here."

"Miss Lucy, I don't think I can. I've tried."

"You have to," Lucy said. "They should hear it from you. You can call me here as well—anytime day or night. Just reverse the charges. Do you have paper and pen?"

Charlotte hung up the telephone and stared at the numbers written on the paper in her hand. She had never made a telephone call, only answered them. Archie would want to know about this development, but she had no way to reach him. She would have to wait until Thursday afternoon when she could get away from the house on her day off and meet him at Mickey's for supper. Four days. And she had not even told Lucy about Archie's proposal or his new position at Mr. Glessner's firm.

One thing at a time. Will and Lucy would be back in Chicago for good after New Year's.

Charlotte did not think she would sleep a single minute all night. How could she? She had accepted Archie's marriage proposal and Lucy's offer to help reclaim Henry all in the space of an hour. But she had to do her part.

She had to speak to the Bannings. Soon.

Charlotte shuffled back through the dining room and into the kitchen, where she picked up her cloak and started up the back stairs. A squeak told her that someone had only a moment's head start on her taking the steps up. The hour was not late. It was probably Lina, or perhaps Elsie, who would be waiting up to help Mrs. Banning undress.

Upstairs, Charlotte sank onto her bed, stunned. It seemed pointless even to undress, because surely she would require the entire night to muster her courage for what she must do tomorrow. Charlotte glanced at the nightstand, where her grandmother's Bible had sat unopened for so many weeks now. When she lifted the volume, it felt more solid than she remembered. Half a dozen strips of cardboard marked various passages. Charlotte had not looked at the verses in years. She slipped a finger under the first bookmark and opened to Joshua. Her grandmother had underlined several verses in the first chapter. Charlotte's eye settled on Joshua 1:9: "Have I not commanded thee? Be strong and of a good courage; be not afraid, neither be thou dismayed: for the Lord thy God is with thee withersoever thou goest."

Courage was exactly what Charlotte needed. She could

not control what would happen when she told the Bannings the truth. But she was tired of being afraid and dismayed. Deep within her, she longed to believe the words she read.

Charlotte knew she ought to acknowledge the knock on her door when she heard the sound a moment later, but she could not find the strength to speak aloud. The knob turned, and Sarah, already in her nightdress, entered.

Charlotte looked up, surprised.

"I heard the telephone ring," Sarah said bluntly. "I know you answered it, and I know it was Miss Lucy."

Charlotte sat up on the bed. "I didn't realize anyone was home."

"She wants you to tell the truth, doesn't she?"

Charlotte nodded.

"You see! I'm right. Archie's right. You have to speak up. Even Miss Lucy thinks so."

Charlotte rubbed her eyes with both hands. "It's not as simple as that."

"Yes, it is," Sarah insisted. "He's your son, and he deserves not to have his mother abandon him. It's as simple as that."

Charlotte had no response.

"When you tell them," Sarah said, "just be sure to let them know right away that Lucy already knows. They won't argue about it if they know it's what she wants—getting him back, I mean."

Charlotte had to admit Sarah was right. Lucy's support knocked out the last pillar of fear threatening her cobbled life.

"Thank you, Sarah," Charlotte said. "You were kind to speak out and encourage me to do something I'm afraid to do."

Sarah's eyes widened. "Don't you hate me?"

Charlotte shook her head. "No, I don't hate you. Maybe you're not just here because of Lucy. Maybe God sent you here to help me after all."

"I never thought of that. Are you sure that's not far-fetched?"

"I'm not sure of anything anymore."

As Sarah turned and left the room, Charlotte closed the Bible and pressed it against her chest.

Her grandmother was the last person Charlotte was sure had loved her. Until Archie. Her parents had shown the confines of their love when they gave her to Lathan Landers to protect themselves, and Lathan never made any pretense of true affection. But her grandmother's eyes had always lit up when Charlotte entered the room, and the touch of her hand was always welcoming and gentle.

Because of her, I know love. Because of her, I can love. She believed that God loved her. Maybe it's true that God loves me.

Charlotte closed her eyes, breathed deeply, and thought perhaps she might sleep after all.

Charlotte was in the dining room early in the morning, having been up for hours. She outlined the day in her mind. Mr. Banning would be in a hurry to get to the office on a Monday morning, and Mrs. Banning would most likely call for a tray to be brought to her room much later, so Charlotte did not try to persuade herself that breakfast would be the backdrop for her announcement. She simply served the meal as she always did, pouring coffee, scooping eggs, stirring fruit. The morning would pass quickly enough with chores, and Mr. Banning would be home for luncheon as he usually was on Mondays, and she would tell them together.

As luncheon ended a few hours later, Mr. Penard gave Charlotte the eye signal that she should clear away the remaining dishes. She nodded, but rather than clear the last of the plates, she straightened her apron and spoke.

"Mr. and Mrs. Banning, I wonder if I might have a word with you on a personal matter."

Flora and Samuel both looked up. Leo, who only rarely was home for the midday meal, was a friendly face to Charlotte. Mr. Penard, on the other hand, was already turning shades of infuriation. Charlotte merely turned her gaze away from the butler.

"What is it, Charlotte?" Flora asked. "You're not in any trouble, are you?"

"It's about the baby."

Penard cleared his throat.

"I don't want to talk about the baby," Flora said, "unless you have discovered something that would help us get him back."

"Yes, ma'am. No, ma'am. I mean . . ."

"What is it, Charlotte?" Samuel pulled out his pocket watch and studied it.

Archie knocked on the back door, where the kitchen opened to the courtyard. He would start his new position soon. He was not returning to beg. But he had to know how Charlotte was. Sarah opened the door.

"You can't be here," she said.

"Yet here I am. I need to see Charlotte."

"It's your neck if Penard discovers you." Sarah stepped aside and let him in. "He and Charlotte are in the dining room."

"Where's Mrs. Fletcher?" Archie asked.

"Gout. Charlotte and I are to clean up."

Archie glanced at the clock. "Luncheon is usually over by now. Mr. Banning goes back to the office."

Sarah gulped. "You don't think—"

He nodded. "Yes, I do. She's telling them. I should be with her."

When he started to walk across the kitchen, Sarah jumped into his path.

"Have you lost your mind?" she said.

"I'll just listen from the butler's pantry." Archie moved Sarah aside with one arm.

Archie pushed into the narrow pantry, then quieted his step as he approached the door that connected to the dining room. He pushed it open a fraction of an inch, relieved that he could see Charlotte as well as hear her. Sarah, he noticed, was right behind him, straining to hear.

Charlotte took a deep breath. "He's my son. His name is Henry."

Flora waved a hand. "Whatever do you mean, Charlotte?"

"Wait a minute." Leo pushed his chair back and stood up. "How could he be yours?"

"He was just a newborn when I came." Charlotte's words rushed out. "Miss Lucy helped me hide him until we found Mrs. Given. She takes in orphans from St. Andrew's, and Lucy arranged for her to take Henry."

"Aha!" Leo pointed a finger. "I knew there was a connection to the orphanage."

"Yes, sir. I didn't know it, but Miss Lucy was paying for Henry's board." Charlotte found breath at last.

She surveyed the faces in the room. Mr. Penard's was frozen in a deep red, a bulge on one side of his neck above his stiff collar. Samuel Banning still held his gold watch in his hand, but he tilted a scowl toward Charlotte. Flora Banning's complexion made Charlotte think she should run for the smelling salts.

Archie listened as Charlotte calmly told her story—why she had come to Chicago with Henry, how Lucy had helped, why she sent the baby away with Emmaline, and the truth about her supposed husband.

"She's doing the right thing," Sarah whispered.

"Shh." Archie pushed the door open another fraction of an inch.

"Penard?" Samuel finally said.

Penard stepped forward. "Words cannot express my astonishment, and my deep regret. I will of course take the necessary action."

"And what would that be?" Leo asked. "Are you talking about Charlotte's employment, or getting the child back?"

"Under the circumstances," Penard said, "I assume her employment should be terminated."

Archie pushed the door open wide. Sarah sprang back as heads turned toward the butler's pantry.

"Mr. Shepard, you are not to be on the premises," Penard said. "Mr. Banning, I am sorry for my own failures to manage the household properly."

"Let him in," Leo said. "I have a feeling there is more to this story."

"I have asked Charlotte to marry me, and she said yes."

Archie moved into the dining room and extended a hand to Charlotte. She stepped toward him immediately and clasped his hand with both of hers. "No matter what you decide, Charlotte will know that someone cares for her. We are going to get Henry back. Charlotte is going to have a happy life."

Penard shuffled his feet slightly. "I am profoundly sorry for this intrusion. Perhaps I should retire to the kitchen with Mr. Shepard and Miss Farrow and attend to the details there."

"What details?" Leo asked. "Charlotte has served faithfully in this household for over a year. Let me remind you, when her child turned up in our home, we all agreed to do what Lucy would want. I see no reason why that principle should not apply now."

35

Hand in hand, Charlotte and Archie approached the corner of Wells and Harrison, pausing at the base of the clock tower that rose turret-like above the mammoth conglomeration of brick, brownstone, and granite. The arched carriage court facing Harrison Avenue signaled the flow of travelers that came and went all day at Grand Central Station.

"How do you feel?" Archie asked.

"I'm not sure what to expect," Charlotte responded, "so I don't know what to feel."

"You feel what you feel, Charlotte. Whatever it is, that's all right."

She lifted her shoulders and squeezed them against her neck. "Then I feel nervous. Excited. Sad. All rolled together."

"Sad?"

"For Miss Emmaline."

Archie nodded and let his breath out slowly. "Let's go wait inside."

They sat together on one of the long wooden benches in the cavernous hall, holding hands. Every few minutes, Archie squeezed his grip and Charlotte smiled in answer. The ceiling spanned twenty-six feet above them, and the marble floor gleamed endlessly in all directions. At the far end of the hall, a rank of stained-glass windows sifted and shimmered the outdoor light. In other circumstances, Charlotte might have gaped at the extravagance of the railroad station. But under these circumstances, all she cared about was the roll of announcements of incoming trains.

"Did we come too early?" she asked. "Or too late? What if we're too late?"

"We're not too late," Archie said. "We're right on time. It's the train that's late."

"He'll be so big," Charlotte said softly. "I know it hasn't even been six weeks, but children change so fast."

"He'll still be your baby."

"He can probably outrun me by now."

"Then I'll catch him for you."

"What if he doesn't remember me?"

"He will."

"He might not. Miss Emmaline already had him calling her 'mama' when they left here."

Archie shook his head. "Charlotte Mae Freeman—soon to be Shepard—you are determined to find something to fret about."

"I guess I've had the habit for a long time."

"It's time to break that habit."

"It's not as easy as it sounds."

"Try. Courage, remember."

"Courage," Charlotte said. "I've lived so long with fear."

"You are one of the most courageous people I know," Archie said. "If I have to, I will remind you every day of my life that your grandmother was right."

"I am loved. I am not alone. Wherever I go, God goes with me."

Archie nodded. "Henry is going to know that too."

Charlotte sat up straight at the sound of an announcement. "Did he say New York?"

"Platform six." Archie stood and pulled Charlotte to her feet and in the direction of the mammoth train shed. Passengers from the New York train had already begun filtering into the waiting room, laden with luggage. In another moment, the bulk of the passengers were moving en masse away from the train and toward loved ones.

A plume of green bobbed through the crowd.

"There she is!" Charlotte exclaimed. "Her note said she would wear that hat."

"You always said that hat was the most ostentatious thing you had ever witnessed," Archie commented.

"Now I believe it's the most beautiful hat in the world." Charlotte moved toward the green feather, confirming that its wearer was Miss Emmaline Brewster of New Hampshire and that she held in her arms a squirming toddler.

Finally the two women stood face-to-face. By this time, Miss Emmaline had set Henry on his feet and held his hand firmly. At the sight of him, Charlotte's face filled with her tears. When she squatted in front of him, Henry looked at her, befuddled, and leaned into Emmaline's dark green traveling skirt.

Emmaline moved her hand to the back of the boy's head. "You're all right," she murmured. "You're going home."

Charlotte scooped Henry into her arms and pressed his face against her neck. He resisted and pulled his head back far enough to examine her.

"He was responding very well to the name Teddy,"

Emmaline explained as she handed a small valise to Archie, "but I've been making a point to call him Henry the last few days. I think he knows that's who he has always been."

"Miss Emmaline," Charlotte said, "I can't tell you how sorry I am to have put you through this. When I sent him away with you, I truly did not think this moment could ever happen—when I would ask you to bring him back."

Miss Emmaline appeared blanched but composed. "I couldn't for a moment think of keeping him from you after I knew the truth."

"It broke my heart to send him away," Charlotte said, her tears running freely, "and it must be breaking yours to bring him back."

"I shed all my tears in New Hampshire, away from the boy. Perhaps someday you'll tell him about me. I've put his quilt and some of his favorite things in the valise. I hope you don't mind that I had the quilt cleaned and mended."

"Of course not. Thank you."

"That was before . . . well, I thought perhaps someday he would want to have it."

Charlotte nodded. "I'll always be grateful that you loved him and wanted to keep him safe."

From Charlotte's arms, Henry reached a hand toward Miss Emmaline. "Mama!"

Emmaline took his hand, kissed his fingers, then laid them against Charlotte's chest. "This is your mama."

Charlotte smiled and lifted her eyes to Archie standing beside her. "And this is your daddy."

"I'm certain the three of you will be happy together." Emmaline grew more pale by the moment. "If you'll excuse me, I'll just go the hotel to freshen up for my return trip."

Charlotte's eyes widened. "You're leaving right away? The Bannings are expecting you for Thanksgiving dinner tomorrow. We thought you would stay a few days."

Emmaline shook her head. "Of course Flora would be polite and extend an invitation, but I think it would be unwise on all accounts for me to accept. I've reserved a Pullman on the overnight train back to New York."

"Perhaps we could escort you to your hotel," Archie suggested.

"I have a room at the hotel right here at the station. It's just for a few hours."

"Let me walk you to the desk," Archie said.

Miss Emmaline shook her head. "No, thank you. It's better if I'm on my own." She reached out and stroked Henry's head one last time, then turned and clicked her heels quickly across the marble floor.

Archie gestured to a bench. "Let's sit down and have a good look at him."

Charlotte put the child on the bench between them, taking stock of the expensive clothing, including a tiny tweed jacket. "What's this?" she asked, tapping a bulge at the bottom of the jacket.

Archie unbuttoned the jacket and pulled the bulging side open. "There's something sewn into the lining."

"Why would that be?"

"I see a slit." Archie tugged gently, and several stitches came loose, freeing an envelope. "It's from a law firm."

Charlotte turned to look for Miss Emmaline, but she had vanished into the pulsing throng of passengers arriving and departing. "Is it a legal suit of some sort?"

"You're fretting again," Archie said. "Shall I open it and put your mind to rest?"

She nodded.

Archie broke the seal on the envelope and quickly scanned the letter.

"What is it?" Charlotte asked. "Surely she can't . . . not after the way . . ."

Archie shook his head in disbelief. "She set up a trust for Henry. She's providing for his education and a small inheritance when he turns twenty-one."

"An inheritance?" Charlotte choked on the word.

Archie nodded. "It won't be enough to live on Prairie Avenue, but it's enough for him to go to any school he chooses and have a secure beginning when he's a man."

Charlotte closed the boy's jacket and buttoned it in place. "I don't understand. After what I did to her? After what I put her through?"

"She loves him," Archie said softly and simply.

"Yes, she does," said a woman's voice behind them.

Charlotte's head turned instantly. "Miss Lucy! Mr. Will! What are you doing here?"

Lucy grinned and put a finger to her lips. "It's a secret. We came for Thanksgiving."

"We were on the train with Emmaline," Will explained. "After Lucy worked everything out with her, we decided to travel with her."

"She refused, of course," Lucy added. "She was adamant about not wanting even to bring a servant to help with the baby. But it seemed too much to expect her to make this journey alone."

"However, we neglected to tell her we were on the train until after it left New York." Will extended a hand to shake Archie's. "By then she was stuck with us."

"We just wanted to be there if she needed something," Lucy said. "We've had our eye on Henry all this time. She's very good with him."

"She always was," Charlotte said softly, gazing at her son. She looked up again at Lucy. "Your parents will be thrilled to see you."

"What do they think about your engagement?" Lucy asked. "I want all the details."

"I'll hail a cab," Archie said, "and meet you out front." He picked up Henry's valise.

Archie dashed ahead of the others. Lucy put her arm through Will's, and Charlotte carried Henry. He gave her a shy smile and tucked his head under her chin. She let out her breath at the familiarity of his movement.

"Henry," Charlotte said, "let's go home."

Acknowledgments

Once again I must express gratitude to Stephen Reginald as the person who first pointed me to Prairie Avenue and walked the streets of the Prairie Avenue Historical District with me. A docent at the Glessner House Museum, he led me up staircases and through hallways that the average tourist at the museum does not get to traverse. Though we had permission, it felt furtive and sneaky and was terrific fun. He was a constant source of tidbits about life on Prairie Avenue that seasoned this story, and was a bulldog researcher of Chicago history. When you're in a room by yourself writing, it's a tremendous boost to have someone who always reads your emails because he celebrates the developing story even more than you do. I love having a partner with regular access to the setting I have gotten so attached to. Thanks, Steve.

Thank you, agent Rachelle Gardner, editor Vicki Crumpton, and the team at Revell that has embraced the Avenue of Dreams series in just the way authors hope for.

Thank you to my family, who have gotten used to the people stomping around in my head but who also keep me grounded in what matters.

Author's Note

Although the main characters in the Avenue of Dreams series are fictional, the primary historical markers are true. The Ferris wheel on which both Charlotte's fears and dreams turn almost did not happen. Because what George Ferris proposed to build was unproven, organizers of the world's fair hesitated to give him a chance. Eventually, they did, and he surprised the world with an engineering feat that people these days take for granted. Charlotte's ride on the wheel changed her life.

The 1890s were restless years of urbanization. The forty-hour work week, paid time off, organized labor—these all rose from the era of this series. Questions of justice and distribution of wealth polarized political affiliations of both employers and a workforce swollen by immigration and movement to the cities. Archie Shepard, on the cusp of agitation and navigating carefully through tumultuous times, ran straight into the drama of Chicago's mayor being shot over labor sentiments taken to an extreme.

I love writing historical fiction because the stories themselves rise out of well-documented events and personalities. An urban setting like Chicago provides myriad historical trails to explore and opportunities to imagine how events in the newspapers of the time would have impacted the lives of ordinary people. I never get tired of it.

Olivia Newport's novels twist through time to discover where faith and passions meet. Her husband and two twentysomething children provide welcome distraction from the people stomping through her head on their way into her books. She chases joy in stunning Colorado at the foot of the Rockies, where daylilies grow as tall as she is.

I'm imagining you. You walk past as I water my front flowerbeds and we wave. You check the time as we both stand in a long line at the grocery store. You sit in front of me in church. I'm at my table in the coffee shop and you're at yours.

We may smile politely and move on with our separate lives. Or one of us may speak, a simple invitation to conversation, and the words flow between us.

Here the adventure begins. When we meet someone new, we never know where it might lead.

— Olivia Newport